my family,

I first started writing when my mother gave me a writing kit for Christmas, and once I started I just couldn't stop. *Living Dangerously* was my first novel and since then I haven't looked back.

Ideas for books are everywhere, and I'm constantly inspired by people and places around me. From watching TV (yes, it is research) to overhearing conversations, I love how my writing gives me the chance to taste other people's lives and try all the jobs I've never had.

I love being a writer; to me there isn't a more satisfying or pleasing thing to do. I particularly enjoy writing love stories. I believe falling in love is the best thing in the world, and I want all my characters to experience it, and my readers to share in their stories.'

Katie Fforde

A Rose Petal Summer

arrow books

3 5 7 9 10 8 6 4 2

Arrow Books
20 Vauxhall Bridge Road
London SW1V 2SA

Arrow Books is part of the Penguin Random House group of companies
whose addresses can be found at global.penguinrandomhouse.com

Penguin
Random House
UK

First published by Century in 2019
First published in paperback by Arrow Books in 2020

www.penguin.co.uk

A CIP catalogue record for this book is available from the British Library

ISBN 9781784758257
ISBN 9781784758264 (export)

Typeset in 11.54 /15.7 pt Palatino LT Std

Printed S.p.A.

tted to a
ur readers
om Forest

FSC
www.fsc.org

Acknowledgements

There always seems to be a lot of people behind the scenes in my books. I get ideas from the ether, but sometimes the ether has real people creating it and I am extremely grateful to them. Below is a list of some of them. If I have forgotten you, I am really sorry. It wasn't my intention to leave you out!

Thank you to Emmanuelle Moeglin from the Experimental Perfume Club who was such an inspiration and runs great courses.

My son Guy's friend Joby Osman, who talked to me about my idea when I first had it and made it seem possible.

To Jane Wenham-Jones, travel assistant and general wise-woman on all things writerly.

There follows such a long list of writers that people will wonder if I did any of this myself, but plot development is always helped by talking and writers love to talk about writing.

To Kate Riordan for telling me about Les Senteurs as well as helping me develop a plot. To Judy Astley for coming with me to Les Senteurs and asking useful questions. To Jo Thomas, my road-trip buddy and listening ear. She set up the writers' retreat in beautiful West Wales (and did all of the cooking and looking after) where my plot finally clunked into place. Also present was AJ Pearce whose mere presence works magic!

Jill Mansell for knowing very technical brain stuff, to Elizabeth Lindsay for knowing a lot about powers of attorney.

I have an especially wonderful team behind me at Penguin Random House. Starting with my excellent, creative and sympathetic (not to mention her tougher attributes!) editor Selina Walker. To Cassandra Di Bello for her editorial support and Celeste Ward-Best for her genius marketing; Alice Spencer and Sarah Harwood in publicity; Jacqueline Bissett and Ceara Elliot who designed my gorgeous cover; Linda Hodgson and Helen Wynn-Smith who make sure my books actually get to my readers. Thank you to the sales team including Mat Watterson, Claire Simmonds, Laura Garrod, Sasha Cox and Kelly Webster. And always to my beloved Charlotte Bush. We have worked together for twenty years and it is always terrific!

As always Richenda Todd, who was my first editor and now is my copy-editor. She still gets my jokes! And Bill Hamilton, definitely the best agent in the world. No question.

Finally to my family, always so important to me. Thank you.

To my dear friend Jo Thomas, who has shared so many glorious research trips, writing retreats, health farm weekends and bottles of rosé. Thank you!

Prologue

Two decades earlier

Caro pulled her jersey over her knees knowing she should just be sensible and have an early night. She'd said her goodbyes to her friends who were having drinks not far away and she had a cab booked for five in the morning to get her over to the other side of the Greek island where she'd been staying to catch the ferry to the mainland and the airport.

But the beauty of the evening, dark yet full of the sounds of insects and gently lapping waves, was so seductive. The enormous golden moon shone low over the sea like a lantern. A wild rose bush covered an outcrop of rock and pale-pink petals fell from time to time from the tiny pom-pom flowers filling the air with their scent. Somehow she couldn't tear herself away just yet.

'Do you mind if I join you?'

Caro jumped slightly. She couldn't really see who was asking but his voice was nice and her friends were fairly close so she felt perfectly safe.

'Help yourself,' she said.

They didn't speak for several minutes. Caro wasn't really shy but she was aware that the boy who'd chosen to join her was very attractive. Not that she could see him in detail; it was too dark. But he was tall and well made. She sneaked a look at him and saw that he had a strong nose and chin – a good profile.

'The thing I'm going to miss about the Greek islands, when I move on,' he said, 'is the fragrance. The roses – especially here, just now – smell amazing.'

Caro was surprised. She turned to him, struggling to see him in the dark. She really loved aromas too, but her friends seemed to have no sense of smell and couldn't detect anything unless it came in a bottle in the duty-free section of an airport.

'Men don't usually notice fragrance,' she said. 'I think they ruin themselves by over-application of Lynx when they're at school.'

Her companion laughed. 'I'm Xander and I'm interested in perfume in spite of the Lynx,' he said. 'You smell nice,' he added.

She shifted away a little bit, not quite sure how to take this. She only wore scent on special occasions because the only one she really liked was what her mother wore and it was terribly expensive. She didn't have much left, but she'd put some on that evening because she hoped she might get more for her birthday. 'I'm Caro.'

Possibly aware he'd said something a bit odd, he went on. 'So where is home for you, Caro?'

'London,' she said. 'You?'

'A tiny corner of Scotland called Glen Liddell.' He sighed. 'But there's lots of world to be explored before I go back home.'

Possibly because they were in the dark and the night air was so hypnotic they couldn't stop talking. Xander told her how he wanted to study perfume and that his father wouldn't hear of it. She told him how she was feeling pressure to take up her university place but wasn't sure it was what she wanted. They talked about their favourite music, books and films. Sometimes they agreed and sometimes they had to argue the case for some of their more unusual choices. But Caro never felt she had to keep quiet about liking something a bit odd; she knew he wouldn't judge her and would just be interested.

Then suddenly they saw car lights coming along the coast road. It was her cab, dawn was breaking and she had to go.

In the cab on the way to the ferry she realised that tears were trickling out of the corners of her eyes. She'd met a man she felt totally connected with, in every way, and they hadn't even exchanged contact details. How could she have let that happen? And would she regret it for the rest of her life?

Chapter One

'A caravan,' said Caro, looking about her, trying to keep her feelings out of her voice. It wasn't even a nice caravan. It was made of plastic and had a strong old-carpet smell about it.

'Yes, I'm sorry,' said the woman who had shown Caro to her new temporary home. 'There is a cottage but it needs work doing before it's habitable. It's been rented out and has got into a bit of a state.'

The woman, who had introduced herself as Heather, didn't sound quite apologetic enough about this, Caro felt. Heather was late-middle-aged and kindly, her greying hair cut into a neat bob, but she didn't know – couldn't have known – how disappointed Caro was about her accommodation.

At her interview, which had taken place at a London hotel, there had been talk of a typical Highland cottage, which had given Caro ideas of a low, stone building with a tiled roof, or maybe even some sort of thatch. She was hazy about Scotland and thatch but the image had been lovely and, in her head, had only smelt of peat smoke or possibly pine trees. Mrs Leonie Gordon (call me Lennie) who'd conducted the interview had been nice, Caro had thought, and although quite grand was warm and friendly. A smelly caravan had not been part of the deal.

'I'll leave you to settle in,' said Heather, having given the caravan a cursory inspection from the doorway. 'Then come back to the house for sherry. Murdo always has a drink at about six. With luck all the team will be there and you can meet everyone. Though I don't know if Alec will appear. He's been away. That's partly why the cottage isn't ready. So, see you in half an hour? Is that long enough?'

'I should think so,' said Caro. She was feeling gloomy. She knew it was probably because it had been a long journey and parting from her daughter Posy had been difficult but she really hoped it wasn't because she realised that she'd made a dreadful mistake coming up here. Still, it was only for a month or so. Surely she could survive that?

As she patted the bedding to see if it was damp she wondered if she should take a quick picture of the caravan to send to Posy. She probably wouldn't be able to send it for a little while as she doubted the caravan had a signal (although at least the sheets seemed dry) but it might make her daughter laugh.

Posy only knew that her mother had taken a job looking after an elderly gentleman in Scotland (or keeping him out of mischief, more than anything, Lennie, his daughter, had said) because she'd had a lifelong ambition to answer an advertisement in *The Lady* magazine, and also wanted to do something completely different at the beginning of her daughter's trip to Australia, so she wouldn't feel lonely on the Dutch barge they had lived in together in London.

She wouldn't dream of sharing with her daughter the other reason she'd accepted the job because she didn't really like to acknowledge that one to herself.

While she couldn't summon up any enthusiasm for unpacking, Caro made herself look respectable before setting off for 'the Big Hoose', as she thought of it. She didn't go to the lengths she'd gone to for the interview (skirt, knee-length boots, a blow dry she'd paid for and some extra highlights for her dark blonde hair). Now, she made sure her jeans were clean, her make-up was more or less in the right place and scrunched up her hair, which always reverted to curls if not professionally seen to. She added her favourite cashmere poncho on top of her jumper because she felt good in it and was convinced that Scotland was always freezing. Although it felt like winter, it was the end of April and there were signs of spring shyly appearing among the faded bracken, sheltering against the huge granite boulders. As she planned to tell Posy later, there was still quite a lot of snow on the furthest mountains. She'd moved back a season up here; she'd be glad of the jumpers she'd brought with her.

As she walked down the path she examined the Big Hoose, imagining how she would describe it to Posy. She wasn't sure that Posy, who was twenty, would understand what 'Scottish Baronial' looked like but would relate to 'imagine spooky black birds flying out of the turrets to give you the idea, and then take away the spooky black birds – it's huge, it's grey, it has turrets and it doesn't look homely'.

Inside, Caro was hoping for faded tartan carpets, stags' heads and a huge, smouldering fire. She didn't even mind if the fire billowed out smoke from time to time, she just needed to see a flame. Her permanent home, the Dutch barge she'd inherited from her parents, near Canary Wharf, didn't have any sort of burner that had a visible flame and, to her mind, this was one of the few downsides. She made up for the lack with copious candles.

Now, she wished she'd put on her coat and scarf on top of her double layer of cashmere – the wind could 'clean corn' as her father would have said. She also hoped that she wouldn't have to face too much questioning. She was expecting questions from Murdo, Lennie's father, but she didn't want to be grilled by everyone else as well. There was no shame in saying that she'd been a 'shop assistant' and her reason for leaving was that 'the shop closed down' but it didn't sound very inspiring. She was perfect for the job in many ways, after all. She could play bridge and chess, up to a point, she was quite a good cook (her scrambled eggs were considered excellent by many and this was one of Murdo's favourites, she'd been told) and she had, according to Lennie at her interview, a pleasant speaking voice. This was an advantage when it came to reading the newspaper to Murdo, who had very little sight when it came to small print. Apparently it was the letters to the paper that were his favourite, so he could splutter and exclaim or nod and grunt accordingly. She'd passed the first test, and, now she had Lennie's approval, she had to meet the man whose opinion really counted. She banged hard on the door with the stag's head knocker.

Heather opened the door and let Caro into a hall that was satisfyingly Scottish. It was large and gave the impression that it been like this for generations. There were the hoped-for stags' heads on the walls, no doubt stalked by long-dead ancestors, and the faded tartan carpet had rips in it repaired with gaffer tape. Pervading everything was the smell of peat smoke to add the final Caledonian flourish. Caro gave a little sigh of happiness. This was what she'd travelled over four hundred miles north for.

The furniture was a mixture of periods but none of it was new. A leather hall chair was spewing horsehair from where the gaffer tape – obviously used to mend everything – had peeled off. Caro would have liked a few moments to examine her surroundings, but Heather had things to do.

'Now,' she said briskly. 'Himself is in the drawing room. If you'd like to go through and introduce yourself, I'll go and get the drinks.'

As she was 'staff' and not a regular guest, Caro could only comply with this suggestion although it was the last thing she wanted to do. She wasn't particularly shy but the thought of meeting her new employer without any sort of buffer was daunting. However, she obviously couldn't hover in the hall even though she was dying to inspect the ancient framed maps and family portraits. She took a breath and set forth.

The first thing that struck her when she reached the drawing room was the large bay window that had a wonderful view over the loch. The hills and mountains beyond were truly majestic and Caro longed to gaze at them, too. But she was not here for the scenery and standing by the fire, wearing tweed from head to foot, was a formidable old gentleman.

Caro felt a flash of recognition and she realised that he had a look of her father. Piercing blue eyes under bushy, sandy eyebrows, a wind-burnt complexion and a resolute mouth. The fact that he could hardly see didn't seem to affect his penetrating gaze.

Caro realised she had one chance to get this right. Show fear now and he'd bully her into the ground. Lennie had warned her of this at the interview and her own knowledge of old-fashioned gentlemen, used to getting their own way, confirmed it.

'Hello!' she said, walking towards him. 'I'm Caro Fitzwarren.' She took his hand and shook it.

He squeezed it in return. 'So you're m'minder, eh?'

Already half prepared to be evicted from the house and sent back to London on the first train, Caro made a decision. 'Your minder? Oh God! I thought I was here to play a little gentle rummy and lean over your shoulder while you played patience. And possibly read you the less offensive letters to *The Times*. I didn't know you needed a minder!'

There was an agonisingly long pause and then he nodded. The bright eyes produced a twinkle and they both relaxed a little. 'I think you might do,' he said. 'Murdo McLean. Everyone calls me Murdo.'

Just then a little dog of varying breeds ran into the room and up to Murdo.

'This is my dog, George,' said Murdo. 'Disobedient little brute but small enough not to do too much damage.'

George ran to Caro and sniffed her. Then he raised his leg and relieved himself on her jeans.

11

'Oh my God!' she said before she could stop herself.

'He hasn't done it again, has he?' said Murdo, and then roared, 'Heather! Bastard dog! Pissed on a visitor! He should have been put down. I knew he was a bad 'un.'

Caro could tell from this diatribe that Murdo was devoted to George and hoped she too might come to forgive the little dog in time.

Heather came running in. She had a spray bottle and a cloth in her hand. 'Trouble is,' she said, handing the bottle and the cloth to Caro, 'he doesn't do it for months so you forget he might.'

'It means he likes you,' said Murdo gruffly, with no hint of embarrassment.

Caro sprayed and rubbed, knowing only a proper wash would do the job.

'Actually, would you mind if I went back and changed? It won't take a second,' she said.

Heather nodded. 'Bring your jeans back with you and I'll put them in the machine.'

When Caro came back, slightly out of breath, the drawing room seemed full of people. Fortunately, or maybe deliberately, Heather was on hand again to meet her.

'I am so sorry about the dog!' she said, taking the jeans. 'Murdo dotes on him, of course, and it seems to have made George a bit territorial. But he's a grand little dog really.'

12

'I realised Murdo loved George and it's a case of "Love me, love my dog" with him. I'm sure we'll become friends. Eventually,' said Caro.

Heather sighed, as if with relief. 'It's not everyone who could forgive a dog for lifting its leg on them.'

Caro shrugged. 'It's either that, or go home,' she said bluntly.

Heather acknowledged the truth of this with a nod. 'Now let's get you to meet the family.'

'Are they all family?' said Caro, suddenly a bit overwhelmed by the number of people that seemed to be in the drawing room.

'Not all. One or two people work on the estate in some way or other. Now let me take you around and introduce you.'

Caro noticed a girl – mid-teens probably – with a long rose-gold plait over one shoulder. She was strikingly beautiful and looked quintessentially Scottish, Caro decided.

'That's Rowan, Murdo's granddaughter,' said Heather. 'I worry that it's a bit lonely for her up here. Beauty alone isn't enough when you're seventeen.'

Caro nodded. She wouldn't have thought Rowan was older than about fifteen. 'Are her parents here? I'm just trying to work out who everyone is and how they fit in.'

'Skye and Alec will be here later, I think. Skye's a bit ...' Heather paused, obviously thinking of how to describe her without being disloyal to the family. 'Artistic.'

Caro laughed. 'I used to work in an artists' supplies shop. Some of our customers were away with the fairies.'

Heather nodded. 'We'd call her "fey" round here. Alec is more reserved so don't take offence if he doesn't seem friendly. He is very busy and doesn't socialise much. He lives in a but and ben up the glen a bit.'

'So he's Murdo's son?'

'That's right. I'll introduce you to Rab. He runs the smokery. And then there's Ewan, he's my husband, and he does everything on the estate no one else does and a lot besides. Now, what would you like to drink? There's whisky or sherry?'

Caro hesitated. Part of her yearned for something warming and relaxing but she felt she should hold back until she'd talked to Murdo for a bit.

'I'd better go and talk to Murdo first,' she said. 'I didn't get a chance earlier.'

Heather shook her head. 'That wee dog! But Murdo will expect you to be sociable. Have a dram. I'll bring it over.'

As Caro went across to Murdo she realised how grateful she was to Heather. Although obviously dedicated to the family, she would steer her through if things became rocky.

'Murdo? It's Caro.'

The old man turned towards Caro. 'I'm not blind, you know, just a bit less sharp-eyed than I used to be. Doesn't mean I'm stupid, either.'

'Certainly not but we didn't get a chance to talk earlier.' She waited for him to respond. 'So what's the routine? What time would you like me to turn up in the morning?'

'About nine. I have my breakfast and then I like to read the paper. You can help with that. Then we might go for a drive around the estate – check on things, you know. Can you drive a Land Rover?'

'I've never tried but I'm sure I can.'

'This one's a bit of an antique but, like me, it's got plenty of life in it. Takes all the hills, can drive over a stream and up the other side without a bit of bother.'

When Caro had been asked if she could drive she'd got the impression it would be trips to the shops or the doctor's surgery, not serious off-roading. Still, she'd do her best. And if she needed to ask Ewan or someone to give her a crash course in Land-Rover-wrangling, she would.

'Have you met m'son yet?'

'No, your daughter interviewed me, in London.'

'Lennie? She's gone to be with her daughter, in Canada. She's having a baby.'

'She told me. It'll be lovely for her daughter to have her mother with her.' Caro paused. 'Lennie – she did ask me to call her that – explained that you

15

just needed a bit of a hand about the place and you weren't to be nannied.'

Murdo gave a bark that was apparently laughter. 'Wish she knew how to take her own advice! Bossy woman, my daughter.' He paused. 'Though better than my son. He doesn't care a jot about the estate.'

While he was talking, Caro wondered why Murdo didn't have a Scottish accent – he couldn't have sounded more English. It was probably a class thing.

'I've only been here five minutes but it does seem a very beautiful area. I can't wait to explore a bit.'

'I'll show you around,' he said confidently. When she didn't respond instantly he went on, 'M'sight's not as bad as people make out. I know every stick and stone of this land. Was born here, and I'll die here.'

'Amazing,' Caro said, not sure what the right response was.

Then, to her relief, the man who ran the smokery, Rab, came up. 'Good evening, Murdo. How do you do – Caro, is it?'

'Short for Caroline,' she explained.

Rab nodded. 'I hope you'll come and take a look at the smokery while you're here. It's coming along nicely.'

He had a lovely soft Scottish accent, Caro noticed, and she found herself smiling in response. 'I'd love to. Do you do salmon? Or kippers? Or what?'

'Mostly salmon and kippers but we want to expand.'

Murdo snorted. 'Waste of time. It's not making money.'

Caro saw Rab give Murdo a look that was part resentment and part irritation. 'It just needs a bit of investment.' Would he have looked at his boss like that if Murdo had been able to see? Caro wondered.

'This is a sporting estate,' declared Murdo. 'We don't need fancy fal-lals. Making smoked salmon – ridiculous! We're not goddamn shopkeepers!'

Rab gave Caro an embarrassed smile. 'You see we don't agree on this.'

'Nothing wrong with being a shopkeeper,' said Caro, realising too late which one of these men she needed to keep on the right side of. 'I was one myself until recently.'

'Really?' said Murdo crossly. 'Had I known—'

'I still have all the qualifications mentioned in the advertisement,' said Caro, quiet but firm. 'So my recent employment isn't really relevant.'

As she heard the words coming out of her mouth she remembered hoping no one would ask her about what she'd done before and here she was, talking about it for the second time on her first evening. She realised it was because she felt Rab needed supporting. Murdo could indeed be rather a bully, she decided. Still, she only had to put up with him for a month or two. And maybe she would win him round. She didn't want to have to tell Posy she'd failed, and had been mad to come up here just so she could fulfil a very childish ambition.

She was just trying to think of something faintly placatory to say to Murdo when there was a commotion at the door. A dog streaked into the room, found George (who was under the table) and started a fight.

Then a man and a woman appeared: the man in pursuit of the dog, and the woman smiling at everybody dreamily as if there was no altercation.

Rowan got up and went over to the woman, who was obviously her mother. Seeing them together emphasised how alike they were – and how beautiful. The girl didn't take any notice of the dog fight either.

The man reached in under the table and dragged out the larger, younger dog, who appeared to be some sort of spaniel. 'You tell him, George!' he said. 'Skye, you must learn to control your dog.'

'He's Rowan's dog, sweetie,' said the woman. 'She must learn to take responsibility for her things.'

Rowan shot her mother a resigned look and the spaniel wriggled his way free from the man.

Seeing there was going to be more noise (although Caro realised now it wasn't actual fighting, more an old dog telling off a young one) she called to the spaniel, 'Here, boy!'

The dog – and she realised it was hardly more than a puppy – came to Caro, possibly hoping her beckoning hand had something edible in it. She caught its collar and stroked its neck. It was, she decided, adorable.

The man came over. 'I'm so sorry. He's entirely untrained.'

Caro looked up at him. She'd recognised him the moment he'd entered the room but to her relief he didn't seem to recognise her. Of course it had been nearly pitch dark when they'd met and anyway twenty years would have changed her a lot. 'It's fine. He's lovely and he hasn't peed on me.'

Alec laughed and Caro's heart gave a lurch. 'Oh God, did George do that? How embarrassing! My father is no better at dog-training than Rowan is. I'm Alec, by the way.' He turned to his daughter. 'Rowan? Come and meet – Caro, is it? Is that what Heather told me?'

'That's right,' said Caro, wondering why Alec would introduce his daughter before his wife.

Rowan came over. 'Hello,' she said quietly, with the same soft accent that Rab had.

'Is this your dog?' asked Caro, smiling encouragingly.

Rowan shrugged. 'Mum gave him to me. He's called Galahad.'

'Gally for short,' said Alec.

Rowan's mother, Skye, swayed up to join them. 'You must be Caro, come to help with my father-in-law. I gather you're from London. Please don't bring the influence of the city to bear on my daughter.' She smiled winsomely. 'She's led a deliberately sheltered life. I assume I can trust you not to fill my daughter's ears with anything unsuitable?'

Caro thought that Skye's beauty would have been greater had her smile been sincere. She ignored the woman's question and turned back to the girl. 'Rowan, you have really lovely hair.'

Rowan started to smile in response but her mother broke in. 'We don't want to encourage Rowan to think about superficial things like physical beauty. Rowan is very sensitive – vulnerable to the wrong influences. It's why we've homeschooled her: we wanted to set her on the right course. We hope we can trust her to follow it now.'

'Bloody ridiculous!' said Murdo, who somehow managed to overhear this bit of conversation. 'She's seventeen! She's not a child any more. She should go away to finish her schooling.'

'She's far too young to leave home!'

'Nonsense!' said Murdo. 'I went to prep school when I was seven – never did me any harm!'

This was obviously a very well-worn argument. 'If you overlook your complete lack of sensitivity and insight,' said Skye, but so quietly that Caro, who was standing only a couple of feet away, could only just hear it.

'He's a dreadful old man,' Skye whispered. 'Terribly domineering. You'll have to be careful he doesn't bully you.'

But although this was exactly what Caro had been thinking earlier, now she felt protective of him. 'I'm sure I'll cope.'

She felt she was well up for Murdo – he was what she was expecting after all. But what about the rest of the family? They were another prospect all together.

Chapter Two

Caro had very little energy left for emailing when she got in, but she knew Posy would be anxious to hear how her mother was getting on in Scotland. And once she got started, Caro found it cathartic to write down some of her first impressions.

Caro realised she'd have to be careful how she talked about Rab from the smokery, who had kindly escorted her back up the hill to her little plastic home. Posy would want to know if she 'liked' him because she was so keen for her mother to find a partner. Caro did like Rab but not in the way Posy meant it and, anyway, he probably had a wife and family.

She was free to let rip about the caravan not being as expected with a turf fire and stone walls, but being made of plastic and having an odd smell. And she put in how her new boss's dog had peed on her leg because it would make Posy laugh. She rounded the email off with a quick and pithy description of Murdo and then fell into bed. She almost felt obliged to add a PS – that someone had put a hot-water bottle in the bed and that was lovely. It must have been Heather, thought Caro as she cuddled into it. How extremely kind.

Rab had suggested it would be a good idea for her to get used to the Land Rover before she drove Murdo round the estate in it and they'd arranged to meet up so she could have a practice with him. This was after she'd admitted she didn't do a lot of driving as she lived in London, and when she did it was in an ordinary car on ordinary roads.

'He'll want to take you everywhere,' Rab had said, 'and some of the tracks are in very bad repair. He'll swear at you if you crash the gears or slip back going up a steep bank.'

However, she had slept well and felt excited as she left the caravan, wearing pretty much all of her clothes, to find Rab and the Land Rover.

'Well, that was fun!' she said after half an hour of bouncing around the property with Rab roaring instructions – roaring not because he was bad-tempered but so he could be heard over the sound of the engine.

'Now you'd better go in for your porridge,' Rab said, laughing. 'You've done really well.'

'For a girl?' she said, teasing him.

He shook his head. 'For someone who hasn't driven a cranky old Defender before.'

Caro stopped. 'I thought it was a Land Rover?'

'It is! Don't worry. Now I'm away off to the smokery.'

'You're not coming in for breakfast then?'

He shook his head. 'No. I was invited to dinner as part of your welcome. I don't live in the big house. I had breakfast hours ago. I may see you at lunchtime though.'

Caro went in through the back door, as directed by Rab. She liked him, he'd be a good friend, but there was no chemistry there. He was too beardy for her. And besides, although she despised herself for being so foolish, Caro's interest in men was only pointing in one direction at the moment. She was harking back to a man she'd met for one night, over twenty years ago. The fact that Alec was married didn't stop her feeling attracted, but it would stop her letting him guess her feelings, even if her pride alone wasn't enough. But she was realistic and very confident that when she got to know him better she would stop fancying him. Familiarity breeding contempt, and all that. It had always worked for her in the past.

Murdo didn't like small talk at breakfast, she had been told. He did, however, like to read the paper.

As he could no longer read it for himself, it meant Caro had to.

'Morning, Murdo!' she said breezily as she came in.

George, asleep under his master's chair, awoke and thumped his stubby tail in welcome. An improvement on his behaviour yesterday, thought Caro.

'Is it morning? Could be the middle of the night for all I can tell. I'm nearly blind, you know,' said Murdo.

Caro's sigh of frustration was almost silent. 'I promise I won't say another word if it's going to make you so grumpy,' she said.

'Who are you to tell me I'm grumpy?' demanded Murdo.

'I'm the woman hired by your daughter, at vast expense, to keep you amused while she is away, if you really have forgotten.'

'Whisht with your nonsense!' said Heather, putting a large plate of kippers in front of Murdo. 'And let the poor woman have a bite to eat before you jump down her throat.'

The way Heather seemed to ignore Murdo's brusqueness reinforced Caro's opinion that he shouldn't be pandered to. 'Oh, don't worry,' said Caro. 'I'm used to grumpy old men.'

'What?' Murdo was outraged.

'Grumpy old men who can be completely charming if they have a mind to.' She paused. 'I rather like them.'

25

Caro had confirmed it had been Heather who'd put the hot-water bottle in her bed. Heather had brushed it off as not being a big thing to do, but had obviously liked Caro being so appreciative. Caro knew that Heather would have had to run up the hill to the caravan while the house was full of people, most of them wanting food.

While Caro waited for her porridge, she looked at Murdo's kippers dubiously.

She said, 'Will you manage the kippers or would you like me to help you take out the bones?'

'They're fillets, so I just eat them,' said Murdo. 'You can pour the coffee when it comes. I'm not completely helpless.'

Caro started on her porridge, wondering why there were only two places set at the big round table. Last night there'd been a lot of family for dinner.

'Will Alec and Skye and Rowan be joining us for breakfast?' she asked.

'Certainly not. They have their own house. Not sure who lives where now though.' He carried a forkful of kipper successfully to his mouth, only losing a bit of it on the way. 'God knows where the woman lives,' he went on. 'She left m'son, you know, but she still lives locally. I suppose it's handy for young Rowan. Plenty of houses on the estate.' He paused while he loaded up another forkful of kipper. 'Happy with your accommodation, are you?'

Caro suddenly *was* happy with her accommodation. Alec and Skye weren't married any more. That made her very happy indeed. The plastic caravan no longer seemed important. 'It's fine, thank you.' She spooned up her last bit of porridge. 'Tell me when you'd like me to start reading the paper.'

'Just having porridge, are you? Find I'm starving at ten o'clock if I have that.'

'I'll maybe have some toast as well then.' She wanted to cut down on carbs but the news that Alec was single meant she didn't care for a moment. She shook her head to clear it. 'So? Home news? Foreign news? What do you like?'

'Deaths column. I want to know who's dropped off the perch since yesterday.'

'I get that,' said Caro, finding the page. 'It means you've won.'

After that they went on to world events and Caro was given Murdo's opinion of the current government (although Caro realised it wouldn't have mattered who was in power, Murdo's opinion would still have been low). After the obituaries, Caro was free to go.

'Meet you by the vehicle at ten,' Murdo told her. 'You can drive me round the estate. I'll point out the landmarks and the best views to you.'

The sky had cleared while they'd been at breakfast and it was a beautiful day by the time Caro met Murdo by the Land Rover.

She found she really enjoyed driving the big, primitive vehicle – it made her feel a bit like the Queen in the various films there'd been about her, driving over her estate like a pro. Murdo was good company, in spite of his outlandish and outdated opinions. Whether he could see or not, he told her to stop at all the right places, to see the vistas that could be spotted between the trees, showing the loch and the snow-capped mountains in the distance.

'It is a really beautiful estate,' she said to him when they had stopped at a particularly beautiful spot.

He grunted. 'Been in my family for over four hundred years. It's in my blood.'

'I understand why. It must be very precious to you.'

'Like my heart and lungs are precious to me,' said Murdo. 'Just a shame it's not precious to the next generation.' He harrumphed – a sound, Caro had discovered, that could mean various things. It quite often meant 'I want to change the subject'. Now it clearly also meant he was a bit upset.

'Oh, look!' said Caro delightedly, seeing a bright ginger creature leaping through the trees and stopping at the tree nearest to them. 'A red squirrel! In that tree! I've never seen one before. It's so beautiful!'

'For one, I can't look, I'm practically blind,' said Murdo, who obviously liked to rub it in, 'and for a second, we only have reds up here, so we just call them squirrels.'

Feeling foolish and a bit irritated by him spoiling the mood for her, Caro started up the Land Rover and carried on down the track.

'Stop here!' Murdo ordered a few moments later. 'Down there we can see the cottage you're using, right?'

Caro looked and saw the sort of cottage she'd dreamt of staying in. Grey stone, slate roof, painted woodwork. 'Oh yes! I hadn't realised we were so near home.'

'I took you round in a loop,' said Murdo, pleased with himself.

'So you have. I can see the main house now.' She made a decision. 'Actually, Murdo? Would you mind if I popped down to my cottage? I just want to get an extra cardigan.'

'Well, don't be long.'

She ran, determined to steal a few moments inspecting her would-be home. Why couldn't she stay in it? Heather had mentioned building work but there was no sign of scaffolding or ladders or anything like that. She walked all round it. There was a little garden at the back, mostly consisting of moss-covered boulders and low walls. Lichen hung from an old washing line as well as from the trees. It gave the impression of a garden under an enchantment, waiting for the spell to be broken so it would grow again. Caro realised it was probably just winter holding it back. Even at the end of April, spring was hardly apparent here – so late compared to the south of England.

Knowing her time was limited, she peered in through the window, blocking out the light with her hands. In the sitting room all she could see was some furniture.

She walked quickly round to the kitchen and peered in another window. No sign of any building or plumbing work, but where she'd have expected to see a dresser were shelves, and on the shelves were rows of small amber bottles that reminded Caro of a school laboratory. She resolved to come back and see what she could find out. Yes, it was being nosy, but she felt she had a right to know why she was deprived of this Highland gem.

'Did you find your cardigan?' asked Murdo, as Caro arrived back in the driving seat, panting hard from her uphill dash.

'What? Oh, yes thank you.'

'It's just you seem not to have it with you.'

He was blind! How could he see that? 'No! Well, I washed it last night and it wasn't quite dry.'

'What sort of a damn fool thing is that to do?' said Murdo. 'Washing jumpers at night?'

'I spilt something on it on the journey up here,' said Caro crossly, irrationally annoyed at having her actions questioned even though she hadn't actually performed them.

'Give it to Heather to deal with. She's good at those things.'

'I'm sure Heather has more than enough to do without adding my washing to the list,' she replied.

'Don't get snappy with me, missy!'

'Sorry,' said Caro automatically although she was aware she mustn't make a habit of apologising to Murdo. He wouldn't respect her if she did. 'Oh, look, there's Alec. Is he waiting for us? Or should I take the Land Rover round the back?'

'Let's see what he wants. Good-for-nothing scoundrel.'

As she pulled up in front of the big house, Caro noted there was more regret than censure in his tone.

Alec came up to the driver's side and Caro wound down the window.

'Good morning,' he said. 'Did you have a nice drive?'

'Lovely!' said Caro. 'It's so beautiful here. Murdo told me all the best places to stop to admire the view and I saw a red squirrel – squirrel I mean.'

Alec frowned a little. 'Sorry?'

'Murdo told me off for calling them red squirrels when it's the only kind you have here,' Caro explained. She found being near him a bit awkward.

'We stopped at her cottage,' said Murdo. 'Caro wanted a cardigan.'

Alec's eyes opened in alarm.

'But it was wet, so I didn't pick it up,' said Caro quickly. 'The cardigan, I mean.'

'Oh. That was a shame.' Alec's confusion was growing with every word.

'Silly girl washed it,' Murdo went on, apparently determined that Alec should know just how foolish she was.

'I spilt something on it—'

Before Caro could finish her sentence, Murdo interrupted her. 'But she likes the cottage, don't you?'

'Very much,' she said. Alec, she could see, was in agonies. 'I'd better get Murdo inside.'

Alec, who'd been leaning on the Land Rover, moved away, looking strangely at Caro. Had he now recognised her? she wondered. No – that wasn't recognition in his eyes, it was discomfort. He was the reason she wasn't sleeping in a dear little Highland cottage and she could see he felt guilty about it.

'Maybe we can catch up later, Caro?' said Alec. 'I could show you a bit more of the estate.'

Murdo gave a short laugh. 'Didn't know you were interested in it.'

'No, but maybe Caro is,' said Alec calmly. 'And I do actually run it,' he added sotto voce so Murdo wouldn't hear.

'Easy to be friendly when a pretty girl is involved,' said Murdo.

'Murdo! You keep telling me you're practically blind. You have no idea if I'm pretty or not,' said Caro crossly, feeling manipulated.

'You have a very pretty voice, my dear,' said Murdo. 'And that's half the battle.'

Caro closed her eyes and sighed deeply. 'Come on. We'd better get you inside.'

She got down from the Land Rover, forgetting it was higher than ordinary cars, and nearly twisted her ankle. Alec caught her arm. 'I'm so sorry,' he said. 'My father is never going to even approach political correctness.' There was a smile in his eyes that made up for a lot.

'It's OK,' she said quietly. 'I'm used to old men like him.'

Once he'd seen his father safely down, Alec said, 'We'll fix a time when we're both free. Do you like walking?'

'I think so,' said Caro. She walked a lot in London but she realised it probably wasn't the same as the walking he meant.

'Got some walking boots?'

'Er, no.'

'Don't worry. I expect you can borrow some. Rowan's got a couple of pairs, I know.'

'OK,' said Caro, suddenly breathless.

'We'll make a plan, then,' said Alec.

'OK,' said Caro again, feeling more like a teenager than the confident adult she'd been before she arrived here.

Caro and Murdo went in through the back door to be welcomed by Heather. 'Good timing,' she said. 'I'm just making coffee. You two go through and make yourselves comfy by the fire.'

Murdo had gone into the drawing room and Caro was waiting for the tray so she could spare Heather a job, when Rowan and her dog came in. The dog capered round the kitchen, legs flailing, skidding to a halt in front of Caro, wanting to be congratulated on his elegant performance.

'Hello, Gally,' Caro said, 'what are you up to?' She realised she had that very English characteristic where in some situations she found it easier to talk to animals than people. She could never have asked Rowan what she was up to. Fortunately Rowan volunteered the information.

'We're bored,' she said with a shy smile.

'Oh, well, come and talk to me and Murdo,' said Caro. 'Heather, I'll take the coffee. No need for you to wait on me.'

Caro sensed reluctance in Rowan and Heather obviously did too.

'Murdo will have a wee nap after his coffee,' said Heather. 'If you like, you and Rowan can have a chat here. I'll take him his coffee.'

34

Although she was obviously quite shy, Rowan seemed happy with this suggestion and Caro realised that Heather was right when she'd suggested Rowan was a bit lonely. The estate was quite far away from civilisation and it wouldn't be easy for her to have a real-life social life, as opposed to an online one. And Rowan didn't really seem the type to have loads of cyber friends. Rowan was a lot less grown up than Posy had been at seventeen. Caro had always enjoyed young people, so she was pleased to have the chance to chat to her.

'So, can I help with the boredom?' she suggested. 'It seems I'm off the hook for a bit.'

Rowan sighed. 'I don't suppose you can. Unless you're an art teacher.'

'Hmm,' said Caro. 'I got an A in my Art GCSE, if that helps.'

'Oh?' Rowan seemed genuinely interested. 'It might, I suppose. I've been home educated but my mum – well, she's funny about art.'

Hoping she'd find out what this meant exactly, Caro kept her tone light. 'Oh, well, I'm not an art teacher – nothing like – but my last job was in an artists' supplies shop. I could advise you on materials with some expertise.' She smiled to indicate she knew that knowing her way round an art shop probably wasn't all that useful.

Rowan laughed. 'I'm fine for materials, thank you. My family are quite happy to give me wonderful boxes of watercolours or pastels, they just don't want to find me a tutor or let me to go away to study.' She bit her lip and turned away, as if she felt she'd said too much to someone she didn't know.

'Plenty of time for that, surely. Your grandfather told me last night that you're seventeen?'

'That's right. And I'm quite old enough to go away to art college.'

Caro nodded. 'Old enough to think about it, certainly. I hope you don't feel I'm prying, but I've got a daughter of twenty. I've been through all the "where do I want to go to uni?" questions.'

Rowan seemed really interested. 'And where did she go?'

'She didn't in the end. She got a great job working for a local artist and now she's gone to see her dad in Australia.'

'Goodness! How do you feel about that?'

Caro shrugged, touched that Rowan realised this wasn't as easy for Caro as it sounded. 'OK, actually. I miss her, of course. She was living with me on my barge in London – but it was the right thing for her to be doing.' Caro laughed. 'She was worried about leaving me, though.'

'She thought she'd miss you? Be homesick? That's what everyone tells me I'll feel. Well, Mum does.'

'Not at all! She was worried about how I'd cope without her to look after me. One of the reasons I took this job was so she could go and not think about me pining on my own on the barge.'

Rowan sat down at the kitchen table and rested her chin in her hands. She reminded Caro of Gally, who was now eating something at their feet. They were both long-legged, a bit gangly, but with a natural grace that was very charming.

'The barge sounds great!' said Rowan. 'Tell me about it.'

Caro was always a bit surprised at how interested everyone was in the barge. She'd lived on boats all her life and so didn't find them particularly exciting. She loved her home and wouldn't consider moving ashore even if she could have afforded to, but it was just a home to her.

'Well, it's quite large. Not huge for a barge but far bigger than a narrow boat.' She realised Rowan didn't know what a narrow boat was. 'I've got some pictures on my laptop. Shall I pop and get it to show you?'

Rowan nodded. 'I'll go and get some of my pictures too, if you'd like to see.'

'I'd really love that!' Caro replied. 'I'm a bit out of my depth here at the moment but I do know a good picture from a bad one and would be thrilled to see your stuff.'

'Supposing you think it's bad?'

But Rowan had an air of mischief about her, a confidence, that told Caro that she wouldn't think that about her pictures.

*

Back in the kitchen half an hour later, Rowan and Caro had started what Caro described as their 'show and tell'. Rowan was finding pictures of the barge intriguing. 'I can't believe there's so much space on a boat!' she kept saying. 'And a garden on top.'

'It's not really a garden. Just herbs in pots, mostly, and a bit of trellis so I can sit up there with a glass of wine and not have to say hello to everyone. Although I do – say hello to them, I mean. The moorings are very sociable, like a little village.'

'And what's happened to the barge now you're here? Will it be OK?'

'I've got a friend living on it. Suits him, and it suits me. He was there before Posy and I left and he may well stay after I get back. He's used to boats and they don't like standing empty, really.'

'It looks amazing! I'd love to see it!'

'No reason why you shouldn't come and stay when I'm back on it.'

'I'd love that, if I'm allowed. I've never been to London.' Rowan sighed. 'And at this rate I'll never get to go.'

'It's one thing wanting to leave home to live in the Big City, but going to stay with a friend would probably be fine.' Caro didn't know this for a fact but surely it wasn't unreasonable? 'What is it you really want to do in London?'

'Go to art college? Is that asking too much?'

Caro could tell Rowan had asked this question before, probably many times. 'Well, I suppose that depends. London isn't the cheapest place to be a student.' She paused. 'Do you want to show me your pictures?'

Rowan sighed. 'I suppose so.'

She had arrived back in the kitchen with an old portfolio, tied together with fraying ribbon, but she'd kept this down beside her chair, apparently reluctant to show Caro the contents.

'Let's see then!'

Rowan lifted the folder and put it on the table. 'Help yourself,' she said. 'I'll go and check on Murdo.' She didn't want to be present while Caro looked, that was obvious.

Caro untied the strings. Inside was quite a large body of work. There were watercolours – views mostly – and as good as many a painting in a gallery. Then there were pencil studies, of flowers, birds, a pair of squirrels on a branch. There were also pencil sketches of people, obviously swiftly drawn but recognisable. There was Murdo, asleep in his chair, hands folded over his tweed-covered stomach. Heather's hands, obviously making pastry; several of Gally, his head, his folded paws, him lying on his back.

The last sheet was covered in small drawings. It was obviously where she made little doodles, just for fun. There was a pair of old boots, all the creases

39

visible, a close-up of a thistle, a pair of kippers, sides of salmon, obviously freshly smoked. Then Caro noticed a picture of a row of little bottles with dropper tops. An electronic scale. A sheet of paper with a pencil. She couldn't read what was on it but it seemed like a list, with calculations beside it. Was this sketch done in the back room of the cottage? she wondered. And if it was, what was going on? Surely it wasn't some sort of drugs factory? Her heart beat faster suddenly. She was overreacting, she knew she was, but if it was perfectly innocent, why couldn't someone just explain why she couldn't stay in the cottage?

Chapter Three

The back door opened and the noise made Caro jump. She turned and saw Alec and she was startled all over again. 'I was just looking at Rowan's pictures,' she said, sounding as guilty as she felt. 'They're very good, aren't they?'

'I suppose so,' said Alec, sounding stressed and hurried rather than the proud father. 'When would you be free to come exploring with me?'

'Alec, are you so desperate to show me the beauties of Glen Liddell or do you want to talk to me privately? Because you could just do that now.'

He laughed and frowned at the same time. 'You're very upfront!'

'No point in not being. I would absolutely love to explore this beautiful place, but I don't want to do it with someone who'd rather be doing something else.'

Caro was proud of herself for sounding so nonchalant while underneath she was desperate for him to remember her.

'I'm assuming you want me to explain why you can't use the cottage when there's obviously no building work going on,' he said, frowning some more.

'That would be good,' she replied.

He sighed. 'I would really like to take you for a drive and a walk, if you're up for it, and while we're doing that I'll explain about the cottage.'

'So it's not a simple explanation then?'

'No.'

'Let's do that then, when I've got time off. I can't predict when that might be.' She gave him a quick smile. 'Oh, here's Rowan. Does Murdo need me?'

Rowan looked at her father before she answered. 'Erm—'

'I'll just pop and check,' said Caro. 'I don't want to get it wrong on my first day.'

'Before you go,' said Alec, 'let's go on our trip this time tomorrow. I'll clear it with Murdo.'

Caro smiled. 'OK!'

Caro's afternoon was mostly spent struggling to remember how to play two-handed bridge, but when Murdo needed another nap, she went back to her plastic caravan to properly settle in.

She was only going to be up here for six weeks or two months at the most, so it didn't really matter where she stayed. But her curiosity was desperately piqued. If Alec didn't tell her what was going on when they went on their expedition together, she would find out for herself. After all, he did owe her an explanation, and if he didn't give her one, it was his own fault if she investigated.

After supper that evening, while she helped Heather clear up, Caro asked if Heather ever had a day off.

'It's fine,' Heather replied. 'It's only this busy while Lennie is away.'

'I'll take that as a "no",' said Caro. 'But I was employed to do "a little light cooking", which means I can take over from you, at least for an evening.'

Heather regarded her doubtfully. 'I usually just cook with what's in the freezer.'

'And that is?'

'Venison, mostly. We don't have to buy that.'

'That sounds like quite a luxury ingredient, if you watch all the cookery shows on television.'

Heather's laugh was more dismissive than amused. 'Really? Not the sort of meat I get presented with, I don't think!'

'I hardly dare ask, but what kind of meat *do* you get presented with?'

'"Deer" just about covers it. It's why I do so many casseroles.'

'Even so,' said Caro briskly. 'I could do the casserole for you one night. Or lots of nights if Murdo doesn't turn up his nose at my cooking.'

'You were only supposed to make Himself the occasional omelette or scrambled egg,' said Heather.

Caro studied her, and did not try and disguise the fact. The woman before her, although only a little older than she was, seemed tired. The family, as far as Caro had had the opportunity to observe, took her for granted. Her husband, though a good man in many ways, probably wasn't the sort to give his wife a foot rub or ask how her day had been.

Caro came to a decision. 'While I am here, I think you should let me help with the cooking. I would really like to do that.'

Heather sighed. 'Well, I'm not saying I wouldn't be grateful, but it's not expected of you.'

'That's fine. I'll help you tomorrow but when I've learnt my way round your kitchen and store cupboard and freezer, I'm determined to give you a few nights off. While I'm here.'

'To be honest, I'm glad enough of the help you've given me already.'

Caro smiled. 'It's been very little but anything I can do, I'd be glad. After all, Murdo spends a lot of time asleep. He doesn't need me all that much.'

'Well, if you could assist me a bit I'd have more time for baking. Murdo dearly loves a bit of cake but I'm no good at them.'

'I'll take over cake duty. Cakes are easy,' said Caro blithely, before adding, 'What sort of a cooker do you have?' There was a range in front of her but she was hoping for something a bit more controllable. She hadn't used a traditional range before.

'There's an electric cooker in the utility,' said Heather. 'Lennie had it put there so we can use it in the summer if we're running short of oil.'

'Thank goodness for that!' said Caro. 'I thought I'd just shot myself in the foot there.'

Heather laughed. 'You get used to the range but it's better for things that are a bit more flexible on temperature.'

While the dishwasher was running, and they were making tea and coffee, Caro said, 'I'm hoping to go for a drive and a walk with Alec tomorrow.'

'Aye, he told me. He's going to bring a pair of Rowan's boots over for you to borrow. Or there's always mine.'

When they'd discussed walking boots and the merits of thick socks for a bit, Caro asked what she'd been longing to ask. 'Do Murdo and Alec get on? Murdo is always very rude about him, but then he's rude about George, and he obviously adores that dog.

Heather sighed and Caro realised that this much-put-upon woman had a lot of reasons to sigh. 'They didn't speak for a while. Alec went off to study and while he was away Frazer Neale came in as factor and took his place rather. When he came back – Alec, that is – he was resentful. So no, they don't really get on.'

'So whose side are you on?' Too late, Caro realised she should never have put Heather in such an awkward position by asking this. But she couldn't take it back.

There was a long silence. Caro could see Heather's effort not to sigh again. 'It's very difficult. I don't take sides.'

Caro allowed herself a small sigh in reply. 'OK, well as long as I can stay friends with everyone while I'm here, that'll be good.'

Alec came to collect Caro after lunch the following day with two pairs of boots for her to try. He was quite particular about her choice and insisted on doing them up for her. Having him at her feet was quite an odd experience but it gave Caro a chance to study his head for quite a long time.

'There,' he said, straightening up. 'How do those feel?'

'A bit tight, to be honest.'

'In the length, or the width?'

'It's the lacing. They were fine before you did them up.'

'They're supposed to be tight. Don't worry about it.'

'I must remember never to ask you to do up my corset,' Caro said, without thinking. 'I'd probably faint.'

His expression was a picture of bafflement and then amusement, which he tried to conceal. Caro was suddenly sent back in time to a Greek island. It was dark and she and Alec (Xander as he was then) had just met. She'd said something, and she couldn't remember what, but she knew she'd spoken without thinking and what had come out was a bit weird. He'd looked at her then with exactly the same expression he was looking at her with now.

'Sorry, I didn't mean to say that out loud,' she apologised. 'I mean, for some reason I made the connection and I should have just kept my mouth shut. Oh, never mind.'

He looked at her and for a second she thought that perhaps he had recognised her. There was intentness in his gaze.

He moved closer and breathed in. 'Would you mind if I asked you what scent you're wearing?'

'It's Royal Water by Creed.'

'I thought I recognised it. It's unusual.'

'It's also horrendously expensive so I don't wear it all the time,' said Caro. 'My mother and my grand-mother both used it.'

Continuing to study her for a few moments, he frowned and shook his head; and then he smiled. It really was like the sun coming out from behind a cloud, thought Caro. It was impossible not to feel warmed by it.

'Come on,' he said, 'we'd better set off. We don't want Murdo having to watch *Pointless* on his own.'

But although she laughed, as she followed him out to the car she felt instead of drawing a bit closer to Alec she was suddenly much further away. For some reason, he resented her presence. Was it because he felt guilty about the cottage? Surely it couldn't just be that. There must be something else that was wrong.

They didn't speak as they drove. Caro wanted to see the view and Alec obviously didn't want to make lighthearted conversation. But the silence wasn't awkward in any way, they were both happy to be in their thoughts.

He took a different track from the one they had followed when she was with Rab and then Murdo. They were going away from the estate, up through the forest and then down again.

Eventually they came out of the trees and suddenly they could see a lochan.

The change of scene took Caro aback. Where there'd been trees and tracks and the occasional glimpse of a mountain, now there was an expanse of green broken up by the occasional boulder and beyond that the water, and beyond that a distant mountain range, catching the light where the sunshine hit their snowy tops. 'Gosh! What a view.

I wasn't expecting that at all!' said Caro, when she could speak.

'You like it?'

She caught him looking at her, obviously wanting her to like it. 'It's stunning. And such a surprise.'

'I've driven up the track and seen that view my whole life, on and off, and it still takes my breath away.'

'I can imagine.'

'Come on. Time to get out and walk.'

'I can't believe there is still snow on the mountains.'

He smiled at her. 'We have snow on the highest tops until the end of May up here. Early June, some years.'

'Scotland really is a different country, isn't it?'

'It definitely is. I hope you'll come to love it as much as I do.'

She didn't ask him to explain this slightly curious remark – it was nicer not knowing.

Caro was glad of her boots and equally glad they were tightly laced. They made her ankles feel protected, as if they couldn't twist. She strode out with confidence next to him. Considering he was tall and she wasn't, she did well.

They had been walking along a path towards the lochan a little way when they came across a barbed-wire fence.

'Can you manage?' he asked. 'I'll hold the wire up for you.'

'But should we go through it, if the path is blocked? Doesn't it mean it belongs to someone who doesn't want us here?'

'It's part of the original estate,' said Alec. 'It's fine for us to walk on it. Oh, look!' He pointed to a large brown bird of prey. 'A hen harrier. Can you see it? It's a male.'

He handed her a pair of binoculars she hadn't even noticed he was wearing round his neck.

After a bit of searching she saw it. Mostly grey and white, it had a ghostly quality. 'Gosh. I've never seen one before.'

'They're quite rare. We just have to hope this one is safe.'

'Why wouldn't it be? I wouldn't take it on!'

He laughed. 'Nor would I. Those talons are amazingly strong. Currently this is a nature reserve. Everything is protected. But that's going to change.'

Caro was about to ask how when he held up his hand. 'Hear that? Curlews. They'll be going down to the shoreline to feed.'

'I love the sound they make,' she said.

'Yes. The Gaelic word for them is supposedly onomatopoeic and sounds like their cry, but I must admit I've never managed to make it work in my head. Probably because my Gaelic isn't good enough.'

'But you seem to know a fair bit about birds.'

'I know the wildlife of this area well. I've been watching it all my life – with a few gaps.'

He went on to tell her how otters could be seen in the early mornings and at dusk, how deer came down to drink and what a large range of waders and other birds used the area.

'It's very special. I feel very privileged to see it.' Caro didn't add, because it didn't seem necessary, that she also felt desperately sad at the prospect of it all changing.

'Still! I'm sure it will make an absolutely fabulous golf links,' Alec said bitterly.

'I can't believe anyone would do that to a place like this,' said Caro. 'I mean you can play golf anywhere, can't you?'

He shrugged. 'I don't know. I've never played it.' Then he smiled. 'Come on. We shouldn't get gloomy. We must make sure you have a good time while you're here. Even if your accommodation isn't what you expected. It was very kind of you not to tell Murdo about that, by the way.' He paused. 'Why didn't you?'

Caro shrugged. 'I thought there was probably a good reason and now I'm very much hoping that you're going to tell me what it is.'

He looked down at her, his craggy, interesting face half amused, half horribly caught out. 'Would you hate me if I didn't?'

51

'Would it matter if I did?'

'Are you one of those annoying people who always answer a question with a question? The fact is, I'm developing a little business and it's something my father would hate but I can do it alongside running the estate. I worry that if I told you what it was you'd have to tell him if he asked you any probing questions.'

'Is he likely to do that?' She was intrigued and a bit horrified.

'I don't suppose so. I just don't want to take the risk. It's not really so much that he'll shout at me – although they'd hear it in Edinburgh if he did – it's that I don't want him being upset. Being angry isn't good for him now he's so elderly and a bit frail.'

'I'll try not to see that as an excuse for not telling me.'

'It's a reason, rather. Now, let's enjoy our walk while we can. You're not going to be here for ever and possibly neither is this perfect bit of land. I'd like to appreciate both while I've got the opportunity.'

He took her arm and together they negotiated the rocks and small hillocks that were dotted among the grass while she took in the fact that he'd paid her a compliment.

'So your father sold this bit of land, then?' she asked when she felt she could sound casual.

'Yes. It happened while I was away on the oil rigs. I was *persona non grata* with Murdo. But then I came home and found he and his factor had done it, without consulting me.'

'Presumably Murdo needed the money for something. The smokery? Some new enterprise? Everyone needs to diversify these days.'

'The smokery would have managed just fine without the money from this land and the house certainly hasn't seen any of it.'

'There must have been some reason—'

'Indeed. I'm just not sure what the reason is – was. I hope he didn't do it just to prove the estate was his to do what he liked with until he actually dies.'

Alec spoke calmly, without expression but Caro could sense the bitterness. 'That does sound quite extreme.'

'It does. But if that was his reason, it worked. My father was very angry with me for studying chemistry instead of estate management. He didn't think – doesn't think – that there's anything anyone needs to know about the world that can't be learnt here. But I'm afraid my interests do extend a bit beyond all this.' He made a sweeping gesture. 'Although on a day like today, I sometimes wonder at it myself.'

If she'd known him better she might have told him she thought his daughter Rowan felt a bit like that too.

'I don't know why I'm telling you all this,' Alec went on. 'You must be easy to talk to.'

'I am generally considered to be a good listener,' she conceded.

'And I'm probably feeling bad because I won't tell you any more about the cottage.'

'You're worried that my loyalty is to Murdo? And that I might tell him what you're up to?'

He smiled. 'I suppose so.' They walked on in silence for a few paces. 'Your frankness is – refreshing. My ex-wife couldn't be straightforward about anything, even the simplest things.'

'It does get me into trouble sometimes,' admitted Caro. 'My daughter says I don't have a filter and whatever is in my head comes out of my mouth. And yet, actually, I'm very good at keeping secrets.'

Over the next couple of weeks, Caro spent time learning her way round Heather's kitchen and store-rooms (with generally acceptable results), dragging up all she'd ever known about sport, pop music and the periodic table for *Pointless*, helping Rowan with her art (which was mainly saying, 'Golly, you're good!') and sharpening up her chess game.

She also drove and rambled over the estate, getting to know the tracks and the wildlife. She even helped out at the smokery one afternoon.

Then, one beautiful morning in mid-May, she happened to find herself walking through the woods to the cottage. Curiosity overcame her like a disease. She ran up the path and tried the front door. It was unlocked.

Like Goldilocks, she couldn't resist and went in.

The cottage opened directly into the main room which had stone, whitewashed walls and a small window each side. A huge fireplace with a wood burner took up most of one wall and there was a narrow staircase in the corner. A sofa was pulled up near the fire and there were bookcases in the alcoves next to the fireplace. Window seats showed how thick the walls were and long, woollen curtains were obviously designed to keep the cold out. It was her dream Scottish cottage, the little house she had imagined before she came up here. Had she not been invested in her job and the area for other reasons, she might have shed a little tear for what could have been. A plastic caravan was no substitute for this gem.

'The kitchen might be horrible,' she muttered to herself. 'It'll be a little lean-to, cold and ill equipped.'

But it wasn't horrible. It was fairly chilly but there was a range cooker, unlit, and if that had been burning it would have been toasty warm. There was a mantelpiece over it on which were a selection of candlesticks, old plates and some very wood-smoked pictures. There was a scrubbed wooden table, big enough for the four wooden chairs that were drawn up to it. Like the living room, it was perfect.

'Your excuse for keeping me out of here had better be bloody good, Alec McLean,' she said aloud.

She turned and looked back and saw rows of shelves on the wall opposite the window. On the shelves were little bottles with pipette tops, carefully labelled. She leant in and read some of them. 'Hedione', 'Oud', 'Neroli' – what on earth were those?

On a shelf in front of the rows of bottles was a notebook. It was open so it didn't seem as if she'd be prying more than she had been before if she read it. There were mathematical calculations and lists of more strange-sounding ingredients.

'So, what do you think?' said a voice from the back door.

She shot round. Alec was standing there, his hands on his hips. As he had his back against the light it was hard to read his expression but his stance implied annoyance mixed with resignation.

'You couldn't wait for me to tell you what I've been up to in here?'

She did feel horribly guilty but also justified. 'You wouldn't tell me; I had to find out for myself.' She paused. 'Although, to be fair, I'm still none the wiser. What are these strange ingredients for?' But as she spoke she suddenly realised she knew. 'Are you making perfume here?'

His head inclined a little. 'What makes you think that?'

'The ingredients – the labels on the bottles. I couldn't make sense of them at first but now I remember reading something in a magazine about making perfume. It was fascinating!' But really it was because she remembered a young man she could hardly see telling her of his dream, his passion for fragrance. She paused. 'This has been a long-time interest for you, hasn't it?'

He nodded. 'And it's one none of my family can remotely understand. My father ... Well, I don't need to tell you what he thinks about a son of his making perfume – scent, he calls it.'

She laughed. 'I can imagine he'd prefer you to set up business as a professional deer grallocher or something.'

He laughed too. 'If such a profession existed, he would infinitely prefer I did that for a living. Taking the intestines out of freshly stalked deer is very much more his thing.'

Caro wrinkled her nose. 'Tell me about the perfume. How long have you been making it?'

'Not long enough. When I came back from studying it – in France – and had spent a few years on the oil rigs, there was so much to do on the estate I hardly had time. And it's hard enough to start up on your own even if you have your family behind you. And I don't.'

'What about your sister? Isn't Lennie interested in perfume?'

'She's not against me doing it in principle but she doesn't much care about it. She's quite happy to splash a bit of something on if I give it to her, but only as long as she remembers. Skye is the same. And in their hearts they both think I should do something more manly.'

'I remember this magazine article saying that originally only men wore perfume and that women who did were considered prostitutes – or perhaps they were prostitutes.' She smiled. 'I bet Heather is on your side though.'

'What makes you say that?'

'Because she put a hot-water bottle in my bed the first night. She wouldn't have done that if she didn't want to make me feel cherished. Because if I'm cherished I won't grumble about the caravan too much.'

He laughed properly now. 'Poor Caro! Is the caravan really that bad?'

'It smells,' she said. But she'd have put up with it smelling like a sewage farm if it would make him look at her like that again. It was a look full of warmth and sympathy and something that may have been interest. She looked at her watch. 'I should be getting back. Murdo will be needing his tea and shortbread.'

'I know I don't need to ask you—' he began.

'No, you don't need to ask me,' she said quickly before he could ask her anything. 'I won't tell

Murdo, or anyone, about this project. But for the record, I think it's great!'

She turned and went out of the back door without waiting to see his reaction.

When back at the house, although it wasn't quite time for tea, she went to check on Murdo before she put the kettle on.

He was lying on the floor.

Chapter Four

A strange sort of calm came over Caro as she ran to Murdo. She found his pulse and as she held his wrist he started to stir. George, the little dog, tried to get between her and his master.

Polite but firm, she moved George aside.

'Hi, Murdo, you seem to have fallen out of your chair. Are you all right?'

He grunted and George licked his face.

'Can you smile?' She'd had to go through this once with her own father and at the time had been extremely grateful that she'd rehearsed it with him. Sadly she hadn't done this with Murdo; he might not react well to being asked to smile in a non-smiling situation.

Murdo mumbled and turned his head away from the dog's caring tongue.

Caro put a pillow under his head and then pulled out her phone from her back pocket. Praying there was enough signal, she tapped in 999.

She knew it would take a while for the ambulance to get there, so she covered Murdo with a couple of tartan blankets and generally made him comfortable. Then she went to the house phone to call the rest of the family.

No one seemed to be answering their mobiles so she left messages. She'd just signed off from Rowan, having said, 'Your grandfather is ill. It would be good if you could come over,' when Murdo spoke.

'What am I doing lying here?' he said. His speech was a bit slurred but he didn't sound too bad.

'I think you've had a small stroke, Murdo. I won't try to get you up as I'm not strong enough, but I'll try to keep you comfy until the ambulance comes.'

'Ambulance? I don't need an ambulance! Fell out of my chair while I was asleep.'

'Well, the ambulance is on its way. If there's nothing wrong with you, they'll go away again.'

Caro spoke calmly but she knew perfectly well that the ambulance would send him to hospital to be checked over, even if he hadn't had a stroke. 'There is a test we can do now though,' she went on.

'Uh?'

'Can you smile?' He hadn't responded when she'd asked him before.

'What have I got to smile about?' His grumpiness was encouraging. 'I'm lying on the floor and you won't help me up in case you do your back in.'

His usual crisp diction was missing but his emotions all seemed as usual.

'I've called all your family, so one of the men might arrive soon and between us we could get you on to the sofa. Now I'll make the fire up to stop you getting cold.'

'None of me family care about me. If Frazer were still here it would be different.'

It was unlike Murdo to sound sentimental but maybe this softer side should be encouraged. 'Tell me about him.' Caro felt a bit guilty for getting Murdo to talk about Frazer but he had brought the subject up himself and she didn't want him to slip into unconsciousness again while she was on her own with him.

'Like a son to me, he was. Took more interest in the estate than Alexander ever did.'

It took Caro a second to realise he was referring to Alec.

Caro couldn't help sticking up for Alec. Ever since he'd told her that bit of land by the lochan which was so beautiful was going to be turned into a golf course because Frazer and Murdo had sold it, she had been prejudiced against the former factor. 'But that was his job, though, wasn't it? To take an interest in the estate?'

'I suppose so. But he left the moment he heard Alexander was coming home.'

Caro thought about this. She'd thought Alec had to come home because Frazer was leaving. 'Do you ever hear from Frazer? Does he keep in touch? Do you keep in touch with him?'

'No. But I'd like to. I must ask m'daughter if we've got an address for him. When she comes home,' he added, eyeing Caro in a way that clearly said, 'I have not lost my marbles, even if I am lying on the floor covered in blankets.'

'Is there anything I can do to make you more comfortable?'

'Half a tumbler of Glenmorangie would help.'

'No,' said Caro. 'Not even a cup of tea.' She paused. 'My father had a stroke – not a bad one; he recovered completely – but afterwards I read up on it so I knew what to do if it happened again. You mustn't have anything to eat or drink.'

'You're a hard woman. I know Frazer would have given me a drink by now.'

'I'm sure he would,' said Caro, her tone making it clear what she thought about that.

'If you're not going to give me a drink, or even a cup of tea, I might as well continue with my nap. I'm feeling quite sleepy.'

'Sorry. That's not allowed either.'

'What? I only want to go to sleep!'

'I promise I'm only looking after your best interests by keeping you awake. Tell me some more about Frazer. Why did you like him so much?'

'I don't want to talk, I want to sleep!'

'I can't let you.'

'You're a sadist!' said Murdo.

'I know. It's what makes me good at my job. So tell me about the estate. What was it like when you were a boy?'

'Well, it was a hell of a lot better than it is now! Me and m'sisters used to roam around all day on our ponies. No "health and safety" then. The estate was a lot bigger and we didn't have to have a smokery or anything like that on it.'

'So how did it support itself?'

'The shooting, stalking, rents. I inherited a lot of debt and death duties when my father died.'

'Is that why you built the smokery?' Murdo sounded drowsy and Caro was concerned he might nod off in spite of her best efforts.

'That's far more recent. We sold off quite a lot of land. I wanted to keep what was left intact, but Frazer recommended selling off the bit by the lochan so I did.'

'There was no alternative?'

'I suggested a few but Frazer was determined we should sell. He had a buyer. It all went through quite quickly. He knew more about it all than I did.'

'And you made enough to put in order everything that was left?'

'I don't want to discuss it if you don't mind.'

'I'll take that as a "no".' Caro didn't take this personally but it was a bit worrying that he didn't want to talk about the sale. She felt it meant he wasn't really happy about it. Had he been pushed into it for some reason?

To her relief, Ewan, Heather's husband, appeared. After a bit of careful questioning of Murdo and some discussion with Caro, they decided not to try and move Murdo. In spite of his grumblings, he seemed comfortable enough on the floor.

Soon afterwards the ambulance crew arrived. Caro took the opportunity to put the kettle on. Murdo might not be allowed tea but she was desperate for a cup herself. She drank it secretly in the kitchen and then refilled the kettle. There might be more refreshments required. The ambulance people had been so brilliant – if they had time for a quick cuppa she wanted to make sure they got one.

The crew were still doing tests on Murdo when Alec and Rowan arrived.

Alec went straight over to Murdo, obviously very concerned. 'Dad? Are you all right?'

'I wouldn't be lying here if I was all right!' said Murdo brusquely.

Caro had become very fond of her charge but just now she wanted to give him a good talking-to. He'd been perfectly polite to everyone else who'd asked after him; why couldn't he make the same effort with his son?

The ambulance team had finally finished their assessment and were loading Murdo into their vehicle when Skye turned up. Ignoring everything that was going on outside the house she swept into the drawing room.

'I know it must be tricky for you,' she said to Caro, 'but FYI, don't ring me again if Murdo has a fall. He's my ex-father-in-law, and I don't have time to look after him as well as everything else. It's not as if there aren't a zillion people ready to do that!' Her eyes swept the room where Alec, Heather, Ewan, Caro and Rowan were all standing.

'What are you doing here, Ro?' she asked. 'If you've nothing better to do you can help me change beds. I've got twelve people coming for a yoga retreat tomorrow and I'm up to my eyes!'

She swept out of the room and then came back in. 'Well, come on, Rowan! Your grandfather will be just fine, I'm sure!'

Rowan looked at her father for confirmation.

'He will be all right, sweetheart,' Alec said.

'I expect he will be OK, Rowan,' said Caro. 'It seems he's had a little stroke but my father had one like that and completely recovered.'

'But he's not alive now though, is he?' said Rowan, her voice shaking.

'No, but he had his stroke in his seventies and lived to be over eighty,' said Caro.

'I'll call you when he's been assessed in hospital,' said Alec reassuringly. 'You'd better go and help your mother.'

Alec went with his father in the ambulance. Ewan went back to doing what he had been before he got the call, and Heather and Caro went into the kitchen.

'Definitely tea and shortbread,' said Heather.

'I am fairly certain that Murdo will be OK,' said Caro, aware that Heather was also quite upset. 'They're just taking him in to be sure.'

'I know. And I've rung Lennie. She doesn't want to leave her daughter just at this moment but she's going to look at flights and come home as soon as she can.'

'Is her daughter all right to be left with the baby?'

'I think so. She says she can always go back if she has to.' Heather put a mug of tea in front of Caro. 'I'm going to miss you though.' She turned away to find the shortbread tin. 'You seem to have really got the place, if you know what I mean. Not everyone does.'

Caro was touched. Heather wasn't one for showing her feelings on the whole. Yet at the same time she was taken aback for a second or two. Of course, with Lennie coming back her own time here would be cut short. She cleared her throat. 'It's so beautiful here I don't know how anyone could fail to love it.'

'It's also a bit scruffy,' said Heather.

'Shabby chic,' said Caro and then laughed at Heather's expression.

'Then there was the whole fiasco about the cottage,' Heather went on, refusing to be amused. 'Lennie is going to be furious when she finds out you haven't been in it. Alec promised it would all be sorted out in time for your arrival.'

'I've got quite fond of my caravan. The views are amazing and it's cosy once you understand how the heating works.'

'And you've been brilliant with Murdo too. He's not easy.'

'I lived with my father for years before he died. It was a good apprenticeship.' She swallowed to clear her throat of the sudden tears that had gathered there.

'It's easy with fathers and daughter,' said Heather. 'My daughter can get anything she wants from Ewan but my son has to get round me!' She chuckled briefly.

'What are they up to now? Your children?'

'Spreading their wings. They grew up here but they want to see a bit of the world before they decide whether to come back here to settle down. They're young yet.'

'That's the same as my daughter, only she's visiting her father in Australia. He emigrated years ago.' Caro paused, thinking how she'd got together with Posy's father because she was on the rebound from one brief night on a Greek island. 'Selfishly I hope she doesn't settle there, but if she does, well, I'm sure she'll make a go of it.

'It's a shame that Rowan isn't getting the same chance to see a bit of the world.'

Caro realised that Heather must have been shaken up to criticise the family. She was very loyal.

Caro shrugged. 'Rowan is a bit young to go back-packing round South America or anything, I agree. But she should be thinking about her further educa-tion.'

'She is thinking about it!' said Heather. 'Talking about it, even, but her mother doesn't listen. And if Alec—' Heather paused. 'Well, I won't go on.'

'Skye gets difficult?' suggested Caro tentatively.

Heather's pursed lips and disapproving expres-sion gave Caro her answer.

'Rowan's a very talented artist,' Caro went on, to stop Heather feeling awkward about having been critical of Skye and Alec. 'As far as I can judge. She could go to art school in Edinburgh or Glasgow. I know they're not exactly near, but near enough to stop her parents from worrying, I'd have thought.'

'The trouble is, Alec would let her go but Skye thinks she'll go on drugs and get pregnant during her first week at uni.' Heather obviously felt strongly about this. 'But if her parents were agreed on the matter it would help.'

Caro nodded. 'Although I agree that Rowan should go away to study, being so beautiful will make her a bit vulnerable.'

'She wouldn't be so vulnerable if she'd mixed with kids her own age more and had a chance to toughen up a bit!' Heather sighed. 'Anyway, it's nothing to do with us!'

A week after his stroke, Murdo was still in hospital having tests. The plan was to move him from the big hospital in Glasgow to the small hospital that was much nearer Glen Liddell but the paperwork as well as the tests seemed to be taking a long time.

Although he stated he was furious about this, it seemed to Caro, when it was her turn to go in and see him, that he was happy enough. The hospital he was in currently was three hours away and so people took it in turns to visit. It would be much easier for everyone if he were nearer home.

When she went, she read to him out of the paper, listened to his complaints and told him not to grumble. But as she drove home, she realised her role was nearly over and she should plan to go back to London. Lennie would be flying back any day now and apart from visiting Murdo in hospital, there was nothing for her to do, officially. Of course she made herself very useful and was never idle, but would the estate be willing to pay her if she wasn't really needed?

She'd miss being up here terribly, she realised. It was so beautiful, she liked everyone so much, and she still nursed a sort of schoolgirl crush on Alec. Although they had almost shared a moment on their walk together and again when he'd found her in the cottage, since Murdo had been ill, he was so busy she hardly ever saw him. It would be madness to think he might come to return her feelings and even if he did, it couldn't go anywhere, with her in London and him up here. Far healthier for her to accept defeat and go home.

Although she talked about it with Heather, waiting for a chance to officially give her notice in to Alec, the person she felt would miss her most was Rowan, so she thought she'd tell her separately.

She suggested a walk with Gally the following morning. The sun was shining and she hoped that Rowan would bring her sketchbook and lean against a rock and draw. This would give Caro a chance to tell Rowan her plans. George, an older dog, had declined the invitation to join them.

As Caro and Rowan walked along, watching Gally running around, smelling everything, full of joy, Caro discovered that although spring was late to appear in Scotland its shy beauty was breathtaking.

The larches were fuzzed with green and the birch trees were bright with new foliage. The fact that it could snow the following day made it even more special.

'I'm going to have to go back soon,' said Caro when Rowan had pulled a sketch pad out of her pocket and was concentrating on a sprig of larch cones, her pencil recreating nature in front of Caro's eyes. The pencil stopped moving.

'Do you have to?'

'I do. Lennie's coming back and Murdo will be out of hospital soon. I won't be needed when Lennie gets here.'

'I like Lennie but she doesn't understand art like you do. None of my family do. They all just think it's little Rowan drawing pictures.'

'I'm not an expert, Ro, I've told you millions of times, but I do think you're talented. If you like I'll talk to your mother about you going to art college? Reassure her about it a bit?'

'You can try,' said Rowan. 'But if she doesn't go on about evil influences she'll say it's all too expensive.'

'I'm sure there are grants and things. I thought if Scottish students went to university in Scotland they didn't have to pay?'

'But I want to go to London.'

'Honey, art schools won't be any better in London than they are in Scotland.'

'I know, but I really want to go there. And anyway there is money! My grandmother left me some to be spent on my education. My mother just makes excuses.'

'What about your dad? Would he support you? If you really wanted to go?'

Rowan shrugged and went back to her drawing. 'I don't know. He mostly backs up Mum.'

'Try him on the art school thing.'

'Could you talk to him about it?'

'It's not really my place to talk about your education. I'm here for Murdo and it's not as if I'm a professional teacher or anything.'

'My parents have been quite happy to use you, though. Haven't they?' Rowan glanced up at her and Caro realised she was being sketched.

'I've enjoyed your company. It stops me missing Posy so much, having you to chat to.'

'I think Posy is really brave, going all the way to Australia to see her dad when she didn't really know him.'

'All she had to do was sit on a plane for twenty-four hours and be met the other end,' said Caro, laughing. 'Although I did think it was pretty brave of her. But it's all working out really well.'

'I really don't want you to leave,' said Rowan. 'Couldn't you find something else to do up here? You're my friend without being paid to be. Although perhaps you could be my tutor?'

Caro smiled. 'I'm not remotely qualified although I have really enjoyed getting to know you. And I'm going to miss you too. In fact, when I'm settled back on the barge you must come and stay. You can go to London City Airport and I'll meet you. I know it's three hours to Glasgow but Skye will probably be OK about it if she knows you're being met the other end.'

'I'd love that!'

'We could go and visit all the art galleries.'

'And the art schools!'

'Well, you may need a parent for that, but we could certainly go and look at them from the outside.'

'That would be brilliant! I feel if I could just get to London, anything would be possible.'

Caro caught up with Alec when he came back from visiting Murdo. He seemed even more preoccupied than usual but when she started to explain he frowned.

'Come into the drawing room where we can talk.'

She followed him in and sat on the sofa while he made up the fire and poured two enormous glasses of whisky. He handed him hers without asking and then sat down.

'What was it you wanted to say?'

'That it's time for me to leave. Lennie's on her way home. You won't need me when she's here.'

'Won't we? Are you sure? You've been brilliant.'

His praise and his smile were more warming than the whisky.

'I haven't done a lot—'

'You've been great with Rowan and Murdo will miss you too.'

'Is he OK? He was doing well yesterday.'

Alec frowned a little, inspecting the liquid in his glass, not seeing it. 'I'm worried about him.'

'Any particular reason?'

'I don't feel he's right in himself, really.'

'In what way?' Caro took another sip of her whisky, hoping she didn't get too fond of a habit she couldn't afford.

'He's a bit – needy. He and I haven't got on for years but somehow he's a bit clingy now. He keeps talking about Frazer. Wants to talk to him.'

'Just talk? Or is it about something particular?'

'I don't know.' He sighed and took another large gulp of whisky. 'I'm going to track him down and see if he'll come and see the old man. It's what he wants.'

'But you're also worried about Murdo's health?'

'I think there's something else going on that isn't just a mild stroke. But I don't think anyone knows anything for definite so won't say.' He sighed again. 'Lennie might be able to find out more when she comes. She and Murdo get on really well.'

'Fathers and daughters,' said Caro. 'I got on really well with my dad.'

'Although I'm not as close to Rowan as I'd like to be. She's with her mother so much and I don't think Skye obeys the convention that you don't run down the child's parent even if you are divorced.'

Caro laughed. 'I think that one must be hard. I didn't have that problem with my daughter because her father went back to Australia so soon after she was born.'

'Tough on you, though. You were an entirely single parent.'

Caro shook her head. 'I knew we weren't destined to stay together forever and being pregnant meant I didn't have to finish university which I didn't really want to do. So I moved on to my barge with my father. He was a brilliant dad substitute.'

She took another sip of whisky and a deep breath. This could be the moment to tell him that she remembered him as a boy called Xander on a Greek island nearly twenty-three years ago. But she couldn't, not when he didn't remember her.

She could also use this moment of quiet, when it was just the two of them, to get him to talk more about his perfume business, about her own interest in it. But what would be the point? She was going back to London and this would have been a lovely idyll. Not quite as lovely an idyll as the Greek island and Xander had been, but lovely enough.

'So what will you do, when you're back in London?'

'Job hunt.'

'Caro, really I'd love it if you could stay here longer – we all would – especially Rowan, but—'

'It's all right. I understand. You can't justify my wages. It's fine. It's been a really good experience but now it's time for me to go.'

'Tell me when it's convenient for you and I'll organise your flight.'

'There's no need—'

'Of course there is! Lennie would have my guts for garters if I didn't pay for your flight!'

The evening before she was due to leave, Caro, Heather and Ewan were sitting round the table having a cup of tea after supper when Skye came rushing through the back door.

'Where's Rowan?' she said accusingly.

'She's not here,' said Caro calmly. 'Is she with Alec?'

'Alec's disappeared off somewhere. An errand for Murdo, I think. God knows why. He's never been able to stand his father.' Skye seemed really worried.

'Sit down and have a cup of tea,' said Caro. 'She can't be far away.'

Skye flopped down into a chair. 'We had a terrible row yesterday. She didn't come back last night. I assumed she was at Alec's until I texted him and found out he wasn't at home.'

Caro bit back her expression of dismay. Skye was worried enough already; she didn't need more people throwing up their hands in horror.

'Maybe she's gone to see a friend?' she said, aware she'd never heard Rowan talk about any local friends.

'She hasn't got any friends.' Skye looked ashen. 'I think she's run away.'

Chapter Five

Caro met Skye's eyes and for the first time the women connected, united in their anxiety.

'What was the row about?' asked Caro gently.

'What it's always about! Going to London!' Skye pushed her fingers through her hair, obviously distraught.

Caro felt sick. 'Then maybe that's where she is?'

'Don't be ridiculous! How could she get there?' Skye seemed to think this was impossible, but Caro knew it wasn't – she'd told Rowan how to do it!

'Just let me make a call,' she said. 'I think this may be my fault.'

'I knew it!' said Skye. 'Bring in an outside influence and look what happens.'

Heather pursed her lips but didn't speak. Perhaps it had crossed her mind, as it had Caro's, that for someone who didn't like outside influences for her daughter she'd let Rowan spend a lot of time with Caro.

But instead of mentioning this, Caro left the table and went into the corner of the room, hoping for a signal on her phone. She was lucky. She was back at the table within minutes.

'It's OK!' she said delightedly. 'She's safe. She went to the barge in London. My friend Joe is looking after her.' She gave a sigh of relief.

'What?' said Skye, her voice squeaky with disbelief. 'What do you mean, the barge?'

'I live on a barge in London, normally, and I've talked about it to Rowan. I suggested she came to stay with me when I'm back there and told her how easy it was to get to.' A pang of remorse hit her. 'It never occurred to me she'd go when I wasn't there.'

'Well, you must bring her back the moment you arrive home! You're leaving tomorrow, aren't you?'

'But, Skye,' said Caro, 'I can't make Rowan do anything if she doesn't want to do it. If you want her back, you'll have to get her. I have no authority over her.'

'You can tell her you don't want her staying!' said Skye.

'Yes, but supposing we had a huge row and she walked off into the night? She'd be alone in the middle of a big city.'

But Skye wasn't listening. 'And who's this Joe you say is looking after her? Who is he? Is he safe? How do I know he won't rape her?'

'I've known him for years! He used to babysit Posy when she was little—' Of course there were no guarantees of anything, but of this Caro was certain: that Rowan would come to no harm from Joe.

'And you were happy with that arrangement, were you? You were happy for a man to look after your daughter?' Skye was getting more and more worked up. Maybe it was relief that she knew where Rowan was that was making her so unreasonable.

'Yes,' said Caro calmly. 'I knew him – I know him – and I know that Rowan will be in safe hands. It's good that he's there to look after her.'

'I can't believe how irresponsible you're being!' said Skye as if Caro alone had created this situation.

'Tea, anyone?' suggested Heather.

'Yes please,' said Caro. Her mouth had gone dry with the effort of trying to calm Skye down.

'Tea is not going to solve this disaster!' declared Skye, her green eyes flashing impressively.

'It's not a disaster,' said Caro. 'It's a bit unfortunate and obviously extremely worrying for you, but it could have been so much worse.'

'Oh, I doubt that!' said Skye. 'How could it have been worse?'

Caro hesitated. Did Skye really need her to spell out the different dreadful scenarios that could have happened instead of Rowan running to a known destination with someone Caro knew to be kind and caring?

'At least we know where she is,' said Heather quietly, opening the shortbread tin.

Caro longed for a bit of shortbread, made by Heather and known to be delicious. But she couldn't bring herself to crunch away while Skye was so distressed.

'I've got an idea,' said Caro. 'Why don't you come back with me to London tomorrow and stay on the barge for a little while with Rowan? You could visit some art galleries and—' She'd been about to suggest that they checked out art schools but remembered just in time that this wouldn't go down well.

'If you think I've got time to go visiting when I've got a fully booked yoga retreat coming up you must be mad!' said Skye.

'OK,' said Caro, regretting giving up the shortbread when Skye was being so unreasonable. 'Come with me anyway and see if you can get Rowan to come home with you?'

'Are you deaf? Didn't you hear me say I've got a fully booked yoga retreat coming up?' Skye's eyes flashed again and Caro wondered if it was too late for her to learn the technique.

'But surely—'

Before Caro could finish, Skye's phone went off and she answered.

'Hi. Yes, we know where she is. She's in London on—' A tiny hesitation where Caro could almost hear Skye stop herself from calling her 'that woman'. '—Caro's barge,' she said instead.

Caro assumed she was talking to Alec.

'I'll get her to bring Rowan straight back here,' said Skye. There was a brief pause when presumably Alec was saying something and then Skye passed the phone over to Caro. 'He wants to speak to you.'

'Alec?' said Caro. Skye nodded.

'Hi,' he said. 'So sorry you've got involved in all this. Are you really offering to bring Rowan back?'

'No, I'm not,' said Caro, and then moved away from the table so she could speak more privately. 'Skye has only just voiced that idea, but I'm not willing and I don't think it would work.'

'Wouldn't it?' Alec sounded despairing and tired.

'No. Rowan's made the grand gesture, running away from home, why should she meekly go back up to Scotland with me when she's only been in London a day?' She paused. 'Would you come down and get her?'

'I would, but only if I have to. Sorry to sound as if I don't care about my daughter, but I'm on the trail of Frazer and, for my father's sake, I really need to speak to him. He's apparently going off somewhere soon and tomorrow is my only day.' He sighed. 'Can you give the phone back to Skye?'

Heather and Caro studied the table while Skye had quite an audible row with her ex-husband. Eventually she disconnected and threw the phone on to the table.

'He's useless!' she said.

'I tell you what I suggest,' said Caro, who was suddenly filled with a longing to go to bed. 'I go home tomorrow as arranged, and then let Rowan stay with me for, say, a week, and then either you, or her father, can come and collect her. Or I'll bring her home?'

'But why would you bring her home after a week if it won't work if you did it tomorrow?' asked Skye, ignoring the suggestions that she or Alec did the bringing Rowan home part.

'Because she'd have had a week in London, which she longs for! She may be delighted to go home after all that excitement ...' Caro paused. 'Didn't you ever visit London when you were a teenager?'

'Yes!' declared Skye. 'Which is why I'm so determined that my daughter won't now!'

Caro exhaled. 'Look, I understand that it looks as if you're rewarding bad behaviour if you let her stay for a week but she's wanted to go to London for ages. I think a week in all the traffic and noise will cure her of it. Give her a week, then she can come home – on her own – and settle down. Then when she goes to art school in Glasgow or Edinburgh she'll have done London and she'll be fine.'

'She's not going to art school.' Skye was very definite about this.

'Listen, Skye, I'm older than you—'

'Quite a lot older!'

'—and I have a daughter who is a bit older than Rowan. I'm ahead of you on the path of getting them to be sensible adults. And I can tell you that the surest way to make a child really yearn for something is to forbid it. I obviously don't know for sure but I think if you let Rowan go to art school – when she's old enough, an art school you approve of … you could send her to Florence!' Caro threw this in to pay Skye back for implying she was 'a lot older' when really it could only be a couple of years. 'And if she's as talented as I think she is, she'll do well. And if she's totally unsuited to it, as you think, she'll come home after the first term.' Caro finished her now nearly cold tea, hoarse with trying to make Skye see sense.

Skye didn't answer for what seemed a long time, an impression enhanced by the slow ticking of the kitchen clock.

'Very well. I'll do as you ask. But it's against what I think is right for my daughter.'

'I have to say …' Heather said hesitantly. She seemed distressed. '… although it's not really my place, that Caro has made you a very good offer. You should accept it with grace.'

Skye turned her steely gaze on Heather as if she was about to give her a blast of ice and fire but then she sighed. 'You're right. It's a good offer. I'll come and collect her when my yoga retreat is over.'

'And I'll keep her safe and do my best to give her a good time,' said Caro, very tired now.

'But you won't make her want to stay in London?'

'You can't make people feel things,' Caro said gently. 'She'll either fall in love with the bright lights or she'll yearn for the beauty and quiet there is here.'

She knew she'd be yearning for that herself, now she'd experienced it. She'd always loved living in London but wasn't so sure she would now. She didn't feel like quite the same person any more. And it wouldn't only be grey skies and the sound of the curlew she would miss.

Eventually Skye was satisfied and went home.

As she came up the escalator into Canary Wharf Caro mentally congratulated Rowan for finding her way without the detailed instructions she usually gave people. It wasn't a desperately difficult journey but a few pointers were helpful. Although Rowan may have taken a cab from London City Airport it would still be difficult to find the right barge.

Caro had called Joe from the airport to give him and anyone else who was there time to get the mugs into the dishwasher and generally make the place look respectable. It was an old tradition but this time it was also to give Rowan time to get her game face on.

Rowan was waiting for her on deck but for a moment Caro didn't recognise her. Her long rose-gold plait was gone, leaving a shorn but no less lovely girl.

'Oh my goodness, your hair!' said Caro, before she could stop herself. 'But it looks amazing! Maybe we'll get it tidied up a bit at the hairdresser's. Is the kettle on? Let me get on board.'

Rowan wasn't usually talkative but now she had plenty to say. She began as soon as Caro climbed aboard and went down the stairs towards the cabin below.

'Joe's been so kind – taking me in, not shouting,' she said.

'Joe never shouts. It's not his style. And now you must ring your mother—'

'You don't mind me coming here? You did say I could come and stay ...'

'I don't mind at all, love, but did you have to drive everyone mad with worry?' Caro paused before entering the cabin. She put her hand on Rowan's wrist. 'You could have just come and stayed in the normal way.'

87

'You know Mum would never have let me.'

Caro sighed. She was probably right. 'Well, let me get below and settle in.'

Joe had opened a bottle of wine and was stirring something delicious-smelling. He grinned as he saw Caro. 'You're back!'

'I am! And very pleased to see you!' They exchanged one-armed hugs as Joe was reluctant to put down his wooden spoon. 'Thank you for taking in the waif and stray.'

'She's been no trouble so far, although I suppose there's time.'

'Would you like tea or wine?' asked Rowan, suddenly shy and clearly worried that this was Caro's home: should she be offering drinks? On the other hand, Caro had been on a long journey and should be looked after.

'Tea and then wine immediately afterwards,' said Caro. She'd left her case in the wheelhouse, content to just get home and relax for the moment. Unpacking could wait. She collapsed on to the banquette. 'Thanks, Rowan,' she said as the girl handed her the tea. 'What I'm longing to know is how you found the barge?'

Rowan sat down too, obviously proud of herself. 'It wasn't that easy but I knew roughly where it was and what it was called. I got a cab here and then just walked around looking for someone to ask. I started off at the other moorings and met a man doing work on a boat. He knew all the barges and told me where this one was.'

'But how did you get in? You didn't know the code for the gate.'

Rowan bit her lip, a bit sheepish. 'I told the kind man I was visiting a friend and had forgotten the code and he gave it to me.'

'It was Doug,' said Joe, finally feeling free to stop stirring and coming to join them with a glass of wine. 'He does boat safety examinations on all the barges and narrow boats. He knows everyone,' he explained for Rowan's benefit. 'He probably realised Rowan wasn't up to anything bad.'

'I was lucky, Joe was in,' said Rowan. 'I explained to him—'

'And I understood,' said Joe.

He smiled his slightly wonky smile revealing his slightly wonky teeth. At thirty-five he felt too young for Caro to be romantically attracted to, but he was a friend and she trusted him.

'I expect you're wondering about my hair,' said Rowan. 'Actually I cut off my plait before I left. I thought I would be less easily spotted if I didn't have it. And I felt so – fed up. I wanted to do something drastic.'

Caro would have waited a bit before asking these questions but was glad to know. 'So why didn't your mother find it? It would have been a bit of an awful thing to come across, I must say.'

'It's in my knicker drawer.' Rowan blushed a little, possibly because she'd said 'knicker' in front of Joe. Caro was reminded what a very sheltered life she'd led up to now which made Caro admire her even more for making a break for it, in spite of the worry it had caused.

'I'll take you to my hairdresser tomorrow. My colours need doing anyway.'

'Mum says she doesn't understand people who colour their hair. She says it fools no one,' said Rowan, blushing some more in case it sounded as if she was being critical.

'I colour my hair for me, not for anyone else,' said Caro. 'I want to like the reflection I see in the mirror. Besides, your mother is so naturally beautiful that she could go completely grey and completely haggard and still be stunning.' She smiled to show there were no hard feelings. 'Each to their own.'

'Right,' said Joe, 'if you two are ready to eat—'

'I'll set the table,' said Caro.

Joe was a great cook but his talents stopped at the stove. The niceties like table laying – and quite often the clearing up after himself part – were beyond him.

It didn't take Caro long to find candles and paper napkins and a jug of water. She put Joe's bottle of wine on the table too, struggling to remember how Rowan's parents felt about her drinking. She was seventeen but a very young seventeen.

Joe didn't know about Rowan's sheltered background and offered her wine. To Caro's relief, she refused it. It was one thing taking this beautiful naïve creature round the art colleges and galleries but quite another teaching her how much she could safely drink before making a fool of herself.

In spite of drinking only water, Rowan blossomed and came out of her shell during the meal. Joe's signature chilli with all the trimmings was obviously to her taste and as she ate she talked even more.

'I never thought I'd have the courage to run away,' she said, putting a tortilla into the guacamole and scooping up a mouthful. When she'd swallowed and taken a cooling sip of water she went on. 'I'd never even been to Glasgow on my own.'

'I shouldn't encourage you, but you were brave,' said Caro. 'And you were clever – and lucky – to find where I lived.'

'I just knew I had to do something, or I'd be stuck in Glen Liddell forever! I know I'm lucky, it is really beautiful' – she smiled at Joe as this was for his benefit – 'but I want to see more of the world.'

'So you want to check out art schools?' said Joe.

Rowan nodded. 'I know there are loads and I don't know which I should go for.' She looked at Caro.

Caro bit her lip. 'I don't know either, but you are very young – which is a good thing,' she added quickly before Rowan could feel she was being patronised. 'It means you have lots of time to do the research. And' – Caro felt she had to say this – 'don't forget to look at the Scottish art colleges with the same open mind.'

Rowan looked a bit deflated.

'But we'll look at as many as we can from the outside and if you really fancy the Courtauld Institute say – or is that more history of art?' She looked at Joe, who shrugged. 'Anyway, we'll see where you'd like to study and then find out what you need to do to get in. And we'll look at art galleries too.'

'And shops?' Rowan added this shyly.

'Of course shops!' said Caro. 'In fact we can ignore the art stuff altogether if you want.'

It was nice having Rowan there, Caro realised. It stopped her missing Scotland. But was she missing Scotland, or the chance to see Alec? Really, she was thinking like a teenager herself. Was she fit to be looking after one?

'I think you should ring your mum, Ro,' she said again when they were gathering the dishes and Joe had gone out to make music with some mates. 'Just to let them know you're safe and that I'm here and all is well.'

'Couldn't you do it? Mum will go on forever!'

'I know but it'll make you look more adult if you do it. Like you're taking responsibility for your actions.'

Rowan didn't speak for a long time and Caro could see her running the conversation over in her head.

'OK,' said Caro, 'ring your dad. He won't shout and scream, at least.'

'No, he won't – and he can tell Mum everything and if she shouts and screams at least he's used to it.' Rowan seemed relieved at this compromise.

Suddenly Caro felt as if she was ducking out of her responsibilities too, having told Rowan she wasn't allowed to. 'I'll ring Skye. But you speak to Alec.'

Caro was lucky. Skye's yoga students were requiring her attention. 'OK, thanks for ringing. See if you can get her to come home. I haven't got time to collect her,' she said.

'Really? But you were so worried about Rowan going to London.'

'I can't go to London!' Skye sounded shrill. 'There are so many toxins and diesel fumes.' She paused. 'Besides, my best friend was offered drugs the moment she arrived. I can't expose myself to that sort of thing. I have to keep pure!'

Caro sighed. Skye's feelings about London were obviously as ingrained as they were irrational and there was no point in arguing with her now. 'I'll keep her for a week as we agreed,' she said. 'We're going to visit art galleries and the shops.' She left out references to art colleges – now was not the time. 'I expect she'll get exhausted and want to come home very soon.' And she rang off.

'That was quick, for Mum!' said Rowan, impressed.

'She had her yoga students there,' said Caro.

'Oh, that explains it,' said Rowan. 'When Mum's got students she's very hands off. But when she hasn't, I'm her project.'

Rowan seemed relaxed with this state of affairs. 'Would you like me to make you a cup of tea or anything, Caro? If I'm going to be staying, I need to know where everything is.'

Chapter Six

Caro's hairdresser, Trixie, and Caro looked at Rowan after her hair had been properly cut. They were both silent for several minutes. Rowan looked amazing, even without make-up, and wearing very nondescript clothes.

'Can I put some make-up on you?' asked Trixie. 'Just a bit?'

'I don't think—' Caro began and then shut up. Rowan was perfectly able to decide for herself.

'I never wear make-up,' Rowan said, staring wonderingly at herself. 'But maybe I could now I'm in London. Just a bit.'

'I used to do hair and make-up for photo shoots,' explained Trixie, getting out what looked like a medium-sized tool chest. 'I'll go easy on you, seeing as you don't usually wear it. Perhaps just something to bring out your eyes even more.'

'It does really, really suit you short,' said Caro, watching Trixie work her magic with her brushes and pencils – outlining her eyes in grey and blue and amazing mascara. 'But I suspect your mother will kill me when she sees it.'

While the effect was quite subtle, there were a lot of products on Rowan's face. Her eyes looked Bambi-sized only more intelligent.

Rowan nodded. 'She's never let me cut my hair, which is why I did it myself. And she's never let me wear make-up either.'

'Can I take a few photos?' said Trixie. 'It would be good for my portfolio.'

When they came away a couple of hours later, Trixie had refused payment for any of what she'd done for Rowan, and given Caro her highlights at a very reduced rate.

'Now what?' said Caro. 'Shops or art galleries?'

'Both?'

'Perfectly possible. Let's get you an Oyster card then we can hop on and off buses and trains without having to buy a ticket,' she explained.

Rowan had a charming naivety about her that meant she loved going on the top of a double-decker bus and seeing London from up there.

'Another day we'll do the DLR and we can go up the Thames by water bus and end up at Tate

Britain,' said Caro. 'We can get the boat from there to Tate Modern.'

'This is so cool!' said Rowan. She settled back in her seat at the front of the bus.

Caro smiled, delighted to see Rowan's joy in such simple pleasure, until she spotted the man on the opposite seat staring at Rowan. She did look a bit like a supermodel, Caro realised. She wondered if a beanie hat would be a good idea though she suspected covering Rowan's rose-gold hair wouldn't be enough to make her look ordinary. Sunglasses might help, but she didn't want the girl to feel self-conscious, not when she was having such a nice time.

Caro had escorted Rowan along Oxford Street and into Selfridges when Caro realised she needed the loo.

Rowan was reluctant to leave the make-up counter and stayed playing with testers. Caro, scourged with guilt, wondering what Pandora's box she had opened when she introduced Rowan to make-up, nipped off.

Although she was as quick as she could be, inevitably finding the Ladies and getting there and back took longer than Caro would have liked. The shop was full of tourists and she was just making her way through them when she overheard someone say, 'Look, there's David Callaghan!'

Caro kept abreast of celebrity gossip only when she was having her hair done and read the

97

magazines, but even she had heard of David Callaghan. He was the Hollywood film director whom everyone wanted to work with. His films were spectacularly good; they won Oscars and, most important, earned money. She looked at where the woman was pointing and instantly went icy cold and then hot. He was talking to Rowan!

It seemed to take a lifetime of 'Excuse me's and 'Could I just?'s and 'So sorry's before she got through the crowd to where Rowan and David Callaghan seemed to be in deep conversation.

'Hello!' she said, aware that her heart was pounding, partly from exercise and partly from anxiety. 'Rowan! We should be getting home.'

David Callaghan was very tall and well dressed and, although not desperately handsome, had more charm than should be legally allowed. 'You must be Caro. I'm David. Rowan has been kind enough to help me with buying a present for my fiancée.' He had a low voice and the softest American accent.

Caro took a steadying breath. As long as he wasn't asking Rowan to go into a small private space to do this, it might not have been a problem.

'David wants to buy Scarlet some perfume,' said Rowan. 'He asked me for my advice but I said we need Scarlet herself.'

'I know a bit about perfume,' said Caro. 'At least – I know what smells good on people. But we definitely need Scarlet. Is she back in the States?'

'No,' said David. 'She's trying on dresses. She's due to meet me here about now.'

'She may be delayed,' said Caro, warming to him as it became obvious he wasn't after Rowan. 'It always takes twice as long as you think it possibly could.'

'I know,' said David with a resigned smile. Then his expression changed. 'Ah! We maligned her. She's here.'

Scarlet was a good few years younger than David, who Caro reckoned was about her own age. She had black curls and huge brown eyes, a full mouth and a perfect little nose. She was extremely pretty and fizzed with warmth and energy.

'David! I'm sorry if I kept you waiting. I had to wait in line for ages.' She became aware of Caro and Rowan. 'Oh, who are you guys? Are you friends of David's?'

As her question included a very wide smile, revealing perfect American teeth, it was easy to smile back. But Caro didn't know what to say. Was David's perfume-buying a secret?

'Friends as of a few minutes ago. These kind people have been trying to help me and prove that the English are not all stuck-up and snobbish.'

'I'm not English,' said Rowan quickly. 'I'm Scottish.'

'We are both British, though,' said Caro. 'But we're not stuck-up. I'm Caro, and my Scottish friend is Rowan.'

'And I'm David Callaghan,' he said. 'This is my fiancée, Scarlet Lloyd.'

Rowan, usually so shy, seemed happy to carry on. 'It's lovely to meet you both.' She turned to Scarlet. 'You're so beautiful.' And then she blushed, aware it wasn't usual to be so frank about other people's looks.

Scarlet responded by putting her hand on Rowan's arm. 'Oh! Honey! So are you! Just gorgeous! I love your hair!'

The mutual fangirling went on for a few more minutes until Caro felt obliged to break it up. 'I think we should be going, Rowan. David has got Scarlet now and they can choose perfumes without us.'

'Oh no!' said Scarlet. 'If you're not in a rush, we'd love to have help. We've been trying everything and nothing seems right.' She seemed more distressed than not having the right perfume seemed to justify.

'I wanted to give her a very special present,' explained David.

'Fragrance is important to me,' said Scarlet, her enthusiasm for life dimmed for a moment. 'Have you found anything you like, David?'

'You're the one who matters here, honey,' David said. 'No point in me liking something. It's got to work for you.'

'Well, shall we try a few?' suggested Caro. She studied Scarlet thoughtfully. 'I think you need something that isn't too sweet.'

She surveyed the array of perfumes in front of her. Some were classic and some were new. Although there were so many there, none of them leapt out at Caro as being right for Scarlet. She went to a much advertised fragrance that might work. She sprayed some on to a paper wand and flapped it for a few seconds. She sniffed it and then handed it to Scarlet. 'What about this?'

'It's lovely,' said Scarlet, 'but it doesn't seem special enough.'

'Mm.' It was no good finding something that smelt right on Scarlet if she didn't like it on herself. 'Let's try something else.' Caro chose something much more classic from a very old perfume house. 'What about this?'

Scarlet sniffed and shook her head. 'It's a nice fragrance but I don't want to smell like that.' She sighed, tired suddenly. 'Honestly, I've tried so many of these here.'

'And you haven't liked anything?' said Caro. 'As I said to David earlier, I'm quite good at matching fragrance to people. Maybe if I helped you—'

'What I really want isn't available any more,' said Scarlet. 'I'm crazy to even think of trying to find it.'

'Maybe you need something made specially for you?' said Rowan.

Caro caught Rowan looking at her. Alec's daughter obviously knew what her father was making in that little cottage in the Highlands and she was checking to see if Caro did too.

'Can I suggest we go somewhere and have tea?' said David.

Scarlet jumped up and clapped her hands. 'I love it when you go all British on me, David!' she said.

'I had an English grandmother,' he explained.

'I'm afraid we'd better be going,' said Caro again.

'No, no! We want you to have tea with us, don't we David? I don't think tea would be any fun without actual British people to have it with!'

David smiled indulgently. 'That was what I had in mind,' he said. 'Have you two got time for tea?'

Caro had been thinking that Scarlet and David wanted to be on their own but this invitation made it seem they really wanted their company. Rowan was gazing at her pleadingly and Caro really wanted a cup of tea herself. 'Oh, I think so,' said Caro and was rewarded by happy smiles of gratitude.

'Let's have it in the hotel,' said Scarlet.

'We'll find a cab,' said David.

But just as they set off for the exit, Caro was aware of a little group of tourists taking pictures of them. It unsettled her and she turned her back and took Scarlet's arm. She couldn't help wondering what Skye would say if she ever found out about it. She'd be utterly horrified.

*

It was fairly glamorous being driven through London in the back of a cab with such a famous couple and Caro could see that Rowan was really enjoying it. Scarlet was enjoying it too and Caro couldn't help thinking what a nice girl she was. She was living the sort of life other women might dream of, but she still took pleasure in the simple things.

'So, are you guys related?' Scarlet asked.

'Caro is my friend,' said Rowan. 'I'm staying with her.'

'We met when I was looking after her grandfather, in Scotland.'

'Ah, Scotland!' Scarlet sighed. 'I've never been. But I long to go!'

Caro saw Rowan open her mouth to suggest Scarlet went and stayed with her in Glen Liddell and then shut it again. The poor girl hadn't had much opportunity to develop normal social skills so it was good that she realised it wasn't a brilliant idea to invite people you've only known five minutes to stay. Also she might have wondered what her family would make of her new friends.

Eventually the taxi made its way through the traffic and pulled up outside the Ritz.

'Isn't the Ritz famous?' asked Rowan.

'Yup,' said Scarlet. 'David is spoiling me. I like old-fashioned hotels.'

'We won't be able to get tea in the restaurant,' said David. 'We haven't booked. But they'll bring it to us in the suite.'

Caro and Rowan exchanged looks of amazement and joy.

'I can't believe I'm in London and about to have tea in a suite at the Ritz!' said Rowan. 'It's amazing!'

'I know!' said Scarlet. 'It's going to be so fun!'

David ushered his posse of women into the hotel with the aid of the doorman. Then he spoke to the concierge before shepherding them into the lift.

Scarlet showed Rowan the suite: the lavish bedroom, a bathroom and the sitting room. The furnishings were of striped silk, the curtains swagged and draped. There were several separate seating areas with small sofas and armchairs, little tables and lamps. Caro counted at least three antique desks and more than three huge flower arrangements. The lighting was perfect. The rooms were bright but softly lit giving an impression of warmth and luxury.

'It's so British!' said Scarlet with a sigh, sitting down on one of the sofas and indicating the others should do likewise.

'Compared to where I come from, it's amazing,' said Rowan. 'I mean, ours – I mean my grandfather's – is a pretty big house but the carpets are all worn out, and the stags' heads have got some sort of moth.'

'But it sounds so romantic! Stags' heads on the walls!' said Scarlet.

'It is in a really beautiful part of the world,' said Caro. 'I was only there for a short time, but I completely fell in love with it.'

'Did you?' said Rowan. 'I'm so glad.' She smiled briefly. 'Caro lives on a barge here in London.'

'A barge? That's pretty amazing,' said David. 'Whereabouts is it?'

'Canary Wharf,' Caro said. 'People are always excited when I tell them about it but it's always been home to me. I sort of take it for granted.'

'Do you feel safe there?' asked Scarlet. 'I mean – don't you feel a bit vulnerable not having a proper house?'

'Not at all,' said Caro. 'It's a gated community really. No one can get on to the mooring unless they have the code.'

'Oh, well, I'd love to see that too,' said Scarlet. 'When you go to a foreign country – even when you speak the language – it's hard to get to know the people. That's why it's so cool we met you guys.' She smiled up at David. 'Thank you for getting chatting, sweetheart.'

'I just wanted some advice about your perfume,' said David. 'I wasn't being friendly.' He laughed as if absolving himself of something bad.

'We might be able to help you with the perfume,' said Rowan, looking somewhat anxiously at Caro.

'Rowan's father makes it,' she said.

'Is he any good?' said David.

Rowan and Caro looked at each other. Caro made an executive decision which involved taking a lot on trust. After all, she wasn't a professional, she couldn't know for a fact how good at perfume-making he was, but she did believe his passion and she wanted to help him if she possibly could. 'The best. Shall I ring him and ask if he could meet you? He might be able to create a fragrance that is uniquely yours.'

'Oh, that would be perfect!' said Scarlet.

'It would solve the problem of trying to find something that doesn't exist,' said David.

'So should we get in touch with him?' asked Caro.

'Yes, let's,' said Rowan, delighted by Caro's support for her father.

Caro observed three pairs of eyes looking at her with faith, faith she knew could be misplaced. But she had confidence in Alec and if this was misplaced, well, so be it.

'I have to go home in four days' time,' said David. 'Scarlet is staying for about another two weeks – for an acting course. Could he get here by before I leave, do you think?'

'Scotland's not that far away,' said Rowan, slightly defensive.

'If his sister is home and can look after their father, he'll come, I'm sure of it,' said Caro. 'But he has been quite tied up recently. Shall I call and find out how he's fixed now?'

'Yes, do!' said Scarlet. 'I have a dream, something he may be able to make come true.'

'Maybe you should explain further, sweetheart,' said David.

Scarlet took a moment to prepare what she was going to say. 'My grandmother was a dresser to an old movie star.'

'Oh, I didn't know movie stars had dressers,' said Caro, excited. 'I thought dressers belonged in the theatre. My mother told me all about them!' She turned to Rowan. 'A dresser was like a maid, but for actors. They made sure all their clothes were right, helped with make-up and it often became a very close relationship.' She paused, smiling. 'My mother was mad about old actors. She used to read their biographies.'

'It's so cool to find someone who knows what I'm talking about,' said Scarlet.

'Do go on,' said Caro. 'I interrupted you.'

'Well, when my grandmother was a girl she looked after an actress who became a really big movie star. She had a very rich and powerful boyfriend.' Scarlet glanced at David and Caro wondered if the look was significant. 'As a wedding present he had this perfume made for her but no one else was allowed to wear it. The recipe was destroyed so it was only for her.'

'And I want to recreate that part of the story,' said David. 'I'd love for Scarlet to have something no one in the world has.'

After exchanging loving looks with David, Scarlet went on. 'But the rest of it is very sad. She was killed in a seaplane accident. She was pregnant.'

'Was that – Serena Swan?' asked Caro. 'I remember that story. It was so tragic.'

'The perfume originally came in a Lalique glass bottle, shaped like a swan,' said Scarlet. 'And that's the perfume I want. It has so many memories for me: my grandmother telling me the story – all the stories – of Serena Swan who she looked after devotedly. It's why I wanted to be an actress in the first place.'

'But how can it be recreated if there's no recipe?' asked Rowan.

Scarlet shrugged. 'I was trying to find a perfume that was near it. But nothing smells the same.'

'How do you know?' asked Rowan.

Scarlet looked around as if someone might be eavesdropping. 'I have a tiny bit of it. My grandmother kept a small bottle. She saved it after Serena died, that and a silk scarf, to remind her.'

'That's so beautiful!' said Rowan. 'I think I might cry!'

Caro moved to the bedroom to make the call, wondering at how quickly 'I know someone who makes perfume' had become her asking Alec to turn

Scarlet and David's dream into reality. Of course, if it came off, it would be wonderful, and if it didn't, well, no one was any worse off.

Alec answered the phone instantly. 'Is Rowan all right?' he said, without even a 'hello'.

Caro found herself almost laughing. 'She's fine. She called you last night; what could have happened to her since then?' Although quite a lot had happened to her it was all very positive. 'But I'm not ringing about Rowan, I want to talk to you.'

'Oh? What about?'

'Perfume. We met these people – we're with them now. They're a lovely couple – he's a famous film producer and she's his fiancée. He wants to recreate the perfume that was made for an actress who was around in the thirties – I think. She was killed in a seaplane accident. Her husband said that only she was allowed to wear it. This is the perfume that Scarlet wants.'

'Serena Swan. I know that story,' said Alec. 'It's famous. But there were no recipes kept. How could I – or anyone – recreate it?' She could hear that he was interested.

'Scarlet has a sample.'

'She has a sample?' Now Alec was really enthusiastic. 'Then there's a chance.'

'How soon can you get here? David's got to be back in the States in a few days and he wants to meet you.'

'Lennie is arriving tonight. I'll let her recover a bit and then hand over. I could be with you tomorrow night?'

'Perfect. I'll email you details of how to get to the barge.'

'Great.'

There was a tiny pause and then Caro said, 'Goodbye then!' and disconnected.

While Caro had been on the phone to Alec, the tea had arrived.

'Oh wow,' she said.

There were two silver cake stands on a cloth-covered trolley, every layer packed with finger sandwiches, scones, tiny patisserie, fruit cake and teacakes. The cups and saucers looked as if they were vintage porcelain with a delicate floral pattern and the teapots and hot-water jugs were silver.

'Isn't it just darling?' said Scarlet. 'I love all this British elegance.'

'Look at the tiny meringues! And the sandwiches are long and not triangles.'

'That's so you can eat them without losing your lipstick,' said Scarlet. 'Now, Caro, will you pour the tea?'

'And I'll pour the champagne,' said David. There was another tray with an ice bucket and glasses.

'Which should I have first?' said Rowan, looking at Caro.

110

Caro decided she couldn't ruin this lovely experience for Rowan by telling her she was too young to drink. 'I suggest you have a sip of champagne and then drink your tea before it gets cold.'

'That sounds like good advice,' said Scarlet. 'I'm going to do that.'

When everyone had a glass of champagne, David said, 'Let's have a toast. To new friends and perfume!'

Everyone clinked glasses. 'To new friends and perfume!'

Chapter Seven

Feeling very slightly sick after too many cream cakes and sandwiches, Caro got up. 'We really must go but I do have to say, this is the best treat ever. Thank you both so much.'

Scarlet got up too. 'Hey! It was so great meeting you! It's so lovely knowing British people. I won't feel so odd when I start my acting course.'

'Scarlet may feel a little lonely when I go back to the States and she's here doing her classes,' said David. 'And I have to go to a dinner tonight.'

Scarlet smiled in a way that indicated she was not feeling as brave as she sounded. 'You worry about me too much, David. I'll be fine staying here,' she said.

'Well, you must come and visit us on the barge,' said Caro.

Just then, the telephone rang. David answered it and then went through to the bedroom so he could talk.

David came back into the room shortly after-wards, looking serious. 'That was the concierge. Apparently there's a bit of a paparazzi presence downstairs. We were spotted in Selfridges and now they know where we are.'

'Oh God!' said Caro. 'How horrible! I thought I saw someone taking your picture but I assumed it was just a tourist and didn't give it much thought.' She didn't add that because David wasn't an actor she hadn't realised it could be a problem.

'And I'm afraid it's not just us who are in the pictures,' David said to Caro. 'It's both of you, too. So the paps think you're famous!'

'Blimey!' said Rowan.

'What the concierge suggests is that they get you out via the back entrance where a car will be waiting to take you home,' he said.

'But what about you and Scarlet?' said Rowan. 'Will you have to stay in the hotel until they all go home?'

'I have to go to this dinner,' said David. 'But I'm big enough and ugly enough to handle a bit of press. It's Scarlet they're interested in.'

'Oh, honey!' said Scarlet. 'I hate the thought of being here without you, with all those photogra-phers outside.'

'You'll be quite safe. This is the Ritz,' said David.

'I know I'll be safe,' said Scarlet, 'but I'll also be lonely.'

There was a tiny pause and then Rowan said, 'Could Scarlet come with us?' She glanced between Caro and Scarlet. 'We could look after her and she wouldn't be so lonely.'

Scarlet looked at Caro hopefully.

'Yes, of course, as far as I'm concerned,' said Caro, suddenly feeling very maternal towards the young woman who superficially had everything but now just needed some friends.

Scarlet looked up at David. 'I would like to go, but do you think it's a good idea?'

He nodded. 'I do actually. I could come and pick you up after my dinner.'

'It would be an adventure!' said Rowan. 'Before I ran away to London to stay with Caro, I never had any excitement.'

Rowan's habitual shyness had definitely been affected by the champagne, Caro realised.

Scarlet smiled at her sympathetically. 'It's over-rated, hon, but if you guys would take me in this evening, I'd be delighted.'

'So will we!' said Caro, suddenly realising what she'd taken on. 'Only, of course, if you came in the ordinary way I'd have been cleaning and tidying for days. I seem to remember we just left the barge with the breakfast things still on the side.'

'But that's cool,' said Scarlet. 'It means you never have to tidy for me. I'll have seen you at your worst!'

'And there's Joe,' said Caro. 'He's my lodger and he's lovely and a great cook but he's not very tidy.'

'I don't care about things like that.' Scarlet smiled, obviously delighted at the prospect of mixing with normal people who didn't live in a showbiz bubble. 'When can we leave?'

The concierge came up to the suite to lead them through to the back of the hotel where the car would be waiting for them. Rowan was squeaking with excitement and Caro was almost as bad.

'I'm so sorry about this, Mr Callaghan,' the concierge said, 'but there is a way the press don't know about yet. We wouldn't want them following you or your friends.'

'We're just grateful you found out about it,' said David. 'They could have been here for anyone.'

'We keep an eye on social media for our more high-profile guests,' he said.

'It's so good I've got you guys turning this into a fun thing,' said Scarlet to Rowan and Caro. 'And not just a great big PITA.'

'Pain in the arse?' said Rowan.

'Yep,' Scarlet agreed.

'It is a fun thing,' said David. 'I'll come down with you now, but do please call when you reach the barge safely.'

'And you'll be all right going to your dinner?' asked Scarlet. 'I don't want you to feel abandoned.'

'I only ever feel abandoned in a good way,' he said with a wink, and Scarlet laughed.

They followed the concierge through corridors, down service lifts and, eventually, out into a back alley where a limousine was waiting. They piled in, laughing faintly hysterically.

'It's like some sort of bizarre hen-night caper,' said Caro, settling back into the soft leather upholstery. 'I know it's serious but it was lovely seeing behind the scenes at the hotel. And the concierge was brilliant! It was a bit like being in a film!'

'I'm glad you see it like that,' said Scarlet. 'It's all my fault really.'

'I don't see how that can be,' said Caro, who was sensitive about women taking the blame for all the troubles in the world.

Scarlet didn't speak for a while. They were now driving through London and even Caro, the seasoned Londoner, appreciated the beautiful buildings, the lights, the busy streets and sense of excitement.

Eventually, Scarlet said, 'I suppose it's not my fault exactly, but it's because of me. It's a secret but I can tell you two. I've got a big part in David's next film. Of course all of Hollywood will think it's because we're an item – or if they don't think that they'll think we became an item so I could get the part, but it really wasn't like that.'

'I'm sure it wasn't,' said Caro, although she couldn't help thinking about the age gap between the powerful but not hugely handsome man and the extremely pretty young actress.

'You know I'd still be with David if he was a realtor.'

'That's an estate agent,' said Caro to Rowan, who may not have seen as much American television as she had.

'But everyone thinks I'm with him for the parts he can give me, and this part is pretty wonderful, and he is directing the film,' Scarlet went on.

'But why are you worried about the press?' said Rowan.

'Because rumours about me getting the part got out and another – much more established actor – went public about wanting the role and saying it was because David had the hots for me that I got it.' Scarlet shuddered. 'It's why I'm having some acting lessons while I'm here. I've really lost my confidence.'

Caro sighed. 'It's funny; so many people would envy you. You're beautiful, talented and have a man who obviously adores you, and yet your life isn't perfect at all.'

'I'm going to make it work, though,' said Scarlet. 'I'm going to prove I can play the part and do it well. And I'm also going to prove that I love David for him, not for what he can do for my career.'

'That's so inspiring,' said Rowan. 'I ran away from home to look at art schools, to escape from my family, who do really love me, I know that.' She shot a glance at Caro in case she was going to remind her of this. 'But they – well, it's Mum really – they try to protect me too much. I've got to do my own thing – I can't just live the life she wants for me. I just have to have courage.'

'I think you're both remarkable young women,' said Caro. 'I've had life pretty easy really.'

'Didn't you bring up your daughter on your own?' said Rowan, sticking up for her friend.

'Yes, but I lived with my parents – latterly my dad. I wasn't lonely or unsupported. Maybe I'll make my mark somehow, but later than you two.' Caro sank back in her seat and watched London go past. What had she done with her life, really? And was it too late to do something now? She wouldn't let herself think about Alec, but she did acknowledge that helping him get his perfume business going would be an achievement. If she could do that, she could die happy (although not just yet, of course). For while he still hadn't recognised her, she wanted the best for him. That was how love worked.

'Oh my God,' she muttered as she put in the code to get on to the moorings, 'I'm taking a superstar into my home and I haven't even tidied.'

Scarlet giggled. 'We've been through that! I'm not a superstar and I don't care about it being tidy.

I'm just glad not to be stuck on my own in my enormous suite.'

'Sitting on your lovely sofa watching a wonderful widescreen TV ...' The gate swung open and Caro went in, holding it for the others. 'Our TV is very small and I will have to explain about the loo but at least it's safe here.'

'The loo is fine!' said Rowan. 'The barge is lovely. Come on, Scarlet.'

Caro hung back a bit. Rowan seemed to have really come out of her shell since meeting Scarlet – given that the effect of the champagne must have worn off by now – which said a lot for Scarlet's warm and inclusive nature. If Rowan were a bit more aware of the world of showbiz, she'd be terrified of Scarlet; instead she'd just responded to the real person she'd met, and treated her like anyone else.

Scarlet and Rowan were still in the wheelhouse by the time Caro had walked down the pontoon and climbed on to the barge. They were exclaiming with joy at the skyscrapers of Canary Wharf.

'It's like two worlds,' Rowan was saying. 'Down in the barge it's all quiet and homey, but when you come up here you see London, right there!'

'This is so cool!' said Scarlet. 'I love it!'

'You'd better come down below and see the rest of it,' said Caro, pleased the barge was doing so well so far, and hoping too much washing up left around wouldn't let it down.

Scarlet's enthusiasm didn't wane, in spite of the untidiness of the saloon. Joe appeared to be out but had obviously been home because there were greasy dishes thrown in the sink. Scarlet didn't notice those. She saw the built-in sofa covered with throws and sheepskins near a coffee table that bore a little clutch of candles. She saw the built-in book-cases and desk, the way every nook and cranny was used. Caro sometimes felt she wanted to clear everything out and start again but she didn't want to live in a barge that was more like a flat. She liked the way you knew you were on a boat, with the ancient portholes, one of which had a bullet hole from when the barge was in the Second World War. And Scarlet obviously responded to all these things too.

'This is joyful!' she said. 'I just love it!'

Caro opened her mouth to apologise for the mess but then shut it again. It would be wrong to draw attention to something Scarlet seemed not to have noticed.

She already loved Scarlet but her reaction to the barge made Caro love her even more.

Scarlet moved round the saloon, looking at every-thing. 'It's quite big, isn't it?'

'It's not the biggest barge on the moorings, but yes, it's pretty spacious.'

'Compared to my first Manhattan apartment it's huge,' said Scarlet, impressed.

'Can I get you something to drink?' Caro said. 'And then we can think about supper.'

'Do you have green tea?' asked Scarlet. 'Sorry to be so actressy.' She made a face when she said it but, to Caro's delight, she didn't do the rabbit ears with her fingers to signify the inverted commas.

'That's fine, we have green tea – all sorts of different kinds. Joe's very into all that.' Caro paused. 'You don't want alcohol?'

Scarlet shook her head. 'No thank you.' She sat down on the banquette, next to Rowan and looked quite at home.

'I think I might have a glass of red wine,' Caro said, hoping this didn't make her look desperate. 'Rowan? Scarlet's having green tea, what would you like?'

'Peppermint, please,' said Rowan, who was rummaging in her bag. She pulled out her sketch pad. 'Do you mind if I draw you, Scarlet?'

'Go ahead. Just don't sell the drawings to the press, OK?' Scarlet laughed to show she was joking but Caro sensed she was a bit sensitive about it.

'God, no!' said Rowan. 'No one would want them anyway, I'm not good enough, but I certainly wouldn't do anything with your image you weren't happy with. I can't imagine anything worse! My mum told me that once when her best friend came to London she had something put in her drink and she was photographed— Oh, never mind.'

Caro couldn't press her because Rowan obviously found it all horrendous but she longed to know if Skye's best friend was photographed falling out of a taxi or if it was something far worse. If the latter, it would explain Skye's deep hatred of London.

'Hey? Can I look at your work?' said Scarlet, changing the subject. 'Or would that annoy you?'

'Of course – it's only fair if you're letting me draw you. Here – I'll take out a sheet so I can draw but feel free with the others.'

Caro put on some gentle jazz, feeling that music would be soothing, and then began gathering crockery and stacking it in the dishwasher.

While Rowan was drawing and Scarlet was looking at her sketches, her own mind was churning. She was anticipating Alec's arrival the following evening.

It was like waiting for a particularly large firework to explode. There was excited expectation but there was also, for Caro anyway, dread at the thought of the enormous bang the firework would make. Not that Alec was noisy exactly but at the moment everything was peaceful and calm. Could she be calm when Alec was in her space, so near?

Of course she could. She turned the hot tap on to last night's chilli pan. It would be fine. And, in fact, it was brilliant that he hadn't recognised her from that night long ago on a Greek island. This way she could pretend at least that she didn't care about him, and was only interested in getting the right perfume for Scarlet.

The fact that he would have to stay over was a bit of a problem. It meant they'd have to be together last thing at night, and for breakfast.

She left the kitchen area and went to where Rowan and Scarlet were so happily occupied.

'These pictures are amazing!' said Scarlet. 'I can't think why Rowan keeps saying they're not good enough. Good enough for what? Surely good enough to get her into art school!'

Joe came home and obligingly turned leftovers from the previous night's chilli into a surprisingly delicious spaghetti sauce. He was pleased but not overawed to meet Scarlet. He had never heard of her but, being a film buff, had heard of David and, to Caro's relief, approved of his work. Joe was lovely, but he was a bit inclined to say what he thought without adding a filter.

Scarlet disappeared after the meal to take a call from David. She came back a little while later looking worried.

'David says there's a crowd of paparazzi outside the hotel. He wonders if I could possibly stay the night here with you? He thinks it would be safer. With luck tomorrow they will have lost interest in me and be on to somewhere else. He could pick me up when the coast is clear?'

'Of course,' said Caro. 'We'd love to have you.'

Rowan clapped her hands with delight.

'I'll just fetch some bed linen and show you where you could sleep.

It was a pretty single cabin, with a small wardrobe half full of clothes, a little bedside cabinet and a bookshelf.

'It's just darling!' said Scarlet. 'Here, let me do that.' She took the bundle of linen from Caro's arms. 'I'll put the duvet on. I saw this neat thing on YouTube. You turn it inside out …'

'I have to say I wouldn't have seen you as someone who looked on YouTube to learn how to put on duvet covers,' said Caro, watching Scarlet rolling and tucking while she herself put on pillow cases.

'I haven't always been the superstar fiancée of a Hollywood mogul, you know. I used to be a perfectly normal young woman. But I must admit I got led to the site by something quite different. You know what the Internet is like.

'Oh, I do!' agreed Caro. 'Now, can you fit the sheet round that corner? We'll be done in no time.'

When the bed was made, Caro switched on the bedside light.

'It's adorable!' said Scarlet. 'I feel like Anne of Green Gables seeing her bedroom for the first time. Thank you so much!'

Caro went to bed fairly early, and Joe went out, leaving the girls curled up on the banquette with throws and blankets, wearing pyjamas and bedsocks.

'You look like an advertisement for *hygge*,' Caro said on her way back from the shower room.

'What's that?' asked Rowan.

'Scandinavian cosiness,' said Scarlet. 'It's gone out of fashion a bit now.'

'Not on this barge, it hasn't!' said Caro. 'Now goodnight and don't stay up too late.'

'Why not?' asked Rowan.

'Oh, I don't know,' said Caro. 'It just felt like the right thing to say.'

Caro was up early the next morning and had been to Waitrose to buy bits and pieces including croissants and freshly squeezed orange juice. If Scarlet wanted healthy food for breakfast there was plenty in the cupboard.

Although she was trying hard to be calm, she was a bit stressed. It wasn't so much the thought of David coming to collect Scarlet that morning as much as the prospect of Alec being on the barge in time for dinner. She wanted to get the food thought out so she could focus on all the other stuff.

Finding a perfume-maker for Scarlet and David would likely mean the end of her part in their story, she realised now. Rowan would probably go back with Alec after he'd talked to David and Scarlet, even though she hadn't yet had her promised week in London. She, Caro, would be left on the barge feeling, she anticipated, anticlimactic and lacking a project. She'd have to think of something – something to take her mind off Alec, principally.

The saloon smelt of fresh coffee by the time Scarlet came in, rubbing her eyes and looking delightfully ruffled with no make-up and her hair in curls as yet undisturbed by tongs or even a brush.

'I slept so well! It's so quiet,' she said, coming up to Caro and putting her arm round her waist and kissing her cheek. 'I do love a good hotel but they are much noisier than it is here.'

Caro was delighted. 'It's because we're much lower than all the hustle and bustle of Canary Wharf,' she explained. 'The noise just goes straight over us. I still get surprised when I draw back the curtain and see a double-decker bus through the porthole.'

'And that coffee smells so good!' Scarlet stretched, reminding Caro of a kitten. She was completely unaware of her loveliness.

Rowan came in, looking very similar to Scarlet in that they shared the same sleepy beauty while looking quite different from each other. 'We stayed up talking quite late,' she said. 'I do hope we didn't disturb you.'

'My cabin is tucked away in the stern,' said Caro. 'I never hear what's going on in the saloon apart from when the pump goes off. Now, coffee for both of you? Or tea? Orange juice? Then we have croissants, granola made by Joe, eggs, bacon ...'

Scarlet's phone vibrated. 'Oh, excuse me, it's David.' She got up and retired to her cabin. She came back a little while later.

'All right?' asked Caro as Scarlet sat down at the table. She passed over the coffee pot.

'Everything's fine really, but David now says he can't get here until the evening.'

Caro waited for a few seconds. 'And the problem is ...?'

'Would it be OK for me to hang out with you until he can get here?' asked Scarlet.

'Of course!' said Rowan. 'It would be lovely!' Then she looked at Caro. 'I mean—'

'It would indeed be lovely,' Caro confirmed. 'And he can meet Alec. We'll all have dinner together.'

'We could take you out—' Scarlet was still unsure of her welcome.

'Really,' said Caro. 'I'd love to cook for everyone. It's been ages since I've done fancy cooking.' As she said it, it sounded as if this was a pleasure she'd been deprived of but now she thought about it, she was worried that she was out of practice. But as the two younger women were looking at her happily, convinced she was about to indulge in a favourite hobby, she went on. 'It'll be great fun,' she said.

Soon all three of them were sitting round the table eating breakfast as if they were old friends and Scarlet and Rowan were planning their day.

'So are there actual shops round here?' asked Scarlet. 'Or would you like to do something else, apart from shopping?' She was addressing Rowan.

'I'd love to go shopping with you,' said Rowan. 'I hardly ever get to go to the shops. Where I live, unless you're buying a kilt, you're a bit stuck for haute couture.'

Caro laughed. 'Glasgow is about three hours away from where Rowan lives,' she explained. 'You can get all sorts through mail order but actual shops are a great treat.'

'I'd love to hang out with Rowan,' Scarlet said. 'And I want David to see her drawings when he comes and I'd just love to take Rowan shopping – but not in a regular mall. I want something different.'

'Well,' said Caro, having thought a bit, 'if you want different, you could go to Old Spitalfields. It's great and it's different. You could find some lovely vintage stuff and even if you don't you'll have fun.'

'How do we get there?' said Rowan. 'Will you come with us?'

'You could go on the Underground or the bus,' said Caro. 'I could show you where to go, but I really want to stay at home and cook for this evening.'

'Or we could take a cab,' said Scarlet. 'The lazy option?'

This was the option that seemed to most appeal to Rowan and it wasn't long before the two of them set off, Scarlet fairly well disguised in an old hat of Posy's and an unflattering hoodie. No one would ever guess she was a star of interest to the gossip columnists.

Chapter Eight

Caro was very pleased to see Joe on deck, on hand to help her on board with her bags of shopping.

'Joe! Lovely to see you! Good night?'

'Guests still here, I gather, given the amount of food you've bought.' He effortlessly swung several bulging Bags for Life into the wheelhouse.

'Yes, and they're coming back for dinner, with two others.'

Joe peered into a bag. 'That explains you buying a fatted calf among other little luxuries.'

'I really want it to be nice.'

Caro had now joined Joe in the wheelhouse. 'Are you going to be in?' she continued. 'There'll be loads of food.'

'No one could ever accuse you of being an under-caterer,' he said, picking up the bags again to take them down to the cabin.

Caro shuddered. The thought of under-catering made her feel sick. 'Nor you, thank goodness. So, will you be having dinner with us or not?'

Joe shook his head. 'Not really my thing, making conversation with strangers.' He paused for a second. 'But I'll be your sous-chef if you need me.'

'Would you make a pudding?'

He nodded. 'What would you like?'

'Prune and Armagnac tart? You're so good at it.'

He shook his head. 'Prunes may split the crowd. How about pear and chocolate frangipane tart?'

Caro bit her lip. 'Not everyone likes marzipan—'

Joe laughed. 'You're not in the mood to make decisions. Why don't you let me decide?'

She hesitated. She didn't really like not knowing what the pudding would be – it was an important meal – but on the other hand, Joe made brilliant puddings and she had a lot of cleaning to do as well. She decided to let go of some control. 'That would be lovely. Let me know if you need cash for ingredients.'

Joe was peering into the bags. 'You seem to have plenty of those and enough cream to float the *Titanic*. I'll be fine.'

It was mid-afternoon by the time Rowan and Scarlet – almost completely unrecognisable in a different hat that hid her curls and most of her face, staggered down the steps into the saloon showing evidence of 'big bag shopping'.

'Something smells amazing!' said Rowan.

'Quite a lot of things smell amazing!' said Scarlet. 'I hope you haven't gone to too much trouble, it's only us.'

Caro wondered if Scarlet needed reminding that 'only us' included a major movie director but decided that she didn't.

'Us and Dad,' added Rowan. 'I'm going to put my things in my room now.' She then selected several of the bags and carried them off proudly, the spoils of shopping.

'I hope you don't mind,' said Scarlet. 'I treated her to a few things. Everything was so cheap!'

Caro laughed. 'Did you last go shopping in Knightsbridge?' Cheapness was all relative, after all.

Scarlet shrugged. 'Rodeo Drive. What can I say?'

Caro walked over to the kettle. 'Do you want a cup of tea or anything?'

'Mint tea if you have it. And I bought cupcakes from this precious little stall where the girl said she made them all herself. I love markets!'

Although she must have been tempted, Caro realised, Scarlet didn't fling herself on to the banquette and wait for her tea to be served, she went into the galley area and found mugs. 'You'll have tea and cupcakes too?'

'I thought I'd never want to eat cake again after yesterday's amazing feast,' said Caro, adding teabags to the mugs, 'but it's amazing what a good night's sleep does for you. Very happy to have a cupcake.'

'So tell me about Rowan's dad?' asked Scarlet after she had, very impressively, Caro thought, bitten the top off a cupcake in one go.

'Well, you probably know, Rowan's parents are divorced. She mostly lives with her mother, but as they all live on this big Scottish estate, she sees a lot of her father, too.'

'And what is he to you?'

Caro nearly spilled her tea. 'Er – he's not anything to me ...' Really, Scarlet was far too perceptive for a film star who was not very old. Maybe that was one of the things that David loved about her?

'I just got the impression that – well – there was just a bit more to it than him being Rowan's dad.' Scarlet put down the cake, her need for sugar obviously satisfied by several ounces of buttercream. 'You might as well tell me. I'll get it out of you eventually.'

While Caro had lots of friends, the best friend she would have told everything to lived in Cornwall and didn't really do email. And she really liked Scarlet and felt she could trust her.

'There isn't anything to tell, really, except I've got a stupid crush on him.' As this sounded so ridiculous coming out of the mouth of a nearly middle-aged woman, Caro felt obliged to go on. 'We did meet, just for one evening, when we were students, but it was at night. We just talked until I had to run off to catch a ferry – we were on the Greek islands. We didn't give each other contact details, but I remembered the place he said he came from. So when a position came up there, just when I needed a job, it seemed like fate that I should apply for it.' Caro nibbled on a sugar rose. 'I recognised him straightaway but he didn't recognise me. I expect he's forgotten all about it. After all, it was just a summer night spent with a girl he didn't sleep with.'

'But you still want to cook him a nice meal and have everything looking spotless?' said Scarlet.

Caro nodded.

'Well, I can help with set dressing,' said Scarlet. 'My first job in the theatre – "off", as many times as you can be bothered to say it, Broadway – I had to bring things in from home to make the stage look like an apartment.' She looked around. 'You have lots of brilliant props here!'

'Well, if you're up for it!'

'You'll trust me?'

Caro nodded. 'I have a daughter who can be quite bossy. I've got used to relinquishing control over the finer details of the decor.' Food was usually her domain although now it was shared with Joe.

Scarlet gave a little jump and clapped. 'This is going to be so much fun!' Just then her phone pinged. 'It's David! He's early.'

'I'll put the code in your phone for you, so you can go and get him,' said Caro. 'And don't worry about tidying up. It'll be fine.'

'I want to do it,' said Scarlet. 'I've been waited on like a princess ever since I've been in England. Here I can do normal things!'

Caro laughed. 'Well, go and get your boyfriend first then.'

As Caro went to her bedroom to choose what to wear she remembered Posy getting the barge ready for a party. She'd draped red chiffon scarves over the lamps, which not only created a fire hazard but made the place look like a bordello. It had taken all Caro's motherly guile to get Posy to change it. Eventually she made a comment about Posy's make-up and was it the wrong colour for her and then said, 'Oh no! I think it's the lighting – it's making you look about thirty. And me about sixty.'

Now, Caro wasn't worried about her barge looking like a bordello; she doubted that Scarlet would have time to do very much when David was here to look after. She debated for a moment if she should go and greet him herself but decided not to. She really had to get ready.

She glanced at her watch. David was early but Alec was due to arrive at about five. It was now four o'clock. If she didn't shower and dress soon she'd be greeting him in her dressing gown. She sighed. Had that not been faded and stained round the collar with hair dye she might have gone for that easy option. After all, it seemed just as suitable as anything else.

She was clean and wearing make-up but still in her cabin when Scarlet called for her. 'Caro? Do you want a drink? I'm making David coffee. I hope that's OK.'

'Of course it is. I feel very rude not being ready to greet him, but I'm not dressed.'

'Can I help?'

Caro shrugged. 'Maybe!' The dressing gown option was becoming more and more attractive, and she was clinging to it like a lifebelt.

'Hang on,' Scarlet called back. 'Be with you in a minute.'

When Scarlet knocked on Caro's door a few moments later she was carrying a soft parcel wrapped in pale pink tissue paper.

'We bought this for you,' she explained. 'Will it help you choose an outfit?'

It was a pashmina of the softest cashmere you could imagine. It had an abstract pattern containing every shade of red from the palest pink to the deepest vermilion and was beautiful.

'Rowan chose it,' said Scarlet. 'She has a great sense of colour.'

'It's fabulous! I love it. Thank you so much!' She hugged Scarlet and then gave her a kiss.

'But it hasn't helped your decision, right?'

'Not really,' said Caro quietly.

'Can I look at your wardrobe? You do have to keep your clothes in a very small space living on a barge, don't you?'

'I've sort of got used to it—'

'Do you mind if I dive in?'

Twenty minutes later Caro emerged wearing a pair of soft, very worn velvet jeans she could still get on and a fitted and only slightly moth-eaten cashmere jumper. The whole was enhanced enormously by the scarf that Scarlet draped around Caro in a way that looked amazing and that Caro knew she'd never manage to recreate.

'That's perfect!' said Caro, looking at herself in the mirror. 'I look my best but as if I haven't made a huge effort.'

'It is the hardest look,' Scarlet agreed. 'Now, come and say hello to David and let's see what Rowan has put on. I did get a bit carried away buying her things – it was all such a bargain!' Scarlet obviously still hadn't got over the price of things in a London market compared to her usual shopping haunts.

Caro went into the saloon where David was waiting. He stood up and kissed Caro's cheek. 'Thank you so much for looking after Scarlet. It's been lovely for her to be able to hang out with people who just behave normally around her for a little while.'

'It's been a delight,' said Caro. 'I only wish she could stay for longer.'

'Oh!' said Scarlet as Rowan appeared. 'Look at you!'

Rowan looked like a model. An asymmetrical dress with a cowl neckline gave her the look of a gazelle – graceful, vulnerable and incredibly beautiful. Long soft boots enhanced the length of her legs. Caro barely had time to register relief that it was her father whom she was about to see and not her over-protective mother before her phone pinged. Alec was at the gate and needed to be let in.

'It's your dad!' she said.

A flash of panic crossed Rowan's features and then Scarlet said, 'You look great, honey. He'll love your hair.'

'I'm sure he will,' said Caro. 'It does really suit you.' She didn't add that it made her look less like a child and more like a woman. 'I'll go and get him.'

She had no idea what to say to him and trusted that 'Hello', and 'Good journey?' would suffice.

'Make sure nothing burns!' she said to everyone and then ran up the steps to the wheelhouse and from there, on to the pontoon that led to Alec.

As she walked along she realised she'd had a bit of a transformation herself since she'd last seen him. She hadn't usually put on full make-up and tight jeans up in Glen Liddell.

'Caro!' he said when she'd put in the code and opened the gate. He seemed to look at her for a long time and so intently she wondered if he had suddenly recognised her.

'Hello!' she said, trying to sound casual. 'Flight OK?'

He shook his head slightly, as if clearing it. 'Yes, fine.'

But he went on looking at her – he didn't seem to have much in the way of casual conversation either.

'It's this way,' said Caro after a few moments, and set off along the pontoon to the barge. It was hard to stop smiling. Although she'd been very anxious about seeing him, and was worried about what he'd say when he saw his daughter, short-haired and lovelier than ever, she was just so thrilled to be with him. 'It's that one there.' She pointed to the barge with a glimmer of pride. It looked warm and welcoming. Someone had put the lamps on so all the portholes – round not square like many of the other barges – were glowing with light.

Alec stopped. 'It was kind of you to think of me – about the perfume, I mean. I know I'd told you it was my dream but there are several companies who make bespoke perfume; you could have suggested one of them. Considering my little enterprise meant you couldn't stay in the cottage that was meant for you, it was extra kind.' His smile of gratitude had something else in it that made her stomach do a little back flip.

'My sister would have gone mad if she'd found out and if my father discovered his eldest son was doing a woofterish thing like making scent – it would finish him off!'

'How is Murdo?'

'Good, really. Pleased to see Lennie, of course, but missing you, I think.' He paused and smiled again shyly. 'We all miss you.'

'You've hardly had time to miss me!' said Caro, although she was incredibly pleased. 'Now let's get on board and you can see Rowan. She and Scarlet, the young woman who wants the scent, have become very close, very quickly, and in spite of the age gap, I think it's a real friendship.'

'But they've only known each other about a day and a half!' he said.

He had a point. 'True, but Scarlet is so normal.'

'Why wouldn't she be?'

'Because—' Caro stopped. Alec could see for himself when he met her. While he may not realise what a golden couple David and Scarlet were, he would quickly find out how important David was in the movie-making business.

Rowan was in the wheelhouse waiting for her father. When he arrived, she flung herself into Alec's arms. They hugged for several moments.

But at last he let her go and got a proper look at her. 'Oh my God! Your hair! What will your mother say?'

'It's *my* hair, Dad! Don't you like it?'

Alec studied his daughter and then ruffled her head. 'Actually, I think it looks amazing, but your mother was always so proud that you'd never had your hair cut. She will be upset.'

'I needed to take control of my life, Dad. That includes deciding how long my hair should be.'

Caro was impressed by this and wondered if maybe Scarlet had rehearsed her a little. 'I think it looks amazing too, I must say,' she said. 'Now shall we go down? David and Scarlet are there; you can meet them.'

David had his arm round Scarlet and Caro thought it was very obvious that they'd just been kissing. Lucky them to be so in love, she thought.

'Scarlet and David, this is Alec, Rowan's father.'

Immediately the greetings were over, Scarlet said to Alec, 'Don't you just love Rowan's hair?'

'Actually I do,' he said, relaxing a little, 'but it does make her look very grown-up and I dread to think what her mother will have to say about it.'

'There comes a time in every young woman's life when she has to make up her own mind about stuff, and not just do what her mother tells her,' said Scarlet, looking up at David with a quick adoring glance.

'Quite right too,' said Caro, briefly casting her mind back to when Posy was a teenager and remembering that she always seemed to have her own ideas about everything. 'Now, Alec, what would you like? Technically it's teatime but travellers have different rules. There's whisky or wine.'

'Whisky would be grand but only if you'll all join me. I brought a nice malt as a present.'

'We'll have that then.' Caro didn't want to get drunk by any means, but a bit of something to take the edge off her nerves would help.

They ended up having tea and whisky as Scarlet and Rowan didn't like it and didn't fancy wine, although David joined them in a glass of malt.

Whether it was the strong drink or just the easy-going personalities of her American guests, Caro couldn't decide, but everyone seemed to get on very well. She left them to it and went into the kitchen to fiddle about with dinner.

'Unless you really need to be there,' called David, 'come and join us. We want to talk about Scarlet's perfume.'

Caro took a last look at the leg of lamb and then went and sat on the banquette next to Rowan. Alec poured more whisky into her glass. 'I should keep my head until after dinner,' she said, but didn't reject it.

'So, about this perfume?' Alec seemed in charge now. 'Caro said you had a sample of it?'

'Yes,' said Scarlet. 'But I didn't bring it over with me.'

'Oh,' said Alec. 'Then it will be hard to recreate. I mean it will be anyway, but without being able to smell it ...'

'I'm going back to the States soon,' said David. 'Maybe I could fetch it and bring it over?'

Scarlet looked at him, horrified. 'Honey! It's at my parents' house! Like you can turn up there and demand to go through my things! They would never let you into my bedroom even if you got through the front door. They hate you.'

'I'm sure they don't hate me, darling,' said David, 'they just haven't had a chance to get to know me.'

'The age gap,' Scarlet explained to Caro and Rowan. 'It bothers them. They are very conventional people.'

'I don't entirely blame them,' said David. 'I'd probably feel the same if you were my daughter.'

'When are you going back yourself?' said Alec. 'Maybe you could get it then?'

'I don't have an exact return date,' said Scarlet. 'I have my acting classes here and I don't like to visit my parents when they are so horrid about David.'

'What do they say about him?' asked Caro, in case being horrid was merely worrying about the age gap between David and their daughter.

'I don't want to go into detail,' said Scarlet. 'But they don't approve of movies, put it like that.'

'My mother doesn't approve of movies either,' said Rowan. 'Or anything, really,' she added.

Alec cleared his throat. 'She may be a little over-protective but—'

'It's why I had to run away from home,' said Rowan firmly.

'We'll talk about it later, Rowan, but I have to tell you, your mother fully expects me to bring you back home with me.'

Rowan looked mutinous.

Caro broke in quickly, before there could be a row. 'We're thinking about perfume now.' She shot Rowan a quick smile to indicate she was on her side before turning to Scarlet. 'So you're not going to see your parents before you marry David? Have you set a date?'

Scarlet and David exchanged glances. 'We really want to get married soon but we can't decide about the wedding. I mean, my parents, if they could even bring themselves to think about me marrying David, would want one sort of wedding thing, and Hollywood would like another. We don't like either of those options. But whatever, I'm not going back to their house while they are being like this, and I don't want David going there either.'

'Well, it looks like I'll have to manage to recreate this perfume without smelling it then,' said Alec.

'How on earth will you do that?' asked David.

Alec gave a half-smile. 'I may have a secret weapon.'

'What?' asked Scarlet. Everyone looked expectantly at Alec.

'A friend who has an encyclopaedic interest in old perfumes,' he said. 'Trouble is, he lives in Grasse. Which is where a lot of perfume is made,' he added.

'You have to go there!' said Scarlet. 'How exciting! Do you speak French?'

Caro, not allowing herself to think first, said, 'I do! If you need a translator—'

'Oh yes! You should totally go with him,' said Scarlet. 'You speak French, and you know which perfumes I don't like.'

Caro didn't speak. She was regretting inviting herself along on Alec's trip to France and she was hoping he would forget it. It assumed their relationship was far closer than it was.

'Supposing this special perfume doesn't suit you?' asked Alec, who obviously wasn't thinking about anything except the job in hand.

Scarlet sighed deeply. 'I can't believe it won't. I've loved the smell all my life. And if it doesn't, I'll just have to have something else. There are about a million to choose from, after all.' But the prospect of choosing from the million seemed to make Scarlet sad.

'But I want your wedding perfume to be really special, not just something anyone could buy,' said David.

'I could make something for Scarlet,' said Alec. 'But let's focus on working out what is in this old one first. It's such a romantic story.'

For some reason he looked at Caro as he said it and their eyes met. There seemed to be something in his expression that made it significant, she thought. She looked away instantly, worried that she'd got it wrong. It could have been her wishful thinking after all.

'Do you think we should eat?' she said, getting up. Just at that moment she had no idea what time of day it was. It could have been breakfast as far as she was concerned.

She relaxed when everyone was sitting down and tucking in. Scarlet appeared to have no food issues and made enthusiastic comments about everything on her plate.

David and Alec discovered a mutual interest in sailing.

'Scarlet is a little nervous around boats at the moment, but I'm sure we can sort that,' said David.

'The secret is to go sailing with someone who never raises their voice and keeps strictly within the comfort zone of the person who's anxious,' said Alec.

'You have a boat yourself?' asked David.

Alec nodded. 'In Scotland. I never get enough time to take it out though.'

'I've usually sailed in much warmer waters,' said David, 'but I gather the wildlife you see in Scotland is amazing.'

Alec nodded. 'It's well worth putting on a few extra layers for. Whales, dolphins—'

'I'd love to see those,' said Scarlet.

'You must come and stay with us,' said Alec. 'I'll take you sailing and show you Scottish wildlife at its best.'

'We'd love that!' said Scarlet.

'We'll arrange it,' said Alec. He turned to his daughter. 'Now, sweetheart, perhaps it's time we talked about you?'

Chapter Nine

Caro was relieved when Scarlet managed to turn the conversation away from Rowan's immediate future and by the time Scarlet and David went home (the leaving process took half an hour) and Alec had been shown his cabin (recently vacated by a Hollywood starlet) Rowan had also gone off to bed.

Caro and Alec went back to the saloon and sat in silence for a few moments. Caro was tired and she realised it was more for emotional reasons than the normal cooking and cleaning.

Alec seemed happy not to talk too. They obviously had lots to discuss – the perfume, Rowan, Scarlet and David, Murdo – but both were happy just to let things rest.

'Drop more?' Alec held the bottle hovering over Caro's glass.

'Go on, then.' Caro knew she'd probably regret it in the morning but wanted to live in the moment.

'This really is a lovely home,' said Alec, indicating the barge with a gesture. 'It has such a great atmosphere.'

'It's the people who create the atmosphere,' said Caro, although she knew in truth that there was something else provided by this special place that had been home for most of her life.

'But the right atmosphere makes people relax.'

She nodded. And then, without warning, she yawned enormously.

He laughed. 'You're tired! So am I, actually, and tomorrow I'm going to have to talk to Rowan. It won't be fun.'

'She's such a lovely girl. I've loved having her. I like girls. I suppose I miss Posy. Although she's having such a good time I'd be upset if she suddenly wanted to come home.'

'She's a bit older than Rowan?'

She nodded and got up. She was worried if they went on down this path they'd end up discussing Rowan, and Caro felt strongly that Rowan should be present when that happened. 'I think I'll head off to bed now.'

Alec got up too. 'Good idea.'

There was a moment when it looked as though Alec might kiss her. While Caro wanted this, she didn't want their first proper kiss to be at risk of being interrupted, so before he could move closer she fended him off with instructions about the shower and the marine loo. She said goodnight while he was still figuring out the details and shortly afterwards she was in bed, wondering if Alec really had been going to kiss her and what would have happened if she hadn't got nervous and stopped it.

Caro had got up early and felt well ahead with the day before the others appeared. She made pancakes and defrosted blueberries to go with them. A bowl of crème fraîche to go on top and she felt her breakfast was worthy of an Instagram post, had she been that way inclined.

Her houseguests were appreciative. 'This looks amazing!' said Rowan, pulling out a chair and sitting down.

'It does,' said Alec. 'I haven't had pancakes for breakfast for years.'

The pleasant inanities went on as long as Caro felt she could draw them out, but at last she stopped, knowing the difficult conversation couldn't be put off forever.

'Sweetheart? We can't avoid talking about this any more. You're going to have to come home with me,' said Alec.

'I'll leave you to it,' said Caro. 'I need to go and see if there's post, anyway.'

'No!' Rowan grabbed her arm. 'I want you here!'

'There's nothing Caro can do to change what has to happen, darling,' said Alec. 'You're going to have to pack your things and be ready to come home with me tonight. But we can have a lovely day first.'

Rowan's stricken expression made Caro think it was more than just having her fun stopped that was upsetting her.

'Listen, Skye did say that Rowan could stay for a week,' said Caro. 'Why don't you let Rowan stay with me while you're in France? That will give her a few more days and then she can go home with you. There's no reason why she shouldn't, is there?'

'But I thought you were coming with me to France?' Alec seemed put out.

'Well, it would have been lovely but hardly necessary! I was only going as a translator and with your experience I'm sure you speak fluent French.'

He smiled. 'I did study there for some time and so yes, my French is OK.'

'But Scarlet wanted you to go with him!' said Rowan. 'You know what perfume would suit her.'

'I can't be in two places at once, love,' said Caro. 'That would mean you couldn't stay here any longer.'

'Your mother is very keen to have you back,' said Alec.

Rowan made a sound that was half a sob and half a cough. Caro was terribly torn.

'I do understand,' she said. 'But is there any particular reason? Apart from Skye really missing her daughter?'

'She's worried about her,' said Alec. 'She thinks London is the devil's armpit.'

'It's really not!' said Rowan. 'At least, not the bits I go to.'

'Skye would think it's just a matter of time before you start taking drugs and having sex with every man who asks you.' Alec obviously didn't agree with his wife but was stating her case. However, he couldn't hide the fact that he was a little bit worried too.

'Listen, you've obviously got to go back to Scotland now and get your things. Rowan can stay here while you do that. I will look after her,' said Caro earnestly. 'Posy's a London girl, through and through, but while I can't know for certain, I don't think she's ever done the things that Skye is so worried about Rowan doing.'

Alec thought for a moment and then he sighed. 'OK, I'll go home without you, Ro, and explain to your mother why you're not with me.'

Rowan giggled. 'You mean you'll stand there while Mum rants. She's a good ranter.'

'Great to have skills!' said Caro, feeling slightly uncomfortable about what could be thought of as Rowan's lack of respect, although she was probably completely right. 'So what are you two going to do with your day?'

'Aren't you coming with us?' said Alec. Rowan looked anxious too.

'No, I'm going to give you a Tube map and a bus map, and Rowan is going to prove to you, Alec, that she's fine in London without someone holding her hand all the time.' She smiled encouragingly. 'What time is your flight? Don't be late back or I'll fuss.'

She was going to spend her day thinking about what jobs she might go for. She'd had a lovely interlude since Posy had gone to Australia but she needed to make a living.

Caro found she had several options for future employment but none of them excited her. She really wanted to help Alec with his perfume project. She not only loved it herself and had a knack for knowing what scent suited whom, but she loved his daughter. And although the part of her brain that was sensible told her this couldn't be the case, she was pretty sure she loved him, too.

She went shopping in between job-hunting on the Internet and, among other things, bought the ingredients for her favourite chocolate cake and a big tub of cream to go with it. So when Rowan and Alec arrived back, exhausted but happy, she was ready and happy to see them. Chocolate cake, it turned out, was one of Alec's weaknesses. Secretly, she was utterly delighted and was very glad she'd made one. It was after Alec had been seen off to the airport and Rowan and Caro were eating left-over lamb turned into a biryani that Caro felt it was time to do a little tactful probing. They'd all picked over the enjoyable father-and-daughter day together but now Alec had gone, there were things Caro needed to find out from Rowan.

'So.' Caro made sure she had Rowan's full attention. 'I got the impression that it wasn't only that you weren't ready to go home that made you so keen to stay on for a few days?'

Rowan put down her fork. 'I would have told you but not in front of Dad because he'd tell Mum.'

'Is it something bad?' Caro was fairly confident it wasn't or she wouldn't have asked.

'No, it's good!' Rowan's enthusiasm for her plan made her abandon the left-over lamb. 'I'm having an interview at an art school!'

'Oh, that's brilliant!' Caro was about to ask which one but decided it didn't matter at this stage.

'Scarlet helped me. She's so confident. She'd put some of my sketches in her bag and made them agree to see me. Of course I am too young, really, but they agreed to see if I had enough talent and, I suppose, qualifications, for it to be worth me applying.'

'So when is the interview?'

'Next week—'

Caro didn't reply instantly. She had agreed to stay here with Rowan although her heart yearned to go with Alec to Grasse. Rowan's interview had to take precedence over her own desire to go to France. And she'd be more use to Alec taking his daughter to an interview.

'I know you want to go to France with Dad, so Scarlet will come with me instead. She's got her acting course but we could arrange a time to go in her lunch break or something.'

'It's OK, I can take you,' said Caro, sounding calm, feeling devastated. 'Your dad doesn't need me in France and we wouldn't want to make Scarlet miss any of her course.'

Rowan looked put out. 'Scarlet did seem to really want to come with me – and she wanted you to go to France with Dad!'

'Well, let's not talk about it now.' Caro smiled. She knew she didn't need to remind Rowan that next week she might well be back in Scotland with her mother and her best chance of getting to that interview was letting Caro take her.

Caro and Rowan had a very pleasant time together while Alec was back in Scotland. They met Scarlet for lunch on one day and she confessed she was a little anxious about being lonely when David went back to the States.

'Don't forget you could always come and stay with me on the barge,' said Caro, 'although I don't suppose you'd want to. It's fine for a short time but the Ritz is definitely better!'

'And I might have to go back to Scotland next week,' said Rowan.

'Oh no!' said Scarlet. 'But we have your interview!'

'We'll try and persuade Alec to let her stay on for it,' said Caro. 'But we might not be able to swing it.'

Rowan bit her lip and Caro saw she was fighting tears. She realised that Rowan had been very grown up and mature being with her and Scarlet, but she was still very young and having a good cry was a reasonable way to behave at times.

Scarlet obviously spotted this too. 'Don't worry, we'll make it happen somehow!'

'Sorted!' said Caro, not half as confident as she sounded. 'Now, let's get the menu. We don't have to have pudding, but I always have to read about it.'

'Pudding? I love that you call dessert pudding!' said Scarlet. 'I'm definitely having it.'

A few days later, Caro and Rowan were nervously waiting for Alec to come back. They'd thoroughly enjoyed themselves, although Caro felt she never needed to set foot in an art gallery again. They'd also gone on open-topped busses, queued for Madame Tussauds, and generally 'done London'. Now, Caro was tempted to open a bottle of wine to relieve their tension but it was only five o'clock, it would look bad. Alec knew the code to get in so he didn't need to text to say that he was about to arrive, and to Caro's secret disappointment, he hadn't done it anyway.

'The barge is looking lovely, anyway,' said Caro, making conversation. 'You arranged the flowers beautifully.'

'It's only sunflowers in a jug. It's quite easy to make them look like a Van Gogh.'

They fell into silence again.

Caro's nerves were at breaking point when they heard a noise – someone was getting on to the barge. Both women jumped up and teetered, as if they couldn't decide if they should rush up into the wheelhouse or not.

The footsteps coming down the steps were light. They frowned; it couldn't be Alec. Then the door opened and Scarlet came in.

'Hello? Is it really all right for me to come and stay while David is away?'

Caro and Rowan laughed with the relief of tension and Caro fetched some wine. It was so lovely to see Scarlet when they were expecting someone possibly bringing bad news.

Caro had almost forgotten they were expecting Alec when they heard angry voices coming along the pontoon. As they got nearer and nearer Caro noticed there was a distinct Scottish edge to them. They all froze, listening hard.

Rowan went white. 'It's Mum!'

'I think I'll go and use the bathroom,' said Scarlet and fled.

Caro rushed up the stairs to the wheelhouse, almost as if she was repelling boarders.

Skye and Caro arrived in the wheelhouse at the same time. 'You!' she said in furious tones. 'You have corrupted my daughter and put her life in danger!'

Alec followed his ex-wife in, silent now and tight-lipped.

'Where is she?' Skye went on. 'Where is my daughter? Let me see her instantly!'

Caro opened her mouth to speak.

'You're all the same, you London people! Corrupt, wicked, dishonest—'

'Skye!' said Alec sharply. 'Don't speak to Caro like that!'

'Really, there is absolutely no need to be so worked up,' said Caro, keeping a very calm appearance, although she was beginning to shake. 'Your daughter is absolutely fine!' Although Caro did wish Rowan would demonstrate this fineness by coming up to the wheelhouse. Had she discovered the fire escape next to the bathroom and scarpered? She wouldn't blame her, but it would make things extremely awkward.

'Really? I'll be the judge of that!' said Skye, slightly calmer now but just as angry.

'Follow me,' said Caro, and went downstairs.

Rowan was standing in the middle of the room looking like a deer in the headlights, not sure which side of the road to rush to.

Skye rushed to her daughter and took her in her arms. 'My baby! My baby! You're safe!'

'Yes, Mum.' Rowan returned the hug and patted her mother's back. 'I'm quite safe.'

Skye then thrust Rowan away from her so she could get a proper look at her. 'But are you damaged?'

'Of course she's not damaged,' said Alec. 'You can see! She's absolutely fine.'

'Really, Mum, I am,' said Rowan, obviously not expecting to be listened to.

'Apart from your beautiful hair!' wailed Skye.

Caro went into the kitchen. She felt very in the way with all this melodrama going on. She burrowed in her cupboard for some peppermint tea. She thought it would be soothing and she wanted to disguise the fact they'd already had wine. When she'd put the kettle on, she got out the whisky and some glasses. From a hostess point of view, she was ready for anything.

Skye was still obsessed with her daughter's new look. 'You may think you are all right, darling, but how can you be?' Skye's gaze swept the barge with a look that expected to find Sodom and Gomorrah.

'Can I offer anyone any refreshment?' said Caro, aware she sounded like a character from *The*

Archers – Jill Archer, probably. 'The kettle's boiled, or there's whisky. Or wine.'

'Have you been giving my daughter alcohol? May I remind you she's only seventeen?'

Having Skye's furious beauty turned on her was not pleasant, especially as Caro was aware she had let Rowan have wine, just minutes before. However, Caro was determined to remain calm. 'I'm just offering you a drink after a long journey. There's no need for you to get aerated about it, Skye.'

'I don't know how you can talk like that when you think of the harm you've put my daughter in!' Skye obviously hadn't made a resolution to stay calm.

'What danger?' said Caro, pouring whisky into two glasses and handing one to Alec. She then put a peppermint teabag into a mug, added water and gave it to Skye. She obviously did not want alcohol at that particular moment.

'This!' said Skye triumphantly.

Her tone made Caro look up. Skye was brandishing a copy of a newspaper.

'What's that?' asked Rowan.

'It's a picture of you! In the papers! In a very compromising position!'

Caro suddenly felt faint. What had Rowan and Scarlet been up to when she thought they were buying clothes and cupcakes? 'Can I see that?'

Reluctantly, Skye handed over the paper. It was her trump card and she didn't really want anyone else to get hold of it. But she probably realised they needed to see for themselves the ghastliness within its pages.

The paper was folded to the relevant page and Caro took it, her hand shaking. She felt overcome with guilt. She'd been *in loco parentis* and something had happened to Rowan.

It took Caro a few moments to work out what she was looking at and then she realised it was a photograph of Scarlet and David, but she and Rowan were in the picture too. It must have been taken when they were coming out of Selfridges, when they first met. The caption read: 'Who's the beauty with golden couple David Callaghan and Scarlet Lloyd? No one knows but it can't remain a secret long. This sort of loveliness must belong to a star of the future.'

Caro lowered the paper and Rowan snatched it.

'It was taken when we were shopping,' said Rowan. 'But there weren't any paps there.'

Alec had hold of the paper now. 'It was probably taken on someone's phone,' he said. 'And sent to the paper.'

'I don't care who took the picture!' said Skye, her voice still pitched several notes higher than usual. 'I am just appalled that my daughter should be in the paper as if she were a – a—'

The right word eluded her and Alec broke in. 'An extremely beautiful young woman?'

161

'She may be beautiful' – Skye turned on Alec as if he were personally responsible for this disaster – 'but she should not know the meaning of the word "paps" in this context.'

'For goodness' sake, she's not a child,' snapped Alec, losing patience.

'I don't think there's anything to worry about in this picture,' said Caro. 'We were in a department store – a perfectly decent public place.'

'So I should hope!' said Skye, just shy of a shriek. 'But why were people taking your photograph?'

Rowan broke in, possibly trying to protect Caro from her mother's spectacular wrath. 'Only because we were with David and Scarlet—'

Skye turned on her daughter. 'You know these people? The "golden couple" the newspaper talked about?'

Skye made inverted commas with her fingers and suddenly Caro wanted to hit her. 'They're an extremely nice couple we happened to meet,' she said. 'Now, Skye, why don't you sit down and have something to drink? You must be tired.' She was about to offer her use of the bathroom but realised Scarlet might still be in there. If she had any sense, she'd stay there until Skye had left.

'I think you are making a huge fuss over nothing,' said Alec, who'd taken the paper. 'As I said on the plane, there's nothing remotely indecent about any of this.'

Aware that those words were more likely to enrage Skye further, rather can calm her down, Caro almost pushed Skye into a seat. 'Of course you're worried: your daughter has been away from home for the first time. But please let me set your mind at rest. She's always been perfectly safe and with an adult, ever since I joined her here on the barge.' She handed Skye the peppermint tea, trusting it wasn't so hot it would scald her.

'But who are the adults?' Skye took a sip from the mug and seemed to relax just a tiny bit.

'Me, her father or—'

'Scarlet's really lovely!' said Rowan. 'She bought me this top.'

'And is she responsible for the desecration of your beautiful hair?' said Skye.

'No, that was me,' said Caro, not thinking properly for a second. 'I mean, Rowan had cut it herself but I took her to the hairdresser afterwards.'

Skye didn't seem to have heard the bit about Rowan cutting it herself. 'You!' She put down her mug so she could point at Caro, something Caro absolutely hated. 'You had my daughter's hair cut! I have never cut my daughter's hair. I'm going to sue you for damages – damage to my daughter. It's an abuse!'

'No it's not!' said Rowan. 'I cut my hair. It's *my* hair. I can do what I like with it. I had made rather a mess of it so Caro took me to someone who made it look OK.' Rowan seemed crushed suddenly. 'I thought it looked quite nice.'

'It's beautiful, chicken,' said Alec. 'You're beautiful.'

'And it makes her vulnerable!' declared Skye, who then sat back and drank some more tea, exhausted by outrage and budget air travel.

Caro didn't know what to do to calm this situation. While in many ways Skye was being unreasonable, in fact Rowan was a bit vulnerable. She was young and naïve and, yes, beautiful. Caro's last little bit of hope that she might, in the end, be able to go to France with Alec faded. She had to stay in London for Rowan's sake.

'Mum?' Rowan had seated herself next to Skye. 'I know you only want the best for me. I really get that. But the best for me right now is to be here, in London.'

Alec was holding a glass of whisky, staring into it, but not actually drinking it.

'Why?' asked Skye. 'Why isn't your life in one of the most beautiful parts of the world enough for you?'

'I need to broaden my horizons.' Rowan was obviously using an expression she'd heard someone else use. (Caro suspected Scarlet.) 'Not just run around surrounded by wildlife and amazing scenery, although of course I do love that. But actual people, shops, theatres, cinemas, exhibitions.' She paused. 'I'm a teenager, Mum. We need those things too.'

'I thought I'd brought you up not to be materialistic,' said Skye.

'I don't think wanting to go to the movies counts as being materialistic,' said Alec mildly.

'Don't you butt in!' Skye snapped. 'You're an absent father most of the time!'

Alec inhaled sharply and then clenched his teeth. Caro could see him trying hard not to throw this comment back at his ex-wife. She was absent a lot of the time too, doing yoga and other esoteric activities with her clients.

'I do think Rowan's upbringing so far has made her one of the sweetest girls imaginable,' said Caro. 'And also one of the most sensible. Really, she's not dazzled by London, she just wants to take advantage of the good things it has to offer.'

Caro was proud of this little statement. It may have sounded a bit like copy for an ad for the capital, but for something she hadn't thought out previously, it was quite good.

'You mean like drugs? Alcohol? Knife crime? Sex?' Skye raised a sceptical eyebrow in Caro's direction.

Caro sighed and tried again. 'I did specify the good things, Skye. Rowan's shown no interest in any of those other things.'

'You know my daughter better than I do, I suppose?'

Caro wanted to groan. 'No! But I have seen her in the West End. I know she's not into drugs and things.'

'You've exposed to her to them, just to find out?' Skye really had sarcasm down to a fine art. 'I hardly think taking her to a department store is much of a test.'

'Enough, Skye,' said Alec. 'Caro has been incredibly kind to our daughter. Please be polite, at least.'

'Dad's right, you know,' said Rowan. 'Caro has been really kind and she's made sure I haven't got into trouble. She's explained where I shouldn't go and things.'

Skye sighed heavily. 'Very well, I apologise if I've been rude.'

No 'if' about it, thought Caro. 'Look, I do understand about having a teenage daughter. In my experience, they're always a lot more sensible than you think they're going to be.'

She sat down opposite Skye and Rowan, wondering if she could fetch her wine from the kitchen without making Skye think she was a complete alcoholic. 'So, how's Murdo?'

'He's probably going to be fine. Lennie has completely taken over, as usual, and he won't hear of taking anything that isn't utterly toxic. And that includes whisky.' She indicated Alec as she said this.

Then she moved in her seat and turned her full attention on Rowan.

'So,' she said, 'who is this starlet you seem to have taken up with?'

'That would be me,' said Scarlet, who had obviously been picking her moment to enter the saloon. 'I'm the starlet – whatever that means.'

Chapter Ten

Both Skye and Alec seemed hypnotised by the vision that emerged from the door to the accommodation. Caro gripped Rowan's hand, silently warning her not to speak, and to trust Scarlet to say the right things.

Scarlet went up to Skye. 'You must be Rowan's mother? I can see where she gets her looks from, and her sweet nature too, I guess.' She smiled.

Skye found her voice. 'You're the woman in the photograph.' It was a statement but Caro knew that soon it would become an accusation.

'Scarlet Lloyd.' She put out a hand, found Skye's and shook it. 'And I'm afraid I and my fiancé David are the reason Rowan was photographed. We'd only just met Caro and Rowan or we'd have been more careful.'

'Why were you photographed?' asked Alec, who obviously didn't read the right magazines to keep abreast of current celebrities.

'Oh, it's very boring!' said Scarlet with a gesture. 'It's because David is really famous and we're engaged and there's an age gap. Some people just don't have enough to do with their lives.' She sighed.

'Scarlet, what would you like to drink? Tea? Wine?'

'Wine please,' said Scarlet, and sat down.

Skye, no longer so stunned by Scarlet's entrance, began to look suspicious. 'Why were you hiding in that cupboard?'

Caro answered. 'She wasn't hiding or in a cupboard, she came a few minutes before you did and had gone to the accommodation at the front of the barge. Would you like me to show you?'

Skye looked at Caro. 'Why would I want to look at the bedrooms?'

'I was thinking of the bathroom, actually, in case you wanted to freshen up after your flight?' said Caro. Privately she was hoping that Skye's lack of interest in the bedrooms meant she wasn't expecting to stay but as Caro had had no idea she was coming, she had no idea what Skye's plans were. Was there an overnight bag left upstairs in the wheelhouse? She might have to go and have a look.

'I'm not a child,' said Skye. 'If I need the bathroom I'll find it.'

Caro intercepted a look of irritation sent to Skye by Alec. She found it comforting. She glanced up at the old ship's clock fixed to the wall. Soon she'd have to think about feeding these people. The alternative, which was to tell them all to go away, didn't seem to be viable.

'So, Skye,' said Scarlet, 'why have you come here? Is it to visit to Caro on her wonderful barge?'

She did sound a bit like an American newscaster on breakfast television, Caro had to admit, but she was so grateful to Scarlet for making conversation in these difficult circumstances, she wasn't going to criticise, even in her head.

'I am here', said Skye, full of dignity and drama, 'to take my daughter home!'

'This evening?' Scarlet was surprised.

'Yes! In fact – Rowan? Get your things together. We're going!'

'But you can't possibly take her home,' said Scarlet. 'She has an interview next week with a very prestigious art school.'

'Rowan isn't going to art school,' said Skye. 'She has a raw, natural talent and it isn't going to be interfered with by anyone else's idea of what art is!'

'She certainly has talent,' Scarlet agreed. 'But even the best talent has to be nurtured.'

'Not the point,' said Skye. 'She's far too young to go to art school.'

'She is,' Scarlet acknowledged, 'but this is a preliminary interview to see if Rowan is good enough to apply for next year. She's lacking a lot of the qualifications that are normally necessary, owing to her – how did they put it? – "unconventional education".'

'I really need to have this interview, Mum,' Rowan said urgently. 'Either that or take about ten exams before next year.'

Rowan was exaggerating, but she may well have to take a few GCSEs in something other than art, Caro realised.

'Why don't you stay, and go with her to the interview?' said Caro, trusting Skye wouldn't need to be on the barge with her, should she say yes.

'I couldn't possibly! I have a tantric yoga group booked for next week. I need to be at home.' Skye appeared to be insulted just by the suggestion.

'I don't want to go on my own, Mum! And Dad can't – he's got to go to France. He's going to recreate a special perfume for Scarlet. It's his big chance!'

'I don't think your father's little hobby should be allowed to get in the way of your education.' Skye directed a sarcastic smile in the direction of her ex-husband.

Caro was convinced that Skye would never have considered Rowan's interview important if it hadn't given her an opportunity to have a dig at Alec.

'It's not a hobby!' said Rowan. 'This perfume is going to be completely unique. It'll probably make him lots of money!'

'Not really, sweetheart.' Alec shot Scarlet an embarrassed glance. 'The money isn't really the point.'

'Typical of you, Alec. You never do anything for money,' Skye snapped.

'But Skye' – Caro couldn't stop herself – 'I thought you abhorred materialism, money, things like that?'

'There's a difference between having values and allowing your family to starve because you can't earn enough money to keep them!' Skye's eyes sparkled with righteous indignation. It was a look that suited her.

'That's fine,' said Scarlet to Alec. She turned back to Skye. 'I'll take Rowan to the interview.'

Caro stopped herself breaking in to say she would take Rowan. If Skye let Scarlet do it, she might still get to France.

'But she can't stay here alone,' said Skye.

'I won't be alone,' said Rowan, 'there'll be Scarlet and Joe—'

'I'm not leaving you in London with – excuse me – a young woman who is hardly older than you are and a man I know nothing whatever about.'

'Thank you for the compliment,' said Scarlet, 'but I am quite a bit older than Rowan.'

Caro broke in. 'And I definitely remember telling you about Joe when you were so worried about Rowan having come down here. He's totally reliable. He doesn't have an evil bone in his body.'

'Get your things, Rowan, this is ridiculous.' Skye might have been into spiritual practices and inner peace but she could be very steely.

Her tiny spark of hope extinguished, Caro sighed. 'I'm going to be here too,' she said. 'Didn't I mention that?' It was a sacrifice, but it was the only solution.

'But, Caro! You were supposed to go with Dad and do the perfume. He needs you!' Rowan was insistent.

'Well, you need me more,' Caro went on calmly. 'It's fine. I was only going to speak French for him but he can do that perfectly well without me. We'll go to your interview together and have a nice time.'

Skye got up. 'Maybe you could show me the bathroom now?' she said to Caro, making it quite clear that being told it was the last door on the right wouldn't do. She wanted to talk to Caro in private.

The moment the two women were through the watertight door that separated the main saloon from the accommodation, Skye stopped.

'You must know – it's only fair to tell you – that Rowan is always trying to matchmake for her father. He's utterly hopeless – I don't even think he's capable of having a proper relationship. And if he was, I'm afraid it wouldn't be with you.' Skye gave a quick little 'I'm telling you this for your own good' smile. 'He's very obsessed with beauty, and while you are obviously lovely' – another smile – 'he's

173

never going to pick you, not for the long haul. Just so you know.'

'OK, and the bathroom is that door there,' Caro said. 'It has a sea toilet but there are instructions on how to use it. Just so you know.'

Caro felt it would have served Skye right if she hadn't told her where the loo was. The thought of having to have this woman in her space for too much longer was making her feel sick. And she disliked her all the more because she realised she was probably right. Alec wouldn't really go for her when he'd had Skye.

'So, Rowan, things,' Skye said briskly when she was back. 'We need to get going.'

'There's no need for Rowan to leave,' said Caro. 'As I said, I'll be here and see she gets to her interview. I'll be *in loco parentis*.'

'I don't think I believe you,' said Skye. 'I think you'll shoot off to France the moment I'm gone.'

'Even if she did,' broke in Scarlet, indignant at hearing Caro virtually called a liar in her presence, 'I'll be here.'

'Really?' Skye turned to her. 'You won't be jetting off to Hollywood to be photographed half-naked in the pool of a movie mogul?'

Scarlet flushed. Skye was apparently referring to a real incident. 'If you mean will I be going to my fiancé's house and wear a swimsuit while swimming, no I won't, not this time. I'm enrolled on an acting course with Sir Thomas Longhampton and will be in London.'

Skye's hands flew to her face. 'Not *the* Sir Thomas Longhampton?'

'Is there more than one?' Scarlet could well have been channelling Skye, her tone was so disdainful.

'I saw his Hamlet when I was a student,' Skye went on. 'It was magical.'

'Ooh! Something good happened in London, Mum!' said Rowan, sounding very young.

'Stratford-upon-Avon, actually,' said Skye. 'But it was an experience I'll never forget.'

'He doesn't do much teaching,' said Scarlet. 'I was very lucky to get on his course.'

'Or you're just very good at acting,' suggested Alec.

'If she was that good she wouldn't need to take lessons,' snapped Skye.

'Hey!' said a soft voice from the door. 'Sounds like the vibe in here has become a bit toxic. Let's see what we can do about that.'

Caro happened to be looking at Skye when Joe came in and saw her face change from tense and negative to intrigued and interested. Joe was very good-looking and Skye had obviously noticed.

'This is Joe, everyone,' said Caro. 'Skye, Joe is very into shamanism.' She sensed that Skye would like this and hoped it would make her feel better about Joe.

It was as if someone had put Skye into a warm bath. She relaxed and smiled. 'Really?' she said to Joe. 'I've been looking for someone to teach that for me at my Wellness Centre. It needs a more masculine energy sometimes. We should talk.'

'Come in and join the party,' said Caro to Joe, fascinated to see the effect he was having on Skye.

'Have you guys eaten?' said Joe, going into the kitchen area instead. 'I've got some wonderful little cakes made with aquafaba if anyone fancies a vegan dessert.'

'I haven't been near anyone who even knows what that is for years,' said Skye.

Caro felt a flicker of sympathy for her as she thought of the huntin', shootin' and fishin' world Skye lived in on the estate. But then again, she could live somewhere else if she was that bothered.

'So what is it?' asked Alec.

'Chick-pea water,' said Skye.

'Actually if you haven't eaten and would like a vegan meal,' Joe went on, 'why don't I pop out and get a few things? I could cook when I get back.'

'That would be great!' said Caro, resisting the temptation to offer him her purse, something she'd always done in the past if he or Posy were popping out for something for the household.

'I'll come with you,' said Skye. 'I could do with some fresh air.'

Within moments, Skye and Joe had gone.

'She makes me feel as if we've all been sitting here farting and burping,' said Scarlet. 'Sorry,' she added.

Rowan giggled and Caro joined in.

'Joe deserves a medal,' said Alec.

'Oh, I don't know,' said Scarlet. 'Your ex-wife is very beautiful.'

Caro thought he definitely deserved a medal but didn't want to get into a discussion about Skye's beauty. 'More wine anyone? I don't think it's vegan, so maybe Skye won't want to drink it.'

'She's only vegan when it suits her,' said Alec.

'Maybe she fancies Joe,' said Rowan.

'He is very cute,' agreed Scarlet.

'You never mentioned he was cute,' Alec said rather pointedly to Caro.

'I've known Joe so long he's almost like my nephew or something,' said Caro. 'He came to live on the barge when he was twenty and Posy was five. He was the son of an old friend of my dad's and couldn't afford accommodation in London. He was only supposed to stay until he found somewhere else to live but he fitted in so well and was so useful, we just kept him.'

She smiled. Joe *was* useful and naturally suited to life on the barge, but he was a free spirit. He wouldn't have stayed if he hadn't wanted to.

'What about when Posy grew up? Weren't you worried about a girl having a piece of eye-candy like him living here?' asked Scarlet.

'Not at all – she always treated him like a sort of older brother. And Posy told me once that she loved him but they didn't have chemistry.' Caro smiled. At the time she had said it wasn't chemistry she was worried about, but biology. Posy had rolled her eyes and said, 'Mu-um!'

'Now,' Caro went on. 'In case any of us aren't vegan, I've got some rather nice pâté. I'll put it on some crackers.'

Skye and Joe seemed to find more in common than just vegan food and shamanism by the time they got back with bags of shopping. Caro was glad. Skye might have been very irritating but it wasn't unreasonable to be worried about her daughter. Maybe she'd be able to go back to Scotland knowing her daughter was perfectly safe.

Or maybe she'd go back to Scotland thinking about a good-looking shaman who had (Caro had always suspected) a weakness for older women. Just as long as Skye went back to Scotland, and soon, Caro didn't really care.

Skye cleared her throat, just as Caro was calculating if they had enough places for everyone to sit down.

'I've decided,' said Skye. 'I will let Rowan stay for a little bit. Joe convinced me that the karmic energy of London isn't quite as toxic as I thought.'

'Hooray!' said Caro. 'That's really good news. Now let's eat!'

It was a delicious meal, everyone agreed. They all had wine, including Rowan, who had a very small amount out of respect for her mother. And while everyone exclaimed at how delicious and unexpectedly varied vegan food could be, Caro worried. Where was she going to put everyone if Skye needed to stay?

And while it wasn't remotely unreasonable for her to ask if Skye was expecting to say, somehow she couldn't. She decided if the worst came to the worst – and it would be the very worst – she'd have to offer Skye her bed and sleep on the sofa. However well Skye and Joe seemed to be getting on she could hardly ask if they'd bunk up together.

But just as the last vegan macaroon was crunched to destruction by Joe's very white but slightly crooked teeth, Alec and Skye got up from the table.

'I don't think you'll make the plane,' said Alec, looking at his watch, 'but I can get you on the sleeper if you hurry.'

They rushed out of the door, Skye hardly sparing time to kiss her daughter goodbye, and then there was silence.

Scarlet started to giggle. 'Well, that was weird!'

'She's a lovely woman,' said Joe. 'Really interesting.'

'You should go up and visit,' said Rowan. 'You'd love Glen Liddell – although it is tough for a vegan, I expect.'

'Oh, I'm not a vegan,' explained Joe. 'I just like to experiment with different types of food.'

'He has been known to eat roadkill,' said Caro.

'Gross!' said Scarlet and Rowan, almost as one.

'We discussed you going to France with Alec,' said Joe.

Caro, who had been gathering dishes, stopped. 'And?'

'She's OK about it,' said Joe casually.

'Really?' said Caro, her heart beating faster. 'She really said it's OK to leave Rowan here with just Scarlet and you to look after her? She doesn't need me too?'

Joe nodded. 'She took a bit of persuading but she came round to the idea. I think getting to know me a bit has given Skye confidence.' He smiled. 'Besides, she's really keen on having a shamanism workshop at her Wellness Centre.'

'But you wouldn't refuse to do that if she said no to Rowan staying with you and Scarlet? I think that would be wrong.' Caro's passionate need to be fair could sometimes work against her.

'Of course not,' said Joe. 'But she's happy enough about it, and for Scarlet to take Rowan to her inter-view at the art school. We went for a quick drink after we bought the food and talked it all over.'

Caro beamed at everyone as she carried a pile of dishes to the galley area, ecstatically happy. 'I'll just get this lot out of the way and we can sort out beds.'

'I'll help you with that,' said Joe.

'No! You cooked.' She didn't like to add that he'd been brilliant with Skye too, although it was true, because she didn't want to imply Skye was difficult, which was also true.

'We can do beds,' said Scarlet. 'Rowan, do you know where things are?'

'Yup,' said Rowan. 'Though Dad's sleeping in the cabin you had before.'

Caro filled the dishwasher rapidly and then put the kettle on. The others may not need a cup of tea and a nice sit-down but she certainly did.

They were all sitting and relaxing when Alec came back.

'Did Mum get her train all right?' asked Rowan, anxious in case her mother might suddenly spring into view and threaten her plans all over again.

'On the train, safe and sound.'

'And she's really OK with Rowan being here, even if I'm not?' asked Caro. 'You don't need me in France, after all.'

He grinned, suddenly reminding her of the boy she'd spent all night talking to on a beach of a Greek island. 'Actually, I really do! When I was paying for Skye's ticket, I realised I didn't have my driving licence with me.'

Caro couldn't stop smiling. Not only was she going to France with Alec, she had a real, proper reason to accompany him.

'We'd better see if we can sort out some flights then,' she said, trying to keep the joyous excitement out of her voice.

'Lead me to your laptop,' said Alec. He was smiling too.

Chapter Eleven

Although it was late, they agreed Alec should email his friend and Caro should investigate flights. She had to force herself to keep calm. She'd had this treat snatched from her so often (it seemed) and now she was really going to France.

She had just booked two seats for tomorrow's afternoon flight (expensive but convenient) and was looking into car hire when Alec had a reply.

'Pascal is really welcoming!' he said. 'If we meet him at the factory in Grasse, he can put us up for a couple of nights.'

'Lovely!' said Caro, thinking that really she'd prefer a B and B or even a small apartment so she could have her own bathroom. She also wondered a little bit about sleeping arrangements but trusted that Alec would have made it clear in his email they weren't a couple. Or were they? She'd lost confidence in her ability to read his body language and

her own feelings made her flee from intimacy sometimes. She really hoped this trip away from everyone
else close to them would give them a chance to sort
things out.

When she finally got into her own bed that night
she was very glad they hadn't gone for the 5 a.m.
flight. Check-in times at London City were relaxed
compared to major airports but it would still have
been a horrendously early start.

Although it was easy to get to the airport via the
Docklands Light Railway, Alec had arranged a cab.

Caro was very excited. She had her carry-on case
which had wheels and hoped she'd packed the right
things. The trouble with packing was, she felt, that
while you knew you wouldn't wear half what you
had put in your case, you never knew which half.
What would the weather be like in the South of
France at this time of year? But as she had a credit
card and was going to a very nice part of the world,
she felt she'd be able to buy anything vital she might
have omitted.

Alec had a worn leather bag slung over his
shoulder which appeared to contain all he needed.
He was, Caro decided, lucky: he could look informal –
untidy even – in an attractive way. What looked
good on him would look a mess on some other
people.

Little bubbles of excitement kept forming inside
her as they drove through the streets. She was going

to the Côte d'Azur with a very attractive man. Whatever happened or didn't happen between them, that had to be good.

She'd been out with a few people since she and Posy's father had broken up and some of the relationships had been fun. But none had been worth either sharing her barge or leaving it so they could live together. Posy was quite fussy too, and anyone she was remotely sniffy about was sent on his merry way. What would Posy think about Alec, she wondered? At least he had his own hair and teeth – a minimum requirement for Posy. Although, to be fair, she didn't know if he took his gnashers out at night and put them in a glass. She'd probably find out soon enough. She glanced across at his teeth and said, 'Are we nearly there yet?'

He looked confused but did smile. No, those teeth looked healthy, but a bit crooked as well. They were his. She smiled back, slightly more enthusiastically than her small joke deserved.

When they were on the plane, Alec said, 'Let me tell you about Pascal. He's been so important in my life.'

'Go on then,' Caro said.

'We met at uni. We both did chemistry but he always wanted to create perfume. I'm not sure if he gave me the idea, but of course that's what I've always wanted to do too, and after uni Pascal went on to study perfumery at ISIPCA in Versailles.' He paused. 'I asked my father if I could go too, offered to pay my own way, but I'm afraid his reaction was – well – fairly extreme.'

'He threw you out?'

Alec nodded.

'Really?' Caro was shocked. 'I was joking when I said that, sort of. Murdo really threw you out of the house because you wanted to learn how to make perfume?'

'There were a few other things wrong with me of course but that was the icing on the cake.' Alec grinned. 'We'd never got on really well. I just wasn't huntin', shootin' and fishin' enough for him, although I do like fishing. He got on much better with Lennie.'

Caro nodded. 'But that's terrible. I suppose Murdo is from a different generation really, older than his age in terms of being a member of the modern world.'

'No one could ever accuse my father of being modern, that's for sure.'

'So,' went on Caro, aware that it wasn't a long flight and she needed to know about Pascal before they met him, 'how did you learn perfumery? And how did Pascal come into it?'

'In some ways, I was lucky. I got a job on the oil rigs in the North Sea. But I also had Skye and Rowan to support, quite early on. This meant I had to learn about perfumery in my spare time. I'd go on the odd course when I was home from the rigs, but I had a family, I had to spend time with them too.'

'Would you rather not have had a family?' The thought did make him seem rather heartless.

'Nothing could ever make me regret having Rowan, but honestly? Skye and I got married because she was pregnant. But anyway, perfume was always more of a hobby. I'd see Pascal sometimes and he'd talk to me about it, tell me what was going on in the industry, point me to books I could read, short courses I could go on. It all had to be secret, of course.'

'Secret from Skye?'

'Oh yes. She didn't want me doing anything that wasn't all about her.'

'Perhaps that was because you were away so much and she may have felt she spent enough time alone with her baby. She would want you there when you could be.'

'It wasn't about me spending time with Rowan – Skye wanted me to focus on her, not our lovely daughter. But I don't want to tell you my wife didn't understand me – she didn't, but that was my fault, not hers, really.'

'So, the perfume? You managed to learn all about it without going to college?'

He shook his head ruefully. 'I managed to learn a bit about it over the years, and managed to blag my way on to an intensive course. I don't suppose a French perfumier would consider me qualified really, but I know enough to start creating some fragrances, I think. I've always had to have other jobs; I could never devote myself entirely to it. Ironically, now I'm running the estate, I can find a bit more time. And Pascal will help if there's anything I can't do for Scarlet and David.'

'Well, that's brilliant. It makes it even more clever, you having to do it part-time and in secret.'

Alec sighed. 'I just wish Murdo wasn't quite as set in his ways. I'm sure we could get on better if only he hadn't got me down as an airy-fairy waste of space.'

Caro giggled. 'If that's what he thinks about you, what does he think about Skye?'

'Well, Skye gets away with a lot more because she's only a woman and she's pretty. Besides, she gave him Rowan and he adores her.'

'We all do! She's so lovely!'

'And I'm so grateful for everything you've done to help her.'

'No need for gratitude. She's a very talented artist and so sweet.'

He put his hand on hers for a second before there was a call for landing.

'Oh, I love it when you step off an aeroplane and know you're abroad,' said Caro. 'The warmth, the smell, the feeling of being somewhere different.'

Her feeling of elation survived passport control, picking up the car and negotiating her way out of the car-hire car park. She pulled over as soon as she could to get out of the way of cars who knew where they were going.

'You don't mind driving on the right?' Alec asked, getting out his phone and finding the satnav on it.

'Not after a few minutes. I've done it before.'

'Cool. Traffic in towns can be a bit unnerving.'

'I'm used to central London,' said Caro. 'Although I avoid taking the car if I can, when I do, I can get down and dirty with the best of the white vans.'

'You are so multi-talented!'

'I like to think so! Shall I head for the motorway? Towards Grasse?'

'That should do it. I'll give you directions as we go.'

Sharing a car, in these circumstances, was a bit like sharing a bathroom, Caro thought – potentially very threatening to the relationship. Fortunately Alec was a good passenger and navigator. Soon Grasse was appearing on signposts and after less than an hour, they were negotiating the steep and narrow streets of their destination.

'Shall I go to that car park?' asked Caro. 'It would probably be easier to find where we want to go on foot from here.'

'Absolutely.' Alec glanced at her. 'I must say you're a whizz at these little roads.'

'I learnt to drive in London and Cornwall. Traffic for one; narrow, steep and twisty roads for the other. Now, where are we meeting Pascal?'

'I wrote it down somewhere.' He studied his phone for a few moments. 'I think it's this way.'

When they had locked the car and made a note of where they'd left it, he took her hand and they set off.

Caro was feeling like a teenager in love. She wasn't absolutely sure if Alec was holding her hand because he wanted to touch her or if he was just worried about her getting lost but she didn't care. She was in France, the roses were out and she was with the man she loved.

She was aware that the roses were lost on Alec, but she would never forget that night they spent together in Greece. There had been a rambling rose, pale pink with tiny pom-pom blossoms, where they were sitting. It had dropped petals like scented snowflakes, on and off through the hours.

'Pascal works in a very small perfume factory,' Alec explained, still holding on to her. 'Ah! Here it is!'

Caro tuned out a bit as Pascal and Alec hugged and they spoke French at a hundred miles an hour. She did smile at herself offering to be Alec's translator back on the barge – he was so good at it! But as she relaxed she began to understand a bit more. When

Pascal turned to her, held her arms and then kissed her cheeks three times, she was able to greet him in French.

'Ah! *Vous parlez français couramment!*' he said delightedly. 'But will you allow me to practise my English?'

Although pleased that she had held her own up to that minute, Caro was quite relieved not to have to speak French any more. In a couple of days she would have got her ear in and would be happy to focus and speak the language, but just now it was proving quite an effort.

'Let me give you a quick tour and then it will be time for an aperitif,' said Pascal. 'I will show you the laboratory tomorrow but now, come and see our antique scent bottles. *Allons-y.* Of course the perfume museum nearby would deny this, but I think our collection is possibly better than theirs.'

They were works of art. Caro could have spent ages looking at the wonderful porcelain and glass that had once held perfume. It seemed at one time the vessel was as important or even more important than its contents. Animals, people, every sort of house: all were represented. 'Now I see how important the Lalique glass swan that was made for Serena Swan's perfume was,' said Caro. 'It wouldn't have seemed special if it had just been in a generic bottle.'

'It's easy to get distracted,' said Alec, 'but we're looking to recreate the lost perfume created by

Anton Dolinière for one of the most famous film stars of her generation – possibly the most famous.'

Pascal shrugged. 'It will not be easy. Even if you know what you are hoping to achieve, the ingredients will be different today.'

'And unfortunately the only sample we know of is in private hands in America,' said Alec.

'Ah!' Pascal made a gesture that reminded Caro of an old-fashioned magician. 'You are in luck! I know the grandson of M. Dolinière and I strongly suspect that his grandpère would not have obeyed the order to destroy all of his creation. What perfumier would so such a thing? It would be a … a sacrilege! So he may well have a small bottle. But what condition would it be in by now? Who can say?'

'But that would be amazingly good luck!' said Caro.

'Not good luck, but good management, do you not say? In England?'

'Sometimes we do,' Caro agreed.

'It is too late to call on my friend today – he is elderly and he sleeps in the afternoon – but we will see if we can persuade him to let us borrow his bottle tomorrow. If he has one, of course. Although I warn you, he may say no.'

'A sniff of it would help,' said Alec. 'And if we all smell it, we have a chance. And Caro will know if the scent is right for Scarlet or not. She has a very good memory for fragrance and a special instinct about what works and what doesn't.'

Caro felt herself go warm with pleasure. She had been feeling a bit like a third wheel on this adventure and Alec had made her feel important and necessary. If she'd needed any more reasons to love him, he'd just provided one.

'I have a few things to finish up here and then you can follow me home.'

Alec and Caro went back to the museum part.

'I reckon Pascal's old friend does have a sample, don't you think?' said Caro.

'It sounded like it,' Alec agreed. 'I think he's giving the old man a chance to keep it to himself so he doesn't have to share it with us if he doesn't want to.'

'I'd love to see the original swan bottle,' said Caro. 'The containers were obviously such an important part of it.'

'There'll be a picture of it somewhere, I'm sure, but I wonder if Scarlet should have something a bit different for her perfume? It's very unlikely that I'll be able to recreate the fragrance exactly; maybe the bottle should reflect that difference?'

'It's up to Scarlet ultimately. I wonder what she knows about the bottle. I'll email her and find out.'

'It's good to have you here, Caro,' said Alec.

Caro sighed with pleasure. 'It's good to be here! Lovely weather, lovely France, roses out: it's all gorgeous.'

To their surprise, Pascal didn't seem to have a little flat in Grasse, which was what they had both expected. Caro followed him out of town and up into the hills, having to drive just slightly faster than she was comfortable with.

'These must be the Alpes Maritimes,' said Caro, negotiating a sharp bend. 'Beautiful, aren't they?'

'I'm surprised he lives so far from his work though,' said Alec.

'Not that far, he's turning off ... down a long drive,' she added, surprised. 'Alec!' she said urgently a couple of seconds later. 'You didn't tell me Pascal lived in a chateau.'

At the end of the drive was a beautiful building, like a child's drawing of a palace: symmetrical, with shuttered windows on three floors and towers at either end. It was set amongst parkland with outbuildings on either side. There was woodland and, behind, the mountains. Caro stopped the car so she could take it in.

'I swear I didn't know about this,' said Alec. 'He's always had small apartments before. I was rather surprised when he said he could put us up, but this explains it.'

'It's gorgeous!' said Caro. 'And I really hope he bought it with the proceeds of perfume.'

'I'm afraid that is really unlikely. Pascal could get a job with one of the major perfume houses but he prefers to do his own thing.'

Caro sighed. 'Oh well, we get to stay in it, however it was paid for.'

She parked the hire car next to Pascal's little sports model.

'Hey! Pascal! When did you buy this?' asked Alec, gesturing towards the chateau.

Pascal shrugged. 'I didn't buy it. My sister and I inherited it from our uncle. It is a money pit but very beautiful, so we forgive it.'

A woman appeared on the front steps. She was probably in her late thirties, wearing dungarees with a scarf round her head. She had dark hair and was very attractive and French-looking. She spoke to her brother in rapid French, shooting apologetic glances towards Alec and Caro as she did so.

'I am so sorry,' she said in highly accented English. 'Pascal is not supposed to have guests unless he gives a lot of notice. The rooms we have are not ready. They are full of spiders and smell of damp.'

Before Caro could somehow extricate them from the situation, the woman went on.

'But if you are true friends, you will forgive a little mess, *non*?' Her smile was wide and very warm.

'It's so kind of you to have us,' said Caro. 'But if it's at all difficult, we could go and find a hotel or a B and B in town.'

'*Pas du tout!*' said the woman. 'We are going to offer *chambres d'hotes* – we can practise on you.'

Pascal seemed to find this all very amusing. 'This is my sister, Amalie. Amalie, this is Alec, my old friend, whom you have heard about, and this is Caro.'

There was a lot of kissing and hand-shaking and Caro realised that Amalie was actually very pleased to see them.

'We have one room finished,' Amalie explained as she led them up a beautifully curved staircase with a highly polished bannister that just asked to be slid down. 'And next to it, we have a work in progress. I think I will call *all* the rooms "work in progress" when we have paying guests. Then they cannot complain if they are not perfect.'

Pascal, who was following with the bags, said, 'Nothing will ever be perfect enough for my sister, which is why having a chateau is good for her. She will have to learn to live with imperfections.'

'But it's so beautiful,' said Caro, in awe. 'No one would care about anything crumbling or not being finished.'

'That is my master plan!' said Amalie, twinkling. 'I see it is working already! *Et voilà!*'

She opened the door to an enormous bedroom. From the door Caro could see a huge sleigh bed, a wonderful view from the windows and some antique wallpaper behind a huge, ancient mirror.

'Alec? I suggest you take this room.' Amalie revealed a slightly smaller room. As yet there was no wallpaper but the bed was huge and the view was as stunning.

'Come down to the *terrasse* at the back when you're ready,' said Pascal. 'We will have champagne to celebrate seeing our old friend and meeting Caro.'

'Wow!' said Caro when she and Alec were alone. 'I feel a bit overwhelmed!'

'Don't be. They are really lovely people. You've seen how warm and friendly they are. Why don't you wash your hands or whatever, while I have a quick word with Pascal? Will you find your way? Or would you like me to come and fetch you?'

In her heart, Caro felt she would like him to come and get her, but she just smiled. 'I'll follow the sound of corks popping and find you.'

Caro took her bag into the larger room. She allowed herself a few moments to take in its grandeur. It was sparsely furnished but it was all antique and high quality, from the chaise longue draped with a pale-pink mohair blanket to the gilt dressing table that had three mirrors and three little drawers.

There was an open door that led to an en-suite which was as modern as the bedroom was period.

Caro felt that putting on more make-up might look a bit wrong when Amalie was so enchantingly dressed in her work clothes. So she just washed her hands, wiped the mascara that had moved under her eyes, crunched her hair a few times and decided that would do. Then she took a breath and set off for the terrace.

Chapter Twelve

They had all had a glass of champagne, the conversation was general – about the journey, the wonderful weather, the history of the chateau. But when Pascal had refilled the glasses, Amalie got up.

'Caro? I know from experience that these boys want to talk about old friends and what is new in the world of perfume. Would you like a tour instead? We can take our drinks. I am longing to show off my efforts to someone who appreciates the finer points of wallpaper and fabric.'

Caro got to her feet. 'That sounds like me. I'd love a tour!'

'Come, then.'

Caro happily followed as Amalie led the way back through the salon with the double doors and into the hall.

'This is gorgeous.' Caro gestured to her surroundings. 'That candelabra is amazing.'

'We found it in one of the old barns. It took a lot of sweat and effort to restore it and even more to hang it.' Amalie looked up with a satisfied smile.

'I love restorations,' said Caro. 'When my father was alive I used to help him do up boats and barges. I was mostly the finisher; I did French polishing, veneer, things like that.'

'Why don't you do it now?' Amalie studied her as if she was really interested in her answers. 'It sounds as if you miss it?'

Caro shrugged. 'I wasn't interested in taking on my father's business after he died, and I have a daughter, I wanted something a bit more regular. I got a job selling artists' supplies. I really enjoyed that and did it for years, but sadly, the shop closed.' Just for a second she allowed herself to think about Alec's ancestral home. A little subtle restoration would make a huge difference there.

'So how long have you and Alec been together?' Amalie asked.

The question came as a bit of a shock – the assumption that they were a couple. 'We're not really together like that. We're more like – colleagues, I suppose.'

'But you would like to be a couple?'

Amalie's frankness was irresistible. 'Well, I would, I'm not so sure about Alec.'

'I understand. I too am suffering from unrequited love. I had a boyfriend for many years, but he would not commit. I felt I should leave him before my childbearing years were over. But I think of him always. '

'That won't be for years yet, surely? Your child-bearing years, I mean.'

Amalie shrugged. 'I still have to find the father. Come and see the orangery; apart from the floors, it's one of our few completed projects.'

They walked down a corridor the walls of which showed partially stripped wallpaper against ancient plastered walls. It was a finish Caro rather liked.

'It is easy for Pascal,' said Amalie. 'He has a girl-friend. When we have made an apartment for them, she may move in. I hope not. I don't like her. I would prefer him to have been gay with a lovely boyfriend who could help us with the restoration.' She paused. 'But things rarely turn out just right. Here we are!'

The orangery was magnificent. The huge, curved glass roof that became arched windows looked magnificent. The floor had old tiles, a bit uneven and sometimes very broken or even missing, but the effect in the late-afternoon sunshine was that it had all been dipped in gold.

'I love this!' said Caro. 'Are you going to grow oranges and lemons in it?'

Amalie gave a very Gallic shrug. 'Perhaps. We can't decide. We could have events here but the floor is so uneven we would have to take it all up and re-lay it. Expensive. Pascal wants to fill it with trees, for the scent, *naturellement*.'

'Do you need to rent it out, to make money?' Caro didn't need to ask if the chateau cost money to restore and maintain.

'Yes! Our uncle bought it many years ago, for a very few francs, he had us believe. But he never restored it and just lived in the bits that had a good roof. But if we could have weddings here we have a chance of making proper money.'

'Re-lay the floor, then,' said Caro. 'It would still look beautiful if you didn't replace the broken tiles, just made it so they were no longer a trip hazard.'

Amalie laughed. 'I like that expression. I will use it from now on. But now, come into the kitchen. I started there. It isn't finished but I love it.'

Caro loved it too. It was large and had possibly been something other than a kitchen in its past. The walls were a mixture of fine panelling and rough plaster. There were double doors out on to the terrace that wrapped its way all round the house.

The furniture consisted of several large armoires that were obviously old, if not antique. A huge kitchen table with chairs took up the middle. It had a large platter of fruit on it and invited long evenings sitting drinking, putting the world to rights.

There were no fitted units, just a selection of cupboards, some of which had surfaces that could be worktops, set around the walls and on either side of a double sink unit. A magnetic knife rack two feet long was studded with every sort and size of kitchen knife. A rack of chopping boards and a *batterie de cuisine* were set on the rough walls.

'This is fabulous! Just made for cooking in!' said Caro. A wonderful savoury smell added to the charm of the room.

'*Oui.* My boyfriend was a chef so he had a lot of input into the design.' Amalie sighed. 'But he is no longer part of my life now. I must accept it.'

'But you like cooking?' It seemed tragic to think of this lovely kitchen not bringing joy to the cook.

'Oh yes. Of course. How else would we eat tonight? But Pascal also cooks, when he is here.' Amalie went across to the very up-to-date-looking range cooker and took the top off a pot that looked as if it came with the chateau. The delicious smell increased as she put in a wooden spoon, tasted the contents of the pot. 'Another ten minutes. Time to look at the salon. The salon and the rest of the rooms are very much works in progress. There is no floor in the dining room. It has rotted ...'

The following morning, after a slightly too-late night, with slightly too much wine, Alec and Caro set off down the drive towards the town. Pascal had been in touch with M. Dolinière's grandson. 'And yes, in his private collection there is a sample of the famous Swan perfume!'

'Will he let us use it for our mission?' Alec had asked, holding his breath.

Pascal had given a shrug as Gallic as his sister's. 'He has not yet committed himself, but I am hopeful.'

'We'll have to be satisfied with that for now,' Alec had said.

Now, as they drove, he asked, 'How's your head this morning?'

'More or less OK. I did drink a lot of water and took a painkiller before I went to bed,' said Caro. 'What about yours?' Alec and Pascal had stayed up even later, drinking cognac, sorting out the world.

'I've felt better, I must admit.'

'Have a rummage in my bag. There are painkillers and a bottle of water.'

'Thank you,' he said. After he had found what he needed, he said, 'It's good to have you along.'

She shot him a smile. 'Driver, provider of medicaments, general good sort ...'

He smiled and closed his eyes.

Finding somewhere to park wasn't easy but thanks to Alec's sharp eyes and Caro's ability to park in spaces hardly longer than the car, they found somewhere.

'You are a very good parker!' said Alec when, finally, they were able to get out of the car.

'For a woman? Don't even think it!'

'I swear I wasn't! There's no way I could have got into that space.'

'If you drive in London you have to learn to park. Now, where is this apartment?'

This question was answered by Pascal, who was ahead of them, hanging over a balcony. 'There you are! I'll let you in.'

Caro felt she was going back in time and was now in a nineteenth-century novel involving makers of millinery or lace. The stairs were very narrow, twisty and badly lit. As they climbed she wondered how an elderly man would manage them. She was panting slightly when they reached the top.

'*Entrez*,' said Pascal. 'I've explained why we're after the sample. I'll make coffee.'

Monsieur Dolinière looked part of the armchair he was sitting in. He was very bent over and thin and yet had a nobility about him. He had dignity and obviously a strong sense of his place in society. It was all Caro could do not to curtsey when she was introduced. He was very gracious.

Although all the conversation was in fairly rapid French, she found she could understand most of it if she concentrated. When she needed a break she looked around the apartment. It was like a mock-up of an old building that you might find in a museum.

The walls were dark although they had possibly started life as cream. They were entirely covered in shelves on which stood bottles and bottles that had once contained perfume. Some of them still did, she realised, although the dark-brown liquid would surely no longer smell very much like the original. The furniture – a small sofa, a couple of armchairs and a selection of dark-wood tables – was all crammed in the middle of the room.

Yes, Monsieur Dolinière knew of the perfume. And yes, his grandfather had made it. Did he keep a sample when it had been ordered by the powers that be that all samples should be destroyed? *Bien sûr!*

After this statement, pronounced with a flourish, there was a long pause. Finally Pascal asked if they could possibly smell the fragrance.

Caro interpreted most of this through M. Dolinière's body language and finally she worked out he'd said, 'Yes, if you can find it.'

'I will make more coffee,' said Pascal. 'We will need it.'

'I'll make it,' said Caro. 'I find the labels on the bottles quite difficult to read.'

'So do we,' said Alec.

Caro opted to make the coffee nonetheless. She wanted to see M. Dolinière's kitchen. It was tiny and like a section of an antique shop that specialised in kitchenalia. Elizabeth David would have felt at home there. She loved it.

Eventually Pascal said, 'I think this is it.'

M. Dolinière asked to see the vial. 'That is the one,' he declared triumphantly, as if he'd found it himself. 'There was a bottle in the museum of perfumery, of course, but it was destroyed after the accident. This is the only one left.'

Caro didn't mention the sample Serena Swan's maid had kept and first Pascal, then Alec, and finally Caro took a deep sniff. Caro couldn't begin to distinguish any of the original ingredients as the sample just smelt musty.

'It's going to take ages to identify the ingredients,' said Alec, in English.

'Why ages?' said M. Dolinière, also in English. 'I have the recipe.'

Pascal and Alec looked at the old man with their mouths open.

'You kept the recipe?' said Pascal, also in English.

'But I thought the house that originally made it destroyed all copies of the recipe?' said Alec. 'That keeping it was punishable by death, practically!'

M. Dolinière looked extremely smug. 'My father was an apprentice at the time. He worked hard on this *parfum*, fetching ingredients. He kept a *liste de courses*.'

'And you still have this list?' Alec sounded incredulous and Caro saw the old man stiffen.

'*Bien sûr*,' he said, reverting to French. 'And of course you may read it, but not take it away from here. It is precious.'

Caro caught a panicked glance between Alec and Pascal. 'It will be incredibly hard to recreate the perfume if we can't take the recipe to the lab,' said Alec in rapid English.

'I know!' Pascal turned to M. Dolinière. His French was too fast for Caro to follow easily but she could tell from his body language that he was pleading and M. Dolinière was shaking his head, becoming more adamant as Pascal became more beseeching.

Caro was good with elderly gentlemen; it was one of her skills. She gently moved Pascal away and smiled at M. Dolinière. Then, in her best French, she asked if it would be possible to copy the list. 'If we could do that, there would be no need for such a very special and precious document to leave this room.' She smiled again, sensing a slight weakening in the old man's stern demeanour. 'I will do the copying myself and wash my hands very carefully before I start.'

M. Dolinière kept everyone in suspense for a very long time, it seemed, but at last his expression softened, a scintilla of difference Caro wouldn't have spotted if she hadn't been studying him very carefully. 'Very well. You may copy it. But out of respect for my *grandpère*, you must use a proper pen, not a "biro".' Even in French, his distaste for such a newfangled invention was apparent. Caro was glad she hadn't suggested taking a picture of the recipe on her phone. And thinking about her phone reminded her it was plugged into an adaptor, charging up. Never mind, Alec would have his.

'Has anyone got a fountain pen?' Caro asked her companions, slightly desperate.

Alec and Pascal both shook their heads. 'There's a shop in town,' said Pascal. 'I'll buy one.'

Alec and Caro sat while M. Dolinière dozed and Pascal presumably dashed up and down the streets of Grasse finding a fountain pen. Caro fervently hoped he also bought a notebook to write in.

Caro was wondering if she would be able to read and accurately transcribe the list of ingredients. Goodness knows what Alec was thinking about but he looked stressed too.

At last Pascal arrived with a couple of fountain pens so Caro could choose her nib and a hard-backed notebook of the most old-fashioned sort he could find, Caro suspected. He apparently didn't want to risk M. Dolinière taking against anything because it was modern and newfangled.

'Very well, you may copy the list,' M. Dolinière said, in English this time. 'The list is in that book in the corner.'

It took a few false goes before the right book was located and after an awful lot of furniture-shifting and small lamps being found, Caro was able to start.

M. Dolinière, however, did not want to stay and watch her copy even though the list was so important to him.

'Gentlemen, I suggest we go out and have cognac while the lady transcribes the list.'

There was a silence while Alec and Pascal wondered how to deal with this. Then a second later

Alec said, 'Pascal, if you would escort M. Dolinière? I feel I should stay with Caro in case there are difficulties with the handwriting or ingredients whose names are strange to her.'

'That would be very kind,' said Caro, in French.

When they had finally got M. Dolinière out of his chair and down the stairs and Pascal had accompanied him outside, Caro and Alec regarded each other.

'Have you got your phone?' she asked Alec.

'Of course', he said, and produced it. 'Oh. No battery.'

'What? Not any? I just want to take a photo of the list.'

'Not a peek. Where's your phone?'

She winced. 'Charging up in my bedroom.'

'I can't believe this!' said Alec.

'No point in moaning, I'll just have to copy it out. We are so dependent on technology. I can't believe it.'

'I'm tempted to go out and get a bottle of brandy so we can indulge too,' said Alec. 'Do you fancy it?'

'It would be nice but I have work to do and I suspect it won't be as easy as copying out a shopping list should be.' She peered at the paper that had been reverently laid on the table for her to transcribe. 'I can't read the first ingredient,' she said, suddenly daunted by her task. 'This is not going to be easy.'

The trouble was, the list had been written quickly and a lot of the ingredients were abbreviated. Also, the ink was faded and the handwriting hard to read.

'OK, well,' said Alec. 'I'm fairly sure that's tuberose. And at least the numbers are clear.'

'You dictate and I'll write,' said Caro. 'It will be easier for you because you nearly know what you're looking for.'

'It's not easy writing,' Alec said a little later having spent some time studying one particular ingredient. 'This could be "frankincense" but it could also be "I sneezed in my hanky".'

'Let's go with frankincense,' said Caro, 'as it's ever so slightly more likely. Though if something seems wrong later, we'll see if what we need is a bit of snot.'

To her huge embarrassment, Caro's stomach rumbled audibly before they were even near the end.

'I'll go out for sandwiches,' said Alec. 'We've been here hours. There are so many ingredients!'

'And how do we know they are all for this one perfume? If you're fetching ingredients you might get stuff for other perfumes at the same time?'

'It may well all become clearer when we get it to the lab.'

'OK, off you go. I don't want to be caught with half a baguette in my mouth when M. Dolinière comes back. It would look disrespectful.'

'Can't have that! I'll be back in a flash.'

When Alec had returned with encouraging brown bags of delicious things, Caro said, 'Listen, I've been thinking.'

'What?' Alec replied.

'M. Dolinière said he had a recipe, but he gave us a shopping list.'

'Yes?'

'I think he might have the actual recipe, with quantities.'

Alec frowned. 'You may be right. And if he has, it would save us hours and hours of time. After all, the end result is open to interpretation.'

Caro nodded. 'As long as Scarlet feels it's as near to the original as it could be. And likes it.'

'Well, we can certainly make her something she likes.' He handed Caro one of the packages. 'Here, eat this. I spotted Pascal and M. Dolinière having lunch. That should give us time to have ours and then look through his library for the recipe. That was good thinking on your part, Caro.'

Caro crunched into the end of her baguette, trying to ignore the feeling of slight weakness at hearing Alec say her name.

They got the rest of the list jotted down quickly in the middle of the beautiful notebook Pascal had bought so they could remove the pages for their own use. Then they searched systematically through the old notebooks and files on M. Dolinière's shelves.

But there were so many of them. They seemed to represent centuries of the perfumier's art. They weren't even halfway through before they heard Pascal and M. Dolinière returning. When they entered the room, Caro was back with the fountain pen and the hard-backed notebook and Alec was dictating the names of obscure ingredients, most of which were extremely abbreviated.

'You are not yet finished?' said M. Dolinière in English, not notably softened by – going on the brandy fumes – a bibulous lunch.

'No, I am being slow,' said Caro, smiling as apologetically as she could manage.

M. Dolinière inclined his head graciously. 'It's a shame for now you must go. I need a siesta.'

'Would it be possible for me to continue here while you sleep?' suggested Caro. 'And when you awake, I could perhaps make you a tisane?'

M. Dolinière appeared to consider this possibility. '*Non*,' he said, reverting to French. 'You have had plenty of time to write out the ingredients.'

Caro took a deep breath, went across to the chair where M. Dolinière was now sitting, and crouched down at his feet. 'M. Dolinière,' she said in her best, most formal French. 'You and your family are among the most respected perfumiers in the world of perfume. I feel sure, having kept the secret of this great perfume close to your hearts for these many years, that somewhere you have the exact recipe. You would not let this treasure stray far from this centre of great perfume. It is here, and I beg you to let us read it. Perhaps copy it,' she added, pushing her luck and with no clue if all this flattery was doing a bit of good.

'Why should I do this?' M. Doliniere had a very aristocratic air about him.

'If you allow us to recreate this unique fragrance, the name of Dolinière will become as famous as it deserves to be. All the modern perfume houses will pay homage to the greatness of your name.'

Caro wished she'd had time to work on this speech. Quoting a few specific famous perfume houses would have been good but at that moment she couldn't think of a single one. But of course, if she'd quoted the wrong name, that might have made things worse.

The dark, stuffy room seemed like an old sepia photograph: immovable, historic and – for Caro – very, very tense. No one except M. Dolinière seemed to be breathing. Caro's knee clicked, the sound like a pistol shot although it couldn't really have been that loud. It didn't help that she knew she would have difficulty getting up from her cramped position. She might have to tip sideways and get up from the floor using all fours.

'Very well,' he said, sounding sad to be giving in. 'If you promise to acknowledge the house of Dolinière, I will allow you to have this recipe.'

Stiffly Caro got herself upright again while Alec and Pascal thanked the old man a million times in French, English and back again.

He seemed pleased at last. He had allowed himself to let go of the secret he had kept for so many years and it apparently felt the right thing to do.

'You may copy the recipe,' he said. 'And you may take it away to do so. I need to sleep now. Bring it back at four o'clock.' He looked sternly at Caro. 'That will that be long enough, huh?'

'Of course,' said Caro, trusting Pascal had access to a scanner, or at least a functioning mobile phone 'I will be as quick as I can.'

Chapter Thirteen

Pascal had given Alec and Caro the use of his private lab, high up in the attic of his apartment in Grasse.

'What an amazing view!' said Caro, panting slightly after the walk up several flights of stairs.

Apart from the many other rooftops that could be seen from that height, always fascinating to Caro, there were glimpses of balconies with pots of geraniums and climbing plants, cats washing themselves in the sunshine and, lower down, streets with cars crawling along the narrow roads, cafés with waiters putting fresh cloths on the outside tables, teenage girls giggling at groups of teenage boys, men and women with paper-covered baguettes under their arms and exchanging news and views with friends and neighbours. And far away, after miles of countryside that included vineyards, farmland and rivers, were the snow-capped Alpes Maritimes.

But it was very warm, even with the window open and the fan on. Caro really wished she'd worn the one dress she'd brought with her and not the jeans and top which had seemed like summer clothes when she had packed them back in London.

'I might borrow Pascal's lab coat, if you think he wouldn't mind,' said Caro.

'What, put on more clothes, in this heat?' Alec was surprised.

'Not exactly. The loo's down a floor, isn't it?'

Caro came back wearing only the lab coat over her jeans. As it was loose on her it was cooler than her own clothes had been, although the jeans were hot and clingy. Modesty made her keep them on as the last button on the lab coat came halfway up her thighs.

Alec didn't bother with a lab coat and just wore his short-sleeved shirt loose over his long shorts.

They began. First of all Alec replaced civet oil with the base modern perfumiers preferred (for reasons of animal cruelty, Alec explained) and ambergris with the synthetic version. When he was fairly sure his base was right, he went on to recreate the heart of the fragrance.

Caro read out the ingredients and quantities from her copied-out recipe when they were present, but often the numbers were unclear or absent, so Alec had to make a judgement and put in the amount he thought was right. It was very time-consuming.

They'd been at work for a couple of hours when Alec sighed. 'Pascal has been brilliant, letting us use all this' – a hand gestured to the 'perfume organ', a sample of practically every odour known to man and perfumiers – 'but it's still really difficult.'

'We must be nearly there,' said Caro, who'd been writing down the quantities Alec had used each time he added something.

'What do you think of this?' Alec said, waving a paper wand he had dipped in the most recent attempt.

'It's lovely,' she said, 'but I don't think there's any point in creating this perfume exactly as it was if it's not going to suit Scarlet.'

'How are we going to know if it does or not?' said Alec. 'She's not here.'

'I'll know,' said Caro. 'It's a bit weird, which is why I haven't mentioned it, but I've got a memory for scent that is almost spooky. And I can smell things on television. Of course I don't really smell the things but I *think* I do. It's probably just an overactive imagination but if there are sewers or rotting bodies on TV I have to change channels.'

'Oh! That is weird,' said Alec, distracted from his vials, pipettes and scales for a minute.

'I can smell nice things too though. The Chelsea Flower Show is lovely! But more to the point, I can remember what Scarlet needs in a fragrance. I can remember the ones she didn't like and my weird fragrance thing means I know what won't work.'

'So we could just make something up for her and abandon all this faded writing and illegible numbers.'

Caro knew he wasn't seriously suggesting they did this. 'That would be cheating and she'd know it wasn't the fragrance she wants. But I'm sure we could adapt it a bit, to suit her.'

Alec nodded. 'OK. Now I'm going to find us a bottle of water and then we'll press on.'

Caro took the opportunity to take off her jeans. She no longer cared about showing a lot of leg, she just wanted to be cooler. She took off her sandals too and twisted her hair off her neck, securing it with an elastic band she found in a drawer. Now she was cooler, she felt her brain and, more importantly, her nose, could function better.

Sadly for her peace of mind Alec's eyebrows shot up when he came back into the lab with the water. 'You look like a Bond girl.'

This was a shock. 'What?'

'You know, the one who's working for the head of SMERSH or something, before she meets James. Although you should really be wearing oversized glasses.'

Caro found herself blushing profusely. 'I don't know what you're talking about,' she said, hoping this didn't seem disingenuous. They had a job to do; she needed to concentrate, she couldn't let the suggestion that he found her sexy enter her consciousness. Although not being quite so hot did help.

'What do you think of this?' said Alec after another half an hour or so, holding a paper tester under Caro's nose.

'It's lovely. I really like it and I think it's almost right,' she said, thinking hard about Scarlet as she sniffed. 'But I think it needs more of an edge. A hint of bitterness.'

'Some petitgrain maybe.' He extracted a few drops from a bottle. 'Maybe half a gram?'

Caro wrote this down.

'Now, how about this?'

Caro sniffed, her eyes closed. She didn't speak immediately. 'That really is lovely,' she said eventually. 'And perfect for Scarlet. But how like the original do you think it is?'

He sighed. 'I don't know. I suspect it's a bit too modern. It'll settle a bit and we've got another couple of days. The original could have taken weeks to create.'

Caro looked at the clock on the wall. 'Oh golly! It's six o'clock. We should be getting back for dinner.' And then she became aware that Alec was staring at her. 'What?' she asked, a bit anxious.

'Nothing really.' He smiled. 'I was just wondering if what they say about hedione is true.'

'That's the very green fragrance, like jasmine, isn't it?' She'd learnt an awful lot about perfume in the last few hours.

Alec nodded.

'So what do they say about it?'

'That it activates receptors in the nose that are supposed to be a bit of an aphrodisiac for women.'

This could definitely be construed as flirting and Caro began to speak rather too fast. 'I'm never quite sure how I feel about those white flower fragrances myself, like lilies. There's a hint of decay about them which can get a bit too much. Although I don't get decay in this.' She sniffed at the wand again.

'I think we should leave it now and see how it smells in the morning.'

Caro yawned suddenly, overcome by heat and concentration.

'I'm going to take you home now,' said Alec. 'I'm sure there'll be a glass of something fizzy waiting for us at the chateau.'

She couldn't help smiling. 'I can't believe we're staying in a chateau,' she said, although the chateau was only a small part of her reasons to smile. 'But I'd better get dressed first.'

Caro let herself relax as they whizzed through the countryside of the Côte d'Azur. She'd never been one for expressions like 'living in the moment' but she felt now she understood what it meant. All her senses were more finely tuned. It could have been the green, floral scent, the hedione (which sounded a bit like hedonism to her), that was affecting her. Or it could just have been the South of France at its most romantic and a man she fancied very much indeed. Beautiful surroundings and the thought that the man possibly fancied her, just a little bit, was enough to make anyone smile.

Amalie was waiting on the steps of the chateau as they drove up, obviously very pleased to see them. She was by the car door before the gravel had had time to settle.

'Pascal's girlfriend is here. I am so sorry to inflict her on you. She is a not very nice person.' She spoke very quickly and her gaze flicked over Caro through the open windows. 'You have had a very long day and worked very hard. I hope you were successful?'

Alec got out. 'Fairly successful,' he said, before going round to Caro's side and helping her out.

Caro couldn't decide if this was chivalry or if he was finding excuses to touch her. Either was good, she concluded, before realising how sticky and untidy she must look compared to Amalie, who had apparently changed for dinner.

'Come and have a drink,' said Amalie, still urgent. 'I know you want a shower and I promise I'll let you have one, but do come and talk to this woman for a few moments. She is a dreadful snob and has no feeling for old buildings at all. Currently she is

planning to demolish the orangery and put a confer-
ence centre there.' Amalie flashed a desperate smile.
'But the good news is, I have made a new sitting place.
The one thing the chateau is very good at is sitting
places. This one has a fountain. Come with me.'

Caro would normally have felt a degree of discom-
fiture at the prospect of meeting a woman like the
one Amalie had described, but she was so happy
that being sweat-stained with dirty hair didn't
matter. The prospect of meeting a glamorous
Frenchwoman when she was wearing the clothes
she'd put on that morning was nothing. Thanks to
Alec's recent attentiveness and apparent interest in
her she felt sexy and powerful and there was nothing
any Chanel-suited girlfriend could do to make her
feel different.

She wasn't wearing a Chanel suit but Laure's silk
sweater and skinny jeans that appeared sprayed on
to her bony legs, worn with very high heels, were
a casual equivalent. Her chunky gold jewellery probably increased her body weight by several kilos.
Her faint disgust as they were introduced just made
Caro want to laugh.

When the introductions were over, Laure said, 'It
will be a relief for you, no doubt, to discover that I
speak perfect English. I am aware that British people
struggle with languages.'

Caro really hoped that her French was as perfect
as Laure's slightly stilted English. 'Thank you but

no. I have been speaking perfect English all day. Now I want to speak the beautiful language of a beautiful country.'

Laure's exquisite eyebrows raised a fraction and Caro had her reward.

Pascal winked at her as he handed her a glass of champagne and replied in French: 'It is always such a surprise when an English person speaks French. And so charming. But would you permit us to practise our English?'

Caro took the glass and raised it to Pascal. He was a star. He knew she did speak quite good French but that maybe it wouldn't hold up all evening, when she was tired. 'That would be my pleasure.'

But as she sipped her champagne she wondered what Pascal saw in Laure and, watching him, decided he was not quite as enamoured as Laure would have liked. For Amalie's sake, she was pleased.

Caro and Alec had both had showers and changed. Caro had put on her dress – a simple floral number that had been very well reduced in the Boden sale, not caring that it probably said 'shabby chic' instead of the other kind. And yet Caro felt it was more fitting for their surroundings than Laure's high heels and jeans were. She had always felt the combination was a bit tarty, anyway. They were ushered into the dining room.

Amalie, while looking quite as well groomed as Laure, managed to produce a meal that would satisfy the most gourmet Frenchman. Caro wasn't a bad cook herself, but she'd have been looking quite a lot more red-faced and harassed by the time she'd brought that lot to the table.

They started with home-made chicken liver pâté served with brioche toast. After that was a perfect carré d'agneau, pink inside, fat perfectly crisp. And finally, after a green salad, and cheese, was a chocolate mousse.

'I see it is true that Englishwomen enjoy their food,' said Laure, who had eaten the salad and the asparagus that came with the lamb cutlets. She was looking at Caro disdainfully.

'It's certainly true that Englishwoman like to honour the chef by enjoying their food,' said Caro with a smile. She was immune to Laure's barbs, she liked her food and was perfectly happy with her figure, even if it was considerably more substantial than Laure's, who probably thought anything bigger than a size zero was a failure.

'Alec and Caro have been creating perfume all day,' said Pascal. 'It would be disappointing if they were not hungry.'

'And what do English people know of perfume?' Laure asked.

'About the same as the French,' said Alec, 'but then I'm a Scot.'

Laure seemed confused and Amalie drew the meal to a close.

'Go and sit by the fountain,' she instructed. 'I will bring coffee and liqueurs.'

'You must let me help you!' said Caro, getting up. 'You've done enough.'

'No thank you, Caro. It is very kind of you to offer but my kitchen is not tidy. I don't want anyone to see it but family. Pascal? How do you say it? Will you give me a hand?'

'Forgive him,' said Laure, in French, 'but I wish him to show me our apartment, so would you object if he didn't help you?'

Caro guessed that Amalie would forgive her brother but not his girlfriend. She also noticed that the two women were still 'vousvoyezing' each other.

'I shall pour the brandy,' said Pascal, 'coffee can wait.'

So it was that Caro and Alec were alone by the fountain with glasses of cognac, waiting for coffee to be brought. Amalie had insisted that coffee was essential and that she would make it.

The new sitting place was truly lovely. Further from the chateau than other places to sit and enjoy the view, this seemed part of a disused walled garden but one that grew roses as well as vegetables. An old stone arch was covered with them, tiny, pale pink blossoms and large, dark-red velvet ones.

Heavily scented, the fragrance was enhanced by the warm stone.

Someone, presumably Amalie, had placed a wooden bench covered with faded cushions under the arch. The roses enhanced the natural arbour, falling down to almost hide the bench. It was like a room partially hidden by roses.

If Caro had been happy before, she was even more so now. She was entirely relaxed (a couple of glasses of wine had helped) but all her senses were on high alert. She heard the birds, she saw the beauty around her and, most of all, she smelt the roses. She sipped her brandy but didn't speak. The only potential fly in this ointment of bliss was the prospect of Laure and Pascal joining them. But she suspected Amalie of being a matchmaker at heart, determined to bring her and Alec together.

Alec put his arm round her and hugged her to him. Then he cleared his throat. 'This is nice, isn't it?'

'Yes,' she said, wishing he wouldn't talk and kiss her instead.

But in spite of saying 'it was nice' he seemed tense. While Caro felt they'd gone beyond the need for polite conversation, he apparently did not.

'It's been a long day,' he said.

'But a successful one, don't you think? You've very nearly got the perfume right.'

'Mm, not quite near enough.'

'But we've got at least another two days to get it perfect, haven't we?' Caro was beginning to feel impatient. She really wanted them to have a couple of nights sharing the gorgeous bedroom she now had on her own. At this rate it may never happen.

'I'm going to need that and possibly a bit more if I can.'

'I'll have to get back though,' she said. 'Scarlet's course wasn't very long and then she'll have to go back to America. I can't leave Rowan and Joe on their own or Skye will eat me.'

He laughed. 'And me.'

She took another sip of cognac. 'Amalie's taking her time with the coffee. Maybe I should go back and help her.'

He put his hand on her arm to stop her moving. 'Listen! There's something I've got to ask you.' He sounded so urgent that Caro's heart began to pound but with anxiety, not excitement. 'What is it?'

He cleared his throat. 'It will sound a bit weird.'

Caro's heart began to sink. She felt she knew what was coming but Alec did not seem a bit happy about it.

He took a breath. 'Once, when I was a very young man, on a Greek island, I spent the night talking to a young woman I didn't even get a proper look at. I told her everything, all my hopes and dreams. You know in the way people do when you don't think you'll ever see them again.'

Caro was silent. She couldn't think of anything appropriate to say.

'That woman was you, wasn't it?'

She sighed. If only he'd sounded happy about it, she could have been too. On the other hand she couldn't deny it just to make him happy. 'Yes. How did you know?'

'Your fragrance. I kept nearly getting it but it's only now that we've got the roses as well that it's finally fallen into place.'

'So – how do you feel about that?'

'Oh God, Caro,' he breathed and took her into his arms and kissed her.

A few minutes later they broke apart as they heard people coming. They were both breathing deeply and both had ruffled hair. But when they saw Pascal followed by Amalie, they were smiling.

Pascal spoke first. 'Alec? There's been a phone call. It's Murdo. He's collapsed and has been rushed to hospital.'

'What?' said Alec. 'Is he ...?'

'*Non*,' said Amalie. 'Your sister, she telephoned. She sounded very distressed.'

Laure appeared. 'I am so sorry. Your holiday in France has possibly been cut short.'

Alec glanced at Caro but didn't speak. Caro nodded, but didn't comment that they were here working. They all headed back to the chateau.

Chapter Fourteen

As they walked through the scented evening, Caro felt her dreams fall away, one by one, with every step.

The mood she and Alec had shared so briefly – the evening's warmth, the roses, the fountain and the satisfaction of having worked hard all day creating something beautiful – seemed to have gone. Maybe she and Alec would never get together properly now. In his mind, she would always be associated with the night his father died – or at least entered his last illness. And if Murdo didn't regain consciousness, he and Alec would never be reconciled, which would be awful.

It also meant that the perfume may never be made, either, which would be awful for Alec, when they'd got so near it. Scarlet might go off the idea if she couldn't have it in time for her wedding and he might never be able to prove to people that he could do it.

She felt sad about Murdo, too. She'd grown very fond of him in spite of his irascibility and his dog who weed on people. He was stuck in a previous century, probably very similar to his own father, and yet he was somehow special.

The chateau was dark after the sunshine and reflected Caro's despondency.

Alec and Pascal disappeared into Pascal's office, looking up the best way of getting to Scotland in a hurry.

Amalie drew Caro into the kitchen and made a tisane. Caro had distracted her from trying to make tea. Tea was never quite right in France, Caro thought, in her very gloomy mood.

Laure, who had joined them in the kitchen for the tisane, got up. 'I have an idea,' she said, and went to join the men in the study.

Caro sensed that she and Amalie were both thinking that Laure preferred male company to female and that was the real reason she left.

'Will you go with Alec?' asked Amalie, who had poured Caro brandy to go with her peppermint tea. 'Or stay here with me? You would be very welcome. You could help me repair my chateau.'

Caro put a grateful hand on Amalie's. 'That is a lovely offer, but I have duties at home. But if ever you want to come to London, you could stay on my barge.'

'I think it is better if you go with Alec. Strike while the iron is warm.'

'Hot,' said Caro. 'Strike while the iron is hot.'

Amalie nodded. 'Thank you. When your English is good no one tells you when it is not perfectly correct. Then how does one improve?' She threw her arms into the air in a very French way.

Reluctantly, Caro smiled.

They sipped from their mugs, making polite conversation, waiting for news. Caro would have felt better if she had been the one looking up flight details on a laptop, being proactive, but instead she was discussing the advantages of handmade tiles for floors over a more modern finish. It was killing her.

At last Laure came in. 'I have solved the dilemma!'

Caro couldn't help noticing that while Laure's English was awfully good, it was rather formal.

'My father is flying to Paris very early tomorrow morning. You will fly with him, in his private jet. And take the flight to Glasgow later.'

Alec and Pascal followed her into the kitchen. 'It's an amazing piece of luck,' said Alec. 'Laure's father can give us a lift to Paris. There's an early flight. We have to go via Birmingham but that's OK.'

'You want me to come with you?' said Caro.

Alec frowned, as if confused. 'Can't you?'

'Of course!' she said. 'I just didn't want to be in the way.'

'No, we need you.' He looked longingly at the brandy. 'Better not. We have to leave here at four.'

'The hire car is in my name,' said Caro, 'and I'll drive. But how will we get it back?'

'We will do that,' said Pascal. 'It will not be a problem. Leave your car here. I will drive you to meet Laure's father tomorrow morning.'

'Pascal!' Caro protested. 'We can't let you do that!'

Pascal put his hand on Caro's. 'Caro, I insist. Please. Let me do this for you and Alec.'

Caro looked at Alec. 'That is extremely kind,' he said. 'If you really don't mind.'

'It will give me a good, early start to my day,' Pascal said firmly, putting an end to further argument.

'So, Alec,' said Amalie. 'Have some brandy after all. You probably need it.'

Alec smiled in gratitude and took the proffered glass. 'I rang Lennie,' Alec said to Caro. 'Murdo's in hospital, unconscious. But Lennie is in an awful state. Not sure why. It's so unlike her. She's usually so pragmatic and calm.'

'It's normal, no?' said Laure. 'Her beloved papa is ill. I would be devastated.'

Alec nodded. 'My father is very old. He was old when he became a father. My sister is prepared for him to die, we both are. There is something else.'

Caro woke every hour until it was time to get up, conscious of Alec sleeping next door, wishing they could have been together, knowing they'd have been completely distracted by Murdo's situation if they had been.

They met at the top of the staircase so early it felt like the middle of the night. He took her overnight bag from her and they went downstairs.

Pascal was in the kitchen. 'Coffee,' he said.

Caro put several spoonfuls of sugar in hers, so she could cope with the fuel-oil strength of it. But she felt brighter afterwards. Five minutes later they were in the car, speeding towards the private airfield where Laure's father kept his plane.

Caro could have done with the flight from Paris to Birmingham being a bit longer. She'd only just got to sleep when it started to land. She appreciated having Alec with her though so she could just follow him to the departure gate and not have to work out where to go when they finally arrived at Glasgow.

Lennie was waiting for them at arrivals. She wasn't exactly distraught any more, but she fell into her brother's arms and let Alec hug her. She didn't seem able to stop talking once she'd started. 'Caro! Thank God you're here! You'll be so useful! Apart from Dad, Skye's kicking off. It's been hell! There's lots I have to tell you, Alec, but we'll go to the hospital first.'

'Just put me out of my misery,' said Alec from the passenger seat when they were all in the car and on the way to the hospital. 'Is Murdo actually dying?'

'Not necessarily but, frankly, he's not the reason I'm so worried. I've had these really strange phone calls.' She sighed deeply and shook her head as if trying to make sense of things.

This was not the confident, in-control woman Caro had met in London.

'So, who's been calling?' said Alec. 'Was it one person calling more than once, or more than one person?'

'Two people.' Lennie stopped speaking as she negotiated the traffic. 'Actually, can we have this conversation when we get to the hospital?'

'Of course,' said Alec.

'I know how worried you must have been,' said Lennie, sending her brother a sympathetic glance. 'And I wouldn't have dragged you back from France, but I didn't know what else to do.'

'You did right to get us back,' he said. 'You shouldn't have to cope with this on your own.'

At last they found a space in the hospital car park and parked. Lennie breathed deeply, trying to get herself together. 'OK, the phone calls. Well, the first one was from the man we sold the lochan land to.'

Alec nodded. 'Richard Percy. What did he say?'

'He left a message. It said, "I hope there aren't going to be the same problems with this lot of land you're selling that there were with the last lot."'

'But we're not selling any land,' said Alec.

'It seems we are because someone else called about it. I spoke to them directly and this man – I've got his name written down at home – said he didn't want to ring the mobile number the agent gave because he wanted to check the land was actually ours.'

'I can't believe this! So how did you deal with that?' asked Alec.

Lennie shrugged. 'I was non-committal and said my brother was dealing with any land sales.' She paused and made a face. 'I think I managed to stall him but we really need to sort this out.'

'Of course, and we will,' said Alec. 'But what about Dad?'

'I really don't know much. As I said, to begin with it was him I was worried about but now I'm more worried about this land business, although when I let myself think about it I get in a panic about him, too. I think he's been targeted, scammed in some way by some sort of fraudster. I think it's because it's now known that he's not in charge.'

'He's been retired for a while though, surely?' said Caro.

'Yes, but he's always kept a firm hand on the tiller, as he'd say,' Lennie said. 'His was the ultimate word that made things happen – or more often stopped things happening.' She paused. 'But not now.'

There was a long silence before Alec said, 'I need to sort this land thing.'

'Yes,' said Lennie. 'But don't you want to see Dad first?'

'If he's lying there unconscious, I think I should stop our land being sold without us being aware it's for sale. It's the best thing I can do for him.'

Lennie began to protest against her brother's practical approach.

'I tell you what I suggest,' said Caro before brother and sister could start to argue. 'Why don't I go and sit with Murdo and make sure no one can get at him, while you sort out the land issue? It shouldn't take you long, after all. All you need to say is that the land isn't for sale; there's been some mistake. Then you can shoot back in here to be with Murdo.'

'We also need to find out who's put it up for sale,' said Lennie, 'and why they think they can.'

'It's something to do with Frazer,' said Alec.

Lennie frowned. 'Really? He always seemed so fond of Dad.'

'You know how I always felt about him,' said Alec grimly.

'So, shall I go and sit with Murdo then?' said Caro brightly, interrupting, trying not to sound as if she'd been up since 4 a.m. and hadn't really slept before then.

'That would be amazing,' said Lennie. 'If you hold the fort until we get back to hospital I won't need to worry about the old reprobate.' She sounded suddenly tearful.

'You need a bit of rest,' said Caro. 'I'll go and find Murdo so you can relax. Alec will sort out what's going on with the land.'

Although as she walked across the car park to the hospital she was aware that nothing was ever that simple.

By telling the nurse that she was related to Murdo, a process aided by Lennie having phoned from the car and saying something similar, Caro was directed to Murdo's room. He was in a side ward on his own. He had tubes attached to him but he looked very peaceful.

Caro sat down in the chair, wishing she'd brought a book with her. Then she closed her eyes and the next thing she knew, she was being wakened from sleep by a noise.

There was a man at the foot of Murdo's bed. He was reading Murdo's chart but Caro instantly knew he wasn't medical. She decided not to move or say anything. She kept her eyes very nearly closed so she could watch him.

The man read the chart and then put it back. Then he turned to Caro. 'I know you're awake but who are you? And before you try to prevaricate, I know you're not really family.'

She had to think quickly. 'I could ask you the same thing.'

She knew it was the Frazer Neal they'd been talking about but she needed him to tell her that.

'I asked first,' he said, not admitting anything.

'I work for the family sometimes,' she said. She was gratified to notice that he seemed to relax a little on hearing this.

'Me too. Rum lot, aren't they? Murdo could have started the stereotype about Scotsmen being mean.'

Caro suppressed her instinct to stick up for Murdo and just nodded. Frazer wasn't going to reveal anything if he thought she was on the family's side. 'So, who are you? You didn't say.'

'I used to work for them too. Got on really well with the old man' – he indicated Murdo, lying motionless in the bed – 'in spite of his tight-fistedness. It was all going swimmingly until the son came back from wherever he was and I had to leave. The son was jealous. I got on well with Murdo and he didn't.'

Caro nodded as if in agreement. 'So you came back here because you heard Murdo was ill?'

Frazer nodded. 'We were very close, as I said.'

'You wanted to say goodbye? Before he died?'

He almost laughed as if this was a ridiculous idea. 'We weren't that close!'

'So why did you come back? And did you tell me what your name was? I'm Caro, by the way.' She knew Alec had gone to find Frazer and ask him to visit, but she'd never asked if he'd been successful. But Murdo obviously felt that they were very close.

239

It made Caro angry to think about it but she was careful to keep her expression bland.

He studied her, making her aware of her travel-stained jeans, her make-up that had been applied in the pre-dawn, skimpily at that, and she added this to the list of reasons to dislike and distrust him. 'I'm Frazer Neal.' He held out his hand, which forced Caro to get up and shake it. 'You know, it looks like we've got a few things in common. Do you fancy a drink when you've got some time off?'

She didn't fancy a drink and was fairly sure he didn't fancy her, but possibly he needed her, which was more interesting.

She nodded. 'It would be nice to spend time with someone who isn't part of the McLean clan, but I'm not sure when I'll be free.'

He pulled out a business card. Caro got the impression he was the sort of man who'd have a handy business card concealed in his Speedos, while waterskiing, just in case. 'Give me a call.'

She put the card in her jeans pocket. 'I will.' She managed a smile but it was an effort. Then she looked at her watch. 'I'm not sure when I'll be relieved – I'm just here to let the family know as soon as Murdo wakes up.'

'Are they expecting him to wake up?'

'Oh yes,' said Caro, hoping what she said was true. 'They just don't want him to be alone when he does.'

'So you're not here guarding him?' Frazer tried to look quizzical but didn't quite pull it off.

It was Caro's turn to make derisive noises. 'No! Why on earth would he need guarding? He's not a drugs tsar or a spy. What bad thing could happen to him? He's in a hospital!'

Frazer nodded slowly. 'I'll be off then.' He walked to the door and then turned back. 'Don't forget to call me.'

The moment she was certain Frazer was well out of earshot, she called Alec. When she had finished telling him about her encounter with Frazer, he pondered for a moment and said, 'Could you bear to have a drink with him? Much as I hate the thought. He might tell you what he's up to which would be really useful.' He sighed. 'I wouldn't ask you if there was any other way of finding out what we need to know.'

'Of course. It's only an hour or two out of my life after all.' It seemed little enough when the family was in such difficulties. 'Is everything else OK at home?'

'Not really. Skye is kicking off. Rowan wants to stay in London so they've been screaming down the phone at each other. And you must want to have a shower and change your clothes.' He paused. 'I'll come in with Lennie and she can drive you home, then you can rest a bit.'

They disconnected but after a few moments' thought, Caro realised that the logistics of Alec's plan wouldn't work. It was too far for her to return to Glen Liddell and then go all the way back into Glasgow. If she was going to have a drink with Frazer tonight, it would be far better for her to stay in town.

She rang Lennie and told her about the plan. Lennie was horrified. 'Caro! You can't have a drink with that awful man!'

'I don't desperately want to, but I might be able to find out a lot of useful information. So I wonder if you could bear to lend me some clean jeans and a top? I think we're more or less the same size.'

'I do see it would be easier than you going backwards and forwards,' Lennie agreed. 'I'll see if I can find something.'

The same size they might have been but not the same sartorial style. But as long as she felt reasonably clean, Caro didn't really care. At least she had all her make-up with her.

Caro made the call to Frazer while she was waiting for Lennie. Frazer was very happy to be contacted and even happier when Caro suggested meeting up later that evening. 'I don't know when else I might be free,' Caro had explained.

'I'm glad you're keen to work with me. You could be just the person I need right now,' he said, having told her the name of a bar.

Caro hadn't realised she was 'keen to work with him' but supposed it must look like that from his point of view.

Lennie arrived looking a lot better. 'Alec sends his apologies. He wanted to come but was too tied up with sorting all this land-sale business. He's upset about you having to have a drink with Frazer, too, but we agreed if you could bring yourself to, it was for the best.'

'Did you manage to find me a pair of jeans to borrow?' asked Caro tentatively. She wasn't surprised when she saw Lennie suddenly look stricken.

'I did,' said Lennie, 'but I left them behind. I'm so sorry!'

'It's OK,' said Caro. 'It's not as if I care what he thinks of me.'

Lennie brightened up. 'I've found a lovely little B and B for you. It's run by a friend of a friend and is top notch! I'll take you there the moment I've had a word with the nurses about Murdo …'

It *was* a lovely little B and B, as Lennie had promised, and the kindly landlady lent Caro an iron so she could wear the dress she took to France. It would be OK if she put a cardigan with it.

As she ironed it, she couldn't help thinking back to how she'd been feeling when she last put it on, about twenty-four hours earlier. Then she'd felt full of hope, of satisfaction for having done a good day's work with Alec creating a beautiful perfume for a beautiful young woman. She had been in a beautiful chateau in a beautiful part of France. All she'd had to worry about was when

Alec was going to take her by the hand and lead her off to bed.

Now she was preparing to go out with a man who made her feel uncomfortable for so many reasons, and she couldn't be rude to him either. She had to find out what was going on with the Glen Liddell Estate and why someone – probably Frazer – thought they were in a position to sell off chunks of it.

The fact that Frazer was waiting for her at the bar felt like a good sign. He was more eager to meet her than she was to meet him, which gave her the upper hand and confirmed he needed her. What exactly he needed her for, though, remained to be seen.

'Caro,' said Frazer, getting up from his seat and kissing her cheek. 'So glad you could make it.'

'I suggested it, so here I am.' Caro felt she should probably be flirtatious, pretend this was a date, but she couldn't bring herself to. This was business.

'Drink?'

Caro rapidly calculated how long she might need to get the information she wanted. 'A white wine spritzer, please.' She thought having fizzy water on its own might look hostile. It was a sort of date after all.

He ordered a whisky and they sat in silence until their drinks arrived. Caro wasn't going to say anything she didn't really need to say. She was going to give him every chance to show his hand.

After they'd clinked glasses in a way Caro considered completely unnecessary, she looked at him over her glass.

'Well, Caro!' said Frazer, possibly a bit put out by her refusal to make small talk. 'What are you doing here?'

'Having a drink with you?'

'I don't mean that, and you know it. Why did I find you by the bedside of Murdo McLean?'

'Look,' she said, dropping her frostiness in favour of something more confiding, hoping he'd confide too. 'I'm employed to sit with Murdo while they wait for him to wake up. I need the work.'

'And they're expecting him to do that? To wake up?'

Caro shrugged. 'I should imagine so. They just don't want him waking up and finding himself alone. I worked for him for a bit earlier in the year so he knows me. The family have put me in a bed and breakfast so I can be handy for the hospital.'

'So you don't know what's going on at the estate?'

Something about his manner gave the impression that he wanted her to know what was going on so she prevaricated. 'Well, I am in their confidence up to a point. Are you still involved in some way?'

'Yes and no,' he said. 'Let me get you another spritzer and I'll explain. Or would you rather have some white wine on its own?'

'A spritzer is fine, thank you.' Let him drink whisky; she'd keep her own alcohol consumption to a minimum.

'So, can you tell me what's going on back at the house?' he asked when he'd come back with the drinks.

'Sorry, Frazer, but why should I?' Caro tried to sound reasonable, as if she was willing to trade secrets. 'If I give you information, what can you give me in return?'

He seemed to assess her for a long time and not as a woman he might or might not fancy but as a man who was deciding whether or not to do business with the person in front of him.

Caro kept her expression bland. She had no idea how someone who was willing to behave in an underhand way would look. Besides, she'd had a long day and this acting lark was quite exhausting.

'Like I said, I think we could work together, Caro. I certainly need someone.'

'And what do you want me to do? You said you'd explain when you got the drinks.'

Still he hesitated but then he leant forward. 'I need you to be my eyes and ears here while I have to go and attend to some business. This business here isn't urgent yet, but it could become so at any time.'

'OK.' She nodded, encouraging him to go on. 'As long as there's something in it for me.' She hoped her smile indicated her willingness to help if the terms were satisfactory.

'I need to know if anyone has offered on some land that's for sale. On the Glen Liddell estate.'

'The McLeans' land?'

He nodded. 'The thing is, they don't know it's on the market. Yet. But of course they will find out. I need to get this land sold before they can stop it.'

'But how can you sell their land? I don't understand?' This time she was being completely genuine. She'd known, or suspected, he was trying to sell the land but how was a mystery.

'Do you know what power of attorney is?' he asked.

Chapter Fifteen

'So that's his plan.' Caro was lying on her bed at the B & B, talking to Lennie on the phone. 'When he was factor for Murdo, he got him to agree to a power of attorney. In the event of Murdo losing mental capacity he would take over. He advertised the land for sale when he heard about Murdo's first stroke so he could get in quickly before anyone could stop him.'

'I just can't believe it!' said Lennie, for about the seventeenth time. 'Who but Frazer would take advantage of a vulnerable old man he pretended to be so fond of.'

'I know. We're just lucky in a way that he's got so many dirty deals on the go that he has to leave this one to attend to another,' said Caro, also going over old ground. 'And of course I'll tell him he doesn't need to worry as often as I can.'

'Surely you don't need to have any more to do with him?' said Lennie, fizzing with indignation over the phone.

'I may have to keep in touch,' said Caro, 'but obviously, not from choice.' She thought back to the drinks she had shared with Frazer and shuddered. He had tried to kiss her goodnight and her skin crawled again with the memory.

'It's good we don't need to guard Murdo day and night,' said Lennie, 'and I managed to speak to a doctor. He's had a bleed on the brain and they're thinking about operating but of course it's very risky. But if it did go well Murdo could possibly be moved to the cottage hospital near here which would make life so much easier.'

'Oh goodness, yes. Being three hours away from him must make it so difficult.'

'Absolutely.' There was a pause. 'So, what will you do, Caro? You must be longing for the thought of your own bed. The older I get the more I want that.'

'Yes.' Caro sighed. She did want the comfort of home but there were so many more things she wanted, things she hardly dared think, let alone share with anyone.

'We're so grateful to you, Caro,' said Lennie. 'You've done so much for us at this difficult time. I don't know how we can repay you.'

Caro swallowed, suddenly a little tearful. 'I've been glad to help. I think I'll go home first thing tomorrow but do tell me if you need me again. I'm very fond of Murdo, as you know.'

'Of course we'll cover your flights for you. I'll sort it out now.'

Lennie was being kind and obviously appreciated what she'd done for the family, but Caro didn't want gratitude, not really. What she did want was a chance for her and Alec to continue what they'd started in France. But with Frazer's machinations and Alec having to sort everything out, it didn't look as if that would ever happen.

She lay awake for a long time before she finally drifted off, although she had to be up early to get her flight. She had a lot to think about, and one of the things was a text from Rowan. It had arrived at eleven o'clock, and was faintly hysterical. *You've got to help me! Mum is being a tyrant! Please come back to the barge as soon as you can!*

Caro didn't engage, she just told Rowan she was on her way and would be back mid-morning the following day. Then she switched off her phone.

'What's been going on with you lot? I've only been away a couple of days!' said Caro. She had dumped her bag in the wheelhouse and gone straight down to the saloon. There were four people looking at her as if she were a creature from outer space. She knew three of them, but one was a young man who she guessed was the cause of Rowan's distress. 'You were expecting me. I did tell you I was coming.'

Rowan came to, got up and threw herself into Caro's arms. 'I'm going to run away again! There's nothing else I can do!'

'Honey,' said Scarlet, sounding tired, 'don't do that.' She picked up her knitting, which seemed to be a new hobby.

'There's no need to panic about this,' said Joe, 'really there isn't.'

Everyone sounded as if they'd been dealing with Rowan's melodrama for a while. Caro doubted if there was anything she could say that would make things better but she was prepared to give it a go.

'Let me make some tea for you,' said the young man. 'I'm Aaron. I'm an actor. I was on the drama course that Scarlet was on. Rowan came and sketched us at work. I hope you don't mind me being here.'

Caro liked him instantly, and thought she probably would have liked him even if he hadn't offered to make tea. 'That's fine, Aaron. You're welcome.'

When Caro had tea, toast and Marmite set in front of her, she said, 'So what's the story?'

Rowan collapsed next to her on the banquette. 'Mum's being SO unreasonable. She says I have to go back immediately.'

'Honey,' said Scarlet, 'the deal was you could stay with me while I did my course but my course is nearly over now and you should go home.' She had obviously said all this before but Rowan wasn't able to accept it.

'I hadn't met Aaron then!' said Rowan, flinging her hands in the air in a dramatic gesture she might well have picked up from the acting course she'd only supposed to be sitting in on so she could sketch the participants.

Caro ate her toast and drank her tea without speaking. She felt responsible. While she hadn't actually encouraged Rowan to run away from home the first time, she did enable her to stay. She had made it possible for Rowan to visit art schools, to see the world beyond the beautiful glen she had been brought up in. It had never occurred to her that Rowan might fall head over heels in love. But of course he was probably the first good-looking young man she had ever seen and falling in love would be something she'd want to do. It was part of the rebellion of running away to London. 'How did your interview at the art school go?'

'Brilliantly,' said Scarlet. 'They were really impressed with her portfolio.'

'I can't apply until next year though,' said Rowan, 'and I want to spend the time travelling with Aaron. I want to see the world!'

The mother in Caro flew into alarm mode, hastily disguised by another crunch of toast. Was Rowan sleeping with this young man who was hardly more than a boy? And were they taking precautions? 'I can't see that working for Skye, sweetie,' she said as calmly as she could.

'She's gone batshit,' said Rowan, her words revealing that the gently reared girl who'd come down from Scotland had probably gone forever.

'The thing is, love,' said Caro, 'you're awfully young to go backpacking round the world. I'd worry about Posy doing it, and she's twenty.'

'But she *has* gone round the world though, hasn't she?' said Rowan, who obviously had this argument ready prepared. 'All the way to Australia! We want to go to Australia!'

'She went on a plane, to Australia, to spend time with her father,' said Caro. 'It's not the same as backpacking, really it isn't.' Although as she said it she realised that she'd gone backpacking round Europe when she was about that age which was when she met Alec. But she hadn't been seventeen and had been a lot more worldly-wise than Rowan.

'So you asked Skye and she said no?' Caro needed to be clear. Had Skye just gone batshit for no particular reason (not entirely unlikely) or had the words 'backpacking' and 'Australia' cropped up in the conversation?

Rowan sighed dramatically. 'I just said I had a boyfriend – I said we wanted to spend time together. I may have said something about travelling.'

When Caro had first met Rowan she'd been quiet, thoughtful and shy. Now she was very much her mother's daughter, prone to exaggeration and a bit self-obsessed. Maybe London had released this inner diva or maybe it was First Love. Either way, Caro still had a lot of sympathy for her.

'And did you say he was an actor?'

Aaron nodded and Rowan blushed.

'OK,' Caro went on. 'So you rang Skye and said, "Hey, Mum, I've got a cool actor boyfriend and we're going round the world together. Isn't that great?"'

This made Rowan giggle. 'No!'

'But maybe you weren't that tactful? You didn't pick your words?'

'Probably not quite well enough,' said Rowan.

'I'll tell you what I think it is,' said Caro. 'It's fear of the unknown. You've never had a boyfriend before. If she met Aaron, she'd probably feel quite differently about it. Although I don't think there's anything in the world that would make her let you go backpacking before you go to art school.'

'Caro's right, you know,' said Joe. 'If Skye met Aaron, and saw what a beautiful person he is, she'd really like him.'

Caro suspected Joe was talking about Aaron's inner beauty rather than his Hugh Grant forehead and manly nose. Skye, she suspected, would be more womanly in her reaction and just see how gorgeous he was.

'So what are you saying?' asked Rowan.

'That you should do what all good girls do and take your boyfriend home to meet your mum!' said Caro, smiling in an effort to make this seem less daunting.

'What! Take him to that madhouse?' Rowan seemed poleaxed by this simple suggestion.

'It's not a madhouse,' said Caro. 'I don't know about your house; the main house is a bit eccentric, but nothing Aaron wouldn't be able to cope with.' She smiled at him, aware they were talking about him as if he wasn't there.

'I couldn't do that to him,' said Rowan protectively, flinging her arms round his knee, which was the nearest bit of him she could reach.

Caro's patience was being tried. 'He'll cope.' She gave him another inclusive smile so he didn't feel objectified by their conversation. 'Wouldn't you, Aaron?'

Aaron nodded. 'Of course I'll go and meet your mother, Ro – if that's what it takes. And it sounds like a beautiful place.'

'I'd love to go up and see where you live,' said Joe. 'Why don't I go with you both?'

'Brilliant idea!' said Caro. 'Joe will protect you from Skye's wrath.'

'Skye is a very pure spirit,' said Joe, quiet but firm. 'But this is a rite of passage. She will need support.'

Scarlet looked up from her knitting. 'Rite of passage?'

'Accepting that your little girl is finally a woman is a milestone. Not always easy.' Joe smiled his gentle smile and Scarlet put down her knitting.

'I haven't looked at it like that before,' she said. 'And you're right. My mother couldn't bear it when men started looking at me.'

'She was jealous?' asked Rowan, horrified by the idea.

Scarlet nodded. 'But my mum's weird.'

'So's mine!' said Rowan.

'She's just a bit overprotective,' said Caro, who did think Skye was a bit weird.

'Anyway.' Scarlet got up. 'I have to go and get ready. David has come back from the States early and will be here to pick me up soon. Isn't that just great?'

'When?' asked Caro, her eyes whipping round the saloon to check how messy it was before she decided if it was great or not.

'Not until three,' said Scarlet, 'but I have to make myself beautiful for him.'

Caro didn't disguise her laughter at this. 'Darling, you're so lovely, you could borrow Joe's overalls to put on and still look sensational.'

Scarlet blushed. 'Thank you. But you know how it is: he's been mixing with adorable Hollywood starlets, all trying to get his attention. I don't want him to think I feel I've got him now and don't have to make an effort any more.'

'Ridic,' said Caro, hoping she didn't sound desperately out of date.

Caro was sorting out her clothes for washing when her phone went. In spite of generally being a sensible sort her heart leapt and then fell again when she saw it wasn't Alec. It was Skye. Just for a second she allowed herself to consider not accepting the call but she knew Skye would only ring again.

'Skye! Hi! How are things up there?' she said breezily. 'Is Murdo OK?'

'Of course he's OK. He's strong as an ox, even when he's in a coma!' snapped Skye. 'I'm not ringing about that. It's Rowan.'

'Do you want to speak to her? Is her phone out of charge? Teenagers, eh. I'll just call her.'

Caro could almost see Skye's eyes flash with irritated fire via the phone. 'I want to speak to you. I want you to sort out the mess you started. Get her back here immediately!'

'I'll do my best, Skye. I have already told her she should go home. So has Scarlet – you know? The actor who's been staying here? We both impressed on her that she should go home. But she won't without Aaron.'

'The boyfriend? This boy she's known for all of five minutes? Well, she can't! I won't have him in the house.'

'Honestly, Skye, the one bit of advice I'll pass on is, if as a parent you show huge appreciation for the boyfriends they bring home, they go off them very quickly. And Aaron is really sweet. He looks like a young Hugh Grant,' she added, not sure if this would mean anything to Skye.

'Can you promise me that will happen?'

'No, I can't promise you anything, but I can almost promise when you meet him you'll feel better about it.' Skye really was a piece of work, she thought.

'You'd better bring them up, then,' said Skye grudgingly.

'Joe said he wanted to come up, if you don't trust them to manage the airport on their own,' Caro said firmly. 'And I don't see why you can't come and collect them.'

'I'm busy!'

'So is everyone else, Skye. But it seems you don't need to worry. Someone is doing your bidding for you.' Caro stopped trying to hide her irritation. 'Ring back when you've arranged flights.'

'Can't you ...?'

'I could but I'm not going to. Bye, Skye.'

Caro left her cabin and went to join the others in the saloon. Rowan and Aaron had tidied it and Rowan was winding up the flex on the vacuum cleaner. Caro felt a surge of fondness for them and realised she'd miss them even though she'd only just met Aaron.

'Oh, that looks better!' she said. 'And I've heard from Skye. She's fine with Aaron going up to stay with you as long as Joe goes too. Where is he?'

'I think he said he was doing some t'ai chi,' said Aaron.

'I don't know when your flights are,' Caro went on. 'Skye is arranging them.'

'Are you sure?' said Rowan. 'She's never booked a flight in her life. She says going on those websites affects her aura and gives her panic attacks.'

'We all feel like that,' said Caro crisply, 'but we just have to get over it.'

A few hours later, Aaron and Rowan were sitting in one armchair, squashed but happy. Caro was sitting next to Scarlet on the sofa and could feel the excitement fizzing in her as her knee bounced up and down. It was very sweet.

'I know it's silly,' said Scarlet. 'But I haven't seen David for a while and I can't help feeling fluttery.'

'I get that,' said Rowan, sighing.

'I understand, and it's lovely,' said Caro more briskly, 'but why did you want to meet him here? Wouldn't it have been easier for you both if you'd met him at the hotel?'

259

Scarlet shook her head. 'No paps here. And we love the barge.'

'But there are people,' Caro said, looking at Aaron and Rowan.

'That's cool!' said Scarlet. 'You're like my family now.'

David knew the code to get in by now and so Scarlet was listening for his step on the gangway. The moment she heard it she was up and off.

'Like a rat up a drainpipe,' said Joe, who had stopped doing t'ai chi and was making a drink.

Caro giggled. The thought of Scarlet, so beautiful, being described as a rat was funny.

'Will you be lonely when we've all gone?' asked Joe.

Caro nodded. 'For a little while but then I'll enjoy having my own space. It's been so hectic and so strange lately. Normality will be good for me.'

It was a little while before Scarlet and David came down to the saloon. Scarlet looked happily rumpled and David just looked very happy.

'Welcome, David!' Caro allowed herself to be enveloped in a warm hug, smelling slightly of something delicious. 'How are you? Would you like a beer or something?'

'Just a cup of British tea, please.'

While Caro was making this, she listened to David.

'So, honey, what's the most surprising place I can tell you I went while I was back in the States?'

Scarlet gave up guessing quite quickly. 'So where?'

'Visiting your mother.'

There was a small scream. 'You visited Mom? I can't believe it! She let you in?'

'It took some work, I can tell you, but eventually she thought she ought to find out something about the rascal her daughter had set her heart on.'

'I never thought I'd hear those words.' Tears sparkled in Scarlet's eyes.

'And what is more – she let me into your bedroom.'

Scarlet's expression altered a little. 'Why would you want to go into my bedroom?'

'To look for the perfume. And I found it. I have it with me!'

'My oh my,' said Scarlet, sounding very Southern Belle all of a sudden.

'So can I smell it?' asked Caro, thinking about the work she and Alec had spent trying to replicate it. 'I hope it's the same as the one we smelt in Grasse.' Perfume was volatile, it could change and the conditions it was stored in would affect it.

'It's in my big case that's gone to the hotel, but I'll pull it out as soon as I can.' He seemed far too relaxed about it for Caro but she didn't think she could push it.

'Now,' David went on. 'Have you thought any more about the wedding? I really think we should set a date.'

Scarlet tossed her head. 'Don't tell me my parents want to come! Unless you used witchcraft on them. They'd die before they'd witness me marrying you!'

'No witchcraft,' said David.

'I will not countenance my daughter aligning herself to a man involved in "the movies"!' said Scarlet, sounding imperious and very straight-laced. 'Even though Dad's mom was dresser to a movie star.'

Rowan giggled. 'You sound like someone's grand-mother!'

'Just like your namesake from *Gone with the Wind*,' Caro added.

'I have been studying at the feet of one of the great actors' – Scarlet emphasised the 'ors' – 'of our generation. It's affected me.' Scarlet was so happy it radiated from her, almost like a glow from a light source. But then it dimmed. 'I'm sure they'd come round if I agreed to go home and get married by the preacher and had the wedding that they want for me. But people who've known my family forever would just want to come so they can peer at me and say I think a lot of myself.'

'It'll be the same if you have a Hollywood wedding,' said David. 'People you don't know, a zillion snappers taking your picture, all wanting the one where you look a bit tired or you have a wardrobe malfunction. But we'd be sponsored for most of it so it would save me a heap of money.'

Scarlet shook her head. 'I don't want that, David, and nor do you. Rowan, honey? Could you show me your sketchbook again?'

'Ah, the church on the hill,' said David. 'Just people we want there?'

Scarlet nodded. 'And something cheerful like a barn dance.'

'A ceilidh,' said Rowan. 'I know a lovely band.'

'I'd want you as one of my bridesmaids,' Scarlet went on.

'And Aaron as a pageboy?' suggested Caro. 'He'd look great in a kilt.'

'Would everyone have to wear kilts?' asked David.

'Well, you could probably wear what you liked but traditionally, yes,' said Caro. She suddenly found herself having inappropriate thoughts about David in a kilt. He would look magnificent. 'Scarlet would wear a dress, though.'

'We talked about it before,' said Scarlet wistfully.

No one spoke for a few moments and then David said, 'Why don't we go up and see this church? Ask Rowan's family if we can have our wedding there?'

Scarlet flung herself at David. 'Could we? Could we really? Are you sure you don't mind?'

'Of course I don't mind! I just want you to have the wedding you want, without anyone else having an opinion. And if we can't use this little church, we'll find another one, somewhere else in Scotland.'

'Oh no!' said Rowan. 'I mean, sorry! Of course Scarlet must have the church she wants, but really, the Michael Kirk is so charming and in such a beautiful setting. I'd be so upset if she couldn't get married there and have the reception on our land.'

'You might need to convince your family,' said David. 'If they're not used to having their property used as a wedding venue, it might not be something they'd care to do.'

Caro caught Rowan's eye and they both bit their lips to stifle their laughter. 'I think Rowan could talk her family round,' said Caro. 'But the house is quite – how should I put it? Unreconstructed.'

'What are you saying?' asked David.

'It could do with redecorating,' Caro said.

'I think it sounds really romantic,' said Aaron. 'My grandparents' house is a bit like that. I love it.'

'It certainly is romantic,' said Caro, 'and the scenery around it is wonderful, really spectacular.'

'Of course venues are very expensive to hire,' said David, 'and we'd expect to pay the going rate for something so special.'

'That sounds good,' said Rowan. 'We're always broke! Although I don't know why, when Murdo sold that land—'

'Anyway,' said Caro quickly. 'I'm sure you could use the land even if the estate no longer owns it.'

She could only guess at how much the estate could make out of Scarlet and David's wedding but it could really make a difference.

'We need to get going on this really,' said David, pulling out his phone. 'I wonder where is good to stay?'

Aware he didn't expect her to answer this, Caro brought up the subject of something that was worrying her. 'Before you all disappear up north, do you think I could smell the perfume? It's just when I was with Alec – helping him – we made one. I'd like to check we got it more or less right.'

'You managed to make some? I didn't dare ask! It seemed such an impossible thing to do,' said Scarlet.

'She has been dying to know,' said David, 'but refused to say anything.'

Caro laughed. 'That was very tactful of you! But if I could have a sniff of yours ...?'

'Of course,' said Scarlet, 'but, Caro! You must come with us! I want you to be my wedding planner!'

Chapter Sixteen

David and Scarlet carried Caro off to the Ritz in the car that arrived for them, leaving the others to fend for themselves on the barge. Caro was going to have a sniff of the perfume that had been guarded so carefully for some eighty years. She wasn't at all sure about being a wedding planner but she did know she had to do all she could to make sure the perfume was right.

She was aware that David and Scarlet hadn't seen each other for a while and so resolved to make her excuses as soon as she could but she allowed Scarlet to order champagne while David looked for the precious bottle.

He brought it in and handed it to Caro. It wasn't in the beautiful crystal swan made by René Lalique, only one of which had been made, but it was in a very ancient vial. The glass stopper had been secured by an early sticky tape and then again by newer versions.

'You can smell it if you sniff hard,' said Scarlet, sitting next to Caro on the sofa.

'Would you mind if I opened it?'

Scarlet hesitated.

'It's entirely up to you,' Caro went on. 'I just want to check this is the same as the one Alec is making for you. It doesn't matter. I think you'll love Alec's version.'

Scarlet exhaled sharply. 'No, let's open it. It's just I haven't opened it for years; I wanted to keep it safe for as long as possible.'

It took a little while to peel away the layers of tape Scarlet had put on when she was still only a child.

Scarlet took the first sniff. 'It's the same, the same smell I remember sniffing when my grandmother first gave me the bottle.' A tear ran down her cheek.

There was a hiatus as the champagne arrived and was poured and then Caro inhaled. She closed her eyes and cast her mind back to Pascal's stifling laboratory and realised the smell wasn't quite the same.

She wanted time to think how to announce this and wonder if she needed to. After all, Scarlet might not notice the very faint difference. But then again it was very important this scent was right. She took a few sips of champagne. She realised she had to mention it.

'It's not exactly the same as the one Alec is making – we had to leave before it was finished. You have to decide which one you like best: this one that you've known for years and years – or Alec's which is a bit fresher. I think they would both work well for you.'

Scarlet put her hands on her face and closed her eyes. This perfume, Caro realised, was much more than a matter of smelling wonderful; it was a memory.

Caro put her hand on Scarlet's. 'Tell me about your grandmother – but only if you want to.'

Scarlet took a deep breath and then finished her champagne. 'I do want to. She was my rock, my role model – all those things. You see, my mom always had a problem with me. I was the oldest and my two brothers came along quite quickly after me. My mom had always wanted boys and although she liked me to be helpful she always preferred them. I always got blamed for everything, even things that were nothing to do with me.'

'Oh, Scarlet!' Caro felt tears spring to her own eyes.

'But it was fine! My grandmother lived with us and she loved me. She gave me praise, made me feel I was important, and pretty, said all the things mothers say to children, except mine didn't. My mother only wanted me to behave well, do the right thing, sing in church, marry the right person. She didn't want me to be an actor, oh no!' A smile broke through her sad reminiscence. 'But my grandmother had told me that my mother would always have a problem with me, so I had to remember that she was on my side and always would be, even after she'd passed away.'

Caro reached for her glass, glad that David had refilled it. It was tragic, this lovely girl unloved by her mother. 'Then the new perfume that Alec is making should be exactly the same as this is.'

'And you'll come up and help me plan my wedding?' said Scarlet. 'My mother won't be there and even if she was, she'd just take over and I'd hate that.'

Caro took a moment. She wouldn't be so much a wedding planner as a surrogate mother and, although Posy was yet to marry herself, a mother's role when her daughter was getting married was to say, 'I think that would be lovely,' unless she really, really couldn't. 'I'd love to!'

'The thing is,' said David, 'I have to be back in the States in a month. Would that give us enough time to organise a wedding that isn't in a regular hotel?'

'Sweetie, we'd be lucky to find a hotel at such short notice,' said Scarlet.

David smiled indulgently. 'I think if we wanted a hotel one would become available.'

'But if you don't want a regular hotel, I'm sure the McLean family and Glen Liddell House would be able to do something.' Caro didn't know this for sure but there were a lot of willing workers up there; if they were asked to put on a wedding, they would. 'Although of course we'll have to ask Lennie – she's Alec's sister – about it. It's her and Alec's house really.'

'I'll write a note so you can take it to her,' said Scarlet. 'Would that be all right?'

'That would be charming,' said Caro, hoping it would do the trick. She didn't want to say no to Scarlet – she felt quite maternal towards her.

Having refused dinner, but accepting a cab back to the barge, Caro got out her phone to ring Lennie. She needed to tell her what was going on. Then she'd phone or text Alec. She had a good reason to – it wouldn't look needy; it would be fine. But then she remembered Frazer. He was expecting her to keep him up to date on Murdo's well-being. She sent him a quick text. *No change on Murdo so no need to come over. I'll keep you posted.*

His reply came back almost instantly. *What is wrong with him exactly?*

Caro felt extremely reluctant to give Frazer any real information when she didn't know how he might use it. She decided to lie. *Don't know*, she texted in reply. *I'll get back to you.*

Then she rang Lennie and agreed what she would say to Frazer. Five minutes later she texted him again. *Murdo had a fall which caused a bleed on the brain.*

Is he expected to survive? was his reply.

They won't know for another three weeks, returned Caro, without reference to anyone. She just thought it would be good if they could stall Frazer for that long. By then they could have sorted out the legal things that would stop Frazer making free with Murdo's property.

Fine, was his reply. Caro left it at that.

Then she texted Lennie. *I don't want to alarm you in any way, but how would putting on a wedding be for you? For an enormous sum of money, yet to be decided?*

It was a while before Lennie replied. *We can't afford to turn anything down that will make us money, but basically, I'd rather stick pins in my eyes. You'd have to do it.*

When she'd reassured Lennie about the wedding, she texted Alec.

It hadn't been part of Caro's plan to travel up to Scotland with Rowan, Aaron and Joe, but apparently it had been part of Skye's. At least she'd sorted the flights while Caro had to get everyone's passport details (which was the hardest part), and then put in her credit card details.

On the journey Caro had felt very slightly as if she were in charge of a school trip. Rowan was inclined to wander off with Aaron and Joe was a stranger to the concept of sticking to a schedule but somehow they arrived and were greeted by Ewan,

Heather's husband, who Heather had once told Caro did everything that no one else did.

'Hello, Ewan!' said Rowan, flinging her arms round him and giving him a hug. 'Great to see you!'

'Hi there,' said Ewan, nodding almost imperceptibly at Rowan's enthusiasm for seeing him again. 'Alec would have come to pick you up himself but he's gone to the hospital.'

'Murdo?' Caro suddenly wanted to cry and knew it wasn't just the potential death of an old man. 'Is he OK?'

'We hope so,' said Ewan, leading his party of passengers. 'He's had an operation.'

Caro had an idea. 'Could you drop me off at the hospital? I need to talk to Alec about something important.'

'How will you get back from the hospital?' said Joe. 'I thought the estate was quite a long way from Glasgow?'

'I'll get a lift with Alec,' said Caro, feeling calmer and more in control of events. She could talk to Alec about the perfume and tell him the one they had been making was slightly different from Scarlet's sample.

It took a while to track down Murdo as he'd been moved but at last she found him on a side ward, Alec sitting by his bedside studying something.

'Hello,' she said quietly.

He looked at her as if she were a ghost. 'Caro! What are you doing here?'

'I came with Rowan and her boyfriend, and Joe, but I need to talk to you. David went to Scarlet's house and got the perfume. I'm afraid it's not quite the same as the one we sampled in Grasse.'

'Are you sure? Possibly the way it's been stored has affected it, but surely not by much.'

'It is different and you're right, not by much, but I think—' She stopped. He was the perfumier, not her. 'David and Scarlet are coming up here soon and they'll bring it, so you can smell for yourself.'

Caro was aware that Alec didn't completely trust her nose. And why should he? It was a rare gift.

'Why are they coming up? Just to let me smell the perfume?' Alec seemed more confused than ever.

'They want to get married up here. It's a long story.' Caro didn't think Alec wanted the whys and wherefores of David and Scarlet's wedding plans. 'What about Murdo? I heard from Ewan they operated.'

'Last night.'

'Oh my goodness! Was it an emergency?'

'No. Operating theatres never sleep these days. It went well. I'm just waiting for him to come round.'

'Can I get you a drink of some kind? Or would you like to go and get a proper meal? I can sit with him.'

Alec hesitated. Caro could see him deciding.

'How long have you been here?' she asked.

'A couple of hours.'

'Have a quick break. I'll wait with him.'

'But you've just got off a plane ...'

'You're OK, jet lag hasn't kicked in yet.'

He smiled at her attempt at a joke. 'I'll go and get a meal then. Can I bring you something back?'

Caro hesitated. She couldn't think of anything she wanted to eat. 'A cup of tea, maybe.'

'I'll see what I can do.'

It was hard to tell what was going on with Murdo. He looked similar to when he'd been in a coma before the operation. But being with him was peaceful. She'd done so much rushing around recently, sitting in the quiet was calming. She had her Kindle in her handbag, thrust in there at the last minute, but she couldn't be bothered to read.

Alec came back with a bag full of supplies. There was tea, a bottle of water, sandwiches and a selection of chocolate bars. 'I thought you may be hungry if you saw food.'

She was. She started with the tea, and then worked her way through the sandwiches, the water and some of the chocolate.

'That's better,' she said. 'Thank you so much.'

'Well, thank you for coming. I managed to get something to eat and have a quick walk round too.'

He smiled but Caro was aware they were suddenly shy of each other.

'So what are Murdo's chances of recovering?'

'The prognosis is good. The operation went well and if all goes to plan we can have him moved to the cottage hospital in a week or so.'

'That would be handy.'

'It would. Being so far away from home when there's so much happening is difficult.' He sounded tired.

'Is it sorting out the land that Frazer put on the market that's being tricky?'

'Tricky and expensive. But still, the man we sold the nature reserve to will sell it back to us. But for the price he paid, which is more than the amount we actually got for it, because naturally Frazer got paid a backhander.' He went and took up his place at Murdo's bedside.

Caro moved another chair to the other side of the bed and sat down. 'I don't know if it will be enough but Scarlet and David having their wedding up here will bring in something. They're going to see Lennie about it any minute. They'll be staying in the hotel, of course, but they will take up her time. She wasn't at all keen when I texted her about it but also said she couldn't turn down anything that made money.' She paused. Alec was looking slightly horrified at the thought of a celebrity couple having their wedding at his house. 'It would be a great earner.

You can charge more or less what you like. It might even make up the difference between what you've got left from the sale of the land and what the seller wants.'

'Of course it would help, and David will be paying me for the perfume ...'

'If it's right,' said Caro, speaking before she had engaged her brain – it wasn't really the time and place to challenge Alec about how accurate the fragrance was. 'But how much could you charge for it?'

Alec shrugged. 'I don't know but it should lead to other business. We'll find the extra money one way or another.'

Just as Caro was casting round trying to think of something encouraging to say, there was movement from the bed.

Alec sat forward and took hold of Murdo's hand.

'Is that you, Alexander?' said Murdo.

'Yes, Dad, it's me.'

'Good to see you, old chap,' said Murdo. 'It's been a long time.'

His voice was a bit faint but the old Murdo seemed to be still there. But was he referring to the time he'd been unconscious that was a long time, or the time Alec was away from home?

'Well, I'm here now,' said Alec. 'How are you feeling?

'Weak as a kitten, but glad to see you.' Murdo frowned as he looked at Caro. 'Who's this? Your wife? Lovely girl. Didn't like that other one much. Beautiful as the dawn, of course, but sour.'

'This is Caro,' said Alec, obviously embarrassed. 'She looked after you for a bit before you were ill.'

'If it was before I was ill, why was she looking after me?'

Caro took his other hand. 'I was mostly there to stop you getting bored. You used to beat me at two-handed bridge.'

His ancient features indicated this was a happy thought. Then he frowned. 'I've made a lot of mistakes in my long life,' he said.

'I'm sure not many very bad ones,' said Caro, having exchanged anxious glances with Alec. They didn't want him wasting his new-found conscious-ness on remorse. 'I wonder if we should tell the nurse he's come round?' she mouthed at Alec across Murdo's bed.

'Good idea,' said Alec and stood up.

'No! I'll do it. You stay with Murdo.' Caro got up too.

Alec shook his head. 'I'd rather go. I won't be long. You stay with Dad.'

Caro sat down again and took hold of Murdo's hand. It was a bundle of bones and veins and Caro couldn't help thinking of all the things those hands had done over Murdo's long life. Lots of them would be things she didn't approve of, like shooting, killing things, but there'd have been good things too.

Her reflective mood seemed to have infected Murdo. 'I've been a stubborn old fool, Caro,' he said. 'I should have let Alec go his own way. He was never keen on the sporting side of things although he was a damn good fly fisherman.'

'Was he? Did you teach him to fish when he was a little boy?' Caro could picture them, man and boy, thigh-deep in a fast-flowing river, casting flies into the whisky-coloured water.

'I did. But mostly I left it to the ghillie we had then. Had I been closer to him, maybe he wouldn't have wanted to go off and do silly things.'

'I think people are who they are, no matter what we do with them,' said Caro. 'As parents we like to think how we treat our children – train them to say please and thank you, tidy up after themselves, things like that – actually affects their character. But now I don't think it makes much difference. They'll be the people they'll be. As parents all we can do is just try to keep them alive; most of what they achieve is up to them.'

'So it's not my fault Alexander didn't want to take over from me?'

'I shouldn't think so. And while he may not want to only run the estate, he really does love the land.'

'Does he?'

'Yes! He took me to see the bit over the hill? Where the lochan is?' She was about to say 'the bit you sold' when she stopped herself. 'Where the otters go? And the hen harriers?'

'Oh yes.'

'He loves it,' Caro repeated lamely. For the second time she'd engaged her mouth without her brain being consulted. Of all the things she shouldn't have talked to a very frail Murdo about was that piece of land.

'I've trusted the wrong people,' said Murdo after a very long pause. Caro had thought he'd gone back to sleep.

Caro didn't reply. She just rubbed the bony hand with her thumb as she held it. She was very relieved to hear Alec come back with a nurse. She made her excuses and left.

She went to the Ladies and washed her face. Murdo had seemed very frail. It was possible he was about to die. She wanted to support Alec but she didn't want to come between him and his father when they seemed likely to be reconciled.

There was a nurse standing outside the door of Murdo's room when she went back. Rapidly she tried to work out if this was a good sign or not.

'You must be Caro,' said the nurse brightly.

Caro decided it wasn't necessarily a bad sign. 'That's right.'

'I'm Alison. Alec's giving me a lift back to Glen Liddell. He told me he was giving you one, too?'

So that's what she was to Alec, someone he was giving a lift to. 'That's right.'

'I'll pop in and see how Murdo's getting on. It's very good news that he's woken up. I'm off duty in about half an hour.'

Caro waited outside the room, her energy drained, her spirits on the shiny green floor. She knew she'd feel better about things soon. Murdo coming round and having a good conversation with Alec was brilliant.

Losing a parent was the worst thing apart from (she assumed) losing a child, but it would be a lot harder if there was unfinished business between parent and child. If Murdo died respecting Alec, and if Alec knew Murdo really did love him, in spite of him wanting to make perfume, that would help a lot with the grief.

When Alec came out he said abruptly, 'We've got to get him out of there.' Then he set off towards the exit.

'But why?' asked Caro, hurrying along beside him. 'I thought the care seemed fine.'

'Nothing wrong with the care,' said Alec, 'he just needs to be at home.'

'What about the cottage hospital? Isn't he due to go there?'

He stopped suddenly, causing Caro to nearly bump into him. 'A man has a right to die where he wants to die, if it's remotely possible. And he wants to be at home. We can hire nurses, get equipment, but he needs to die in his own house.'

Caro found herself sitting in the back of the car, so for the two-hour drive, in which she'd hoped she and Alec could get back to the intimacy they'd shared in France, she listened to Alison and Alec making small talk in the front. They had a lot of school friends in common, and everyone had to be caught up on, their marriages, children, divorces. Caro wouldn't have minded so much if any of it had been remotely scandalous, but it wasn't.

When they finally dropped off Alison and arrived at the house, Caro wanted nothing more than an enormous whisky and possibly an oatcake.

Lennie was there at the door the moment the car pulled up.

'Oh, thank God you're here, Caro!' she said. 'Skye seems to have run off with a much younger man she described as a shaman and Rowan and someone described as her boyfriend have gone up to the spare bedroom. I expect Rowan is getting pregnant even as I speak!'

Lennie looked as if she was about to burst into tears or laugh but hadn't decided which. To Caro's relief, she opted for the latter and managed a rueful chuckle.

Caro smiled. 'I'm sure it's all fine, Lennie. Just let me get my breath and I'll find out what's going on.'

'We have to talk about Dad, Len. He needs to come home.'

'Oh my God, how much would that cost?' said Lennie. 'And what about this wedding we're supposed to be having?' Then she held up her hand. 'No, don't tell me. We need whisky for this.'

'Hell yes!' said Alec. 'And I'm not sure a blended one will do. Let's go and sit down.' He led the way to the drawing room and went across to the drinks cabinet. 'But, Lennie,' he said as he found glasses and poured whisky, 'although it sounds horrifying, the couple who want to get married here, David and Scarlet, are really nice people, and Caro will be here, won't you?'

'Of course. If you agree to have the wedding here, Scarlet asked me to help her. Her own mother is a bit of a nightmare, I gather,' said Caro.

Lennie's hands flew to her face in horror. 'Talking of which, Caro, you couldn't go up and see what Rowan and that Adonis are getting up to, could you? I can't face it!'

'Let the poor woman have a drink first,' said Alec.

'I'll down it in one and then knock them out with my whisky breath,' said Caro, who was beginning to feel faintly hysterical.

Lennie laughed. 'I'll check the oven. It's stew again but Heather made it, so it should be edible.'

'I'm looking forward to catching up with Heather,' said Caro, thinking fondly of the woman who was her first friend at Glen Liddell House.

'She'll be delighted to see you, too. She's been looking after George for us, since Murdo has been in hospital.'

Caro nodded. 'She's very kind.' She exhaled. 'Now, I'd better tackle Romeo and Juliet.'

As Caro found her way up the worn carpet stuck together with gaffer tape she wondered how much shabby she could convince Scarlet was actually chic ...

Chapter Seventeen

Caro knocked on the door of the spare room. A tearful voice asked her to come in.

Rowan and Aaron were sitting on the bed with their arms round each other in a good impression of orphans in the snow. Rowan was sniffing.

'Mum went ballistic,' she said. 'Kept going on and on about how I'd been corrupted by London. Thank God for Joe, who took her under his wing and carried her away.'

'Like an eagle?' said Caro. Rowan and Aaron both looked bewildered so she carried on. 'Never mind. The thing is, this is all very new to Skye. A few weeks ago you'd hardly set foot off the estate. The next thing she knows is that you're in London. And then your picture is in a gossip magazine. Now you've got a boyfriend. That's not so much a learning curve as a learning arch.'

'You mean it's a lot for her to cope with all at once?' said Aaron.

'Yes!' said Caro, glad at least one of them had got the point. 'But she will be fine, I'm sure. Especially if she's got Joe.'

'Isn't Joe a bit young for her?' asked Rowan.

'I don't think they'll necessarily end up together,' said Caro, thinking how inconvenient it would be for her if Joe left the barge. 'But I think for now, it will be fine.'

'I don't think Mum believes we're going to end up together but we are,' said Rowan. 'And going travelling together will just bind us closer together.'

'Oh, loves! You're just heaping one anxiety after another on your poor mother. All you need to make her ping off into the stratosphere with worry is to say you're pregnant.' Caro was suddenly overcome with how dreadful this would be. 'If you are pregnant, tell me tomorrow.'

Aaron looked a bit shocked and Rowan managed a slightly snotty smile. 'Of course I'm not pregnant. I'm far too young!'

'Being young doesn't actually prevent it from happening, you know.'

Rowan, obviously fully recovered now from her bout of weeping, rolled her eyes. 'Please! Caro! We don't need a lecture on where babies come from.'

'Thank the Lord for that. Now I'm going down to see if supper is ready, and if it is, you've got to come down and have it. Then I'll go and see Skye, with you both, and tell her what sensible and responsible young people you are.' She went to the door, stopping when she'd opened it. 'So make sure you're really playing that part when we see her!'

'I'm not an actor,' said Rowan. 'Only Aaron is.'

'Then you have to be that in real life,' said Caro, and went back downstairs.

An hour or so later, Caro walked over to Skye's house with Rowan and Aaron, thinking how light it was in Scotland and how lovely it was. Something she couldn't identify seemed to scent the air. The leaves on the trees were just unfurling, full of promise. As she watched a family of red squirrels crossed a branch and she could see ferns just beginning to unfurl in the woodland. 'This is an amazingly beautiful place,' she said.

'It is!' said Aaron. 'You are so lucky to have grown up here,' he said to Rowan.

'Say things like that to Skye and she'll come round to you in a second,' said Caro. 'Now, brace yourselves!'

Skye was doing up her top button when she opened the door. She did not look pleased to be interrupted and it was very clear what she and Joe had been doing. Caro was torn between amusement and embarrassment. She hoped that Rowan and Aaron, who were dawdling a bit behind her, hadn't noticed the button, and wouldn't pick up on the body language.

'Skye! How are you?' said Caro, as if they were best friends and this was a social call.

'Hello.'

Caro could see her struggling to stay neutral. She returned this with a wider smile. 'Any chance of anything not full of caffeine to drink? I just need something that won't keep me awake all night.' This was a bit disloyal to Lennie, who did have pepper-mint tea in her cupboard, but it was the best excuse to get herself invited in that she could think of.

Joe appeared. 'Caro!' he said, as if they'd been parted for weeks. He came forward and embraced her. 'You've got Rowan and Aaron with you?'

'Yes. They want to talk to you, Skye, and I said I'd come with.'

Skye opened the door wide enough so everyone could come in and Gally shot out. While she watched the dog show his delight in seeing Rowan again, Caro couldn't help reflecting that it was a bit ironic, Skye having a fit at the thought of her daughter having sex although she hadn't been setting a very good example.

'I'll make tea,' said Skye and disappeared.

Rowan guided everyone into the sitting room and Caro sat down, wondering what she was going to say to Skye. She looked around at the room. She had been expecting a plethora of dream catchers, weird sculptures and pictures, evoking someone whose interests could be described as a bit 'dippy hippy'. There was no television and the room was calm and tastefully decorated. Greys and blues reflected the sky outside and soft, thick throws covered the chairs.

The books were a bit more revealing. They were all on weird alternative subjects, from how to see auras to how to interpret dreams using water.

Skye came into the room with a tray. She had really nice mugs that all matched and rough-hewn biscuits she may well have made herself. Caro could see Joe feeling he'd landed in his spiritual home.

'I know why you've come, Caro,' said Skye, having distributed drinks. 'It's to persuade me it's absolutely fine for Rowan to go backpacking all over the world with a young man she's only just met!'

'Not at all,' said Caro. 'I've come to persuade you that it's fine for Aaron to stay up here for a while, with Rowan. I've already told them I think they're too young to go travelling together.'

Aaron and Rowan exchanged longing glances.

'I was about eighteen when I took off for the first time,' said Joe.

'It's different for boys,' said Skye and Caro nodded.

'I don't see why,' said Rowan. 'I want to go to art school next year, I won't have time if I don't do it now.'

'But aren't there some exams you need to take before art school?' said Caro. 'And art school isn't prison, you can go away in the holidays.'

'That's true,' said Joe.

'And art school will inform your choices about where to go,' said Caro. 'Besides, you may be able to travel a bit in Europe, say, before then?' She looked at Skye. She was looking beautiful but stony. Sex with Joe hadn't softened her for long.

'I just wish you'd never gone to London,' said Skye.

'Hey! Everyone needs to go to London sometime,' said Joe. 'Even if they do live in paradise.' His smile at Skye would have melted a statue.

Everyone sipped their tea. No one said anything, until Caro, who really wanted to go bed, said, 'Why don't we go for a walk together, Skye? We shouldn't talk about Rowan and Aaron in front of them.' She sent them a friendly glance. 'It cramps our style.'

'OK,' said Skye, and got up. Not only was she beautiful to look at but she moved beautifully too. Caro's confidence took a dip.

They walked to the edge of the loch, appreciating the truly beautiful evening. A flight of ducks flew across the sky, adding to the magic. Neither of them spoke for some time; possibly neither of them wanted to spoil things.

Eventually Skye said, 'I expect you think I'm making a big fuss about nothing.'

'No,' said Caro, 'I don't think that at all. I think you've had to accept your beautiful daughter is growing up and she seems to be doing it all at once.'

'That is how it feels, I suppose. I just want to keep her pure.'

'Depending on what you mean by pure, that ship may have sailed, although I don't know for sure.'

Skye sighed deeply. Then she bent and picked up a stone and flicked it into the loch so it bounced several times. 'I suppose I have to get to know this Aaron and hope they get tired of each other.'

'That is the best way,' said Caro. 'Keep them here, in each other's pockets, and they may well decide it's not the real thing. Or they may discover that they really are soulmates.' A yawn suddenly overcame her. 'I'd better get back.' She paused. 'Do you feel a bit better about Aaron staying with Rowan?'

'Do I have to let them share a bedroom?'

'Not if you don't want to. Which is why it's better if they stay with you. Nothing would stop them if they slept at the house.'

Rather to Caro's discomfort, Skye put an arm through hers as they set off home. 'Is there anything you can tell me about Joe?' she asked.

Thinking of the trouble Skye had put her to made Caro wonder if there was a case for saying something snippy about toy boys but she wasn't going to sink to that level. 'He's a really nice man. That's all.' The fact that he was basically a really nice man who liked his independence and hadn't had a serious girlfriend since Caro had known him wasn't something she felt obliged to pass on.

When Caro got back she found Lennie and Alec in the morning room. It was particularly full of mounted heads and dark oak furniture. The curtains hung in ribbons from the window and while it might have got morning sun, it obviously didn't get it at any other time. Nor did it get dusted.

'We'll put Dad in here,' said Alec. He was much more relaxed now, which Caro put down to good malt whisky.

'It'll take a bit of clearing,' said Lennie. She was relaxed too, but a bit more realistic.

'It's perfectly doable though,' said Caro. 'We'll just take out all the furniture and store it somewhere. Give it a jolly good clean and then put back only what there's room for after the hospital-standard bed Murdo will need.'

Alec gave her a broad smile, which Caro also put down to the whisky.

'What about the wedding?' said Lennie.

'Oh! I forgot!' Guilt made Caro blush. 'Scarlet wrote you a card asking about it. You weren't supposed to just get a text from me. But it's in my case. I'll go and get it.'

'No rush,' said Lennie, 'a text from you was fine, but it was sweet of her.' She continued to survey the room. 'Do you think we'll need this room for the wedding too?'

'They'd need everywhere, every inch,' said Caro. 'I mean, I'm only assuming, but the bigger the space they use the more you can charge.'

'What *can* we charge?' asked Lennie.

'We'd have to research it but I think at least ten thousand pounds.'

'That is an awful lot of money,' said Lennie. She sighed. 'But we'll need every penny if we're bringing Murdo home.'

'And buying back the land,' said Alec.

'Maybe we have to do one or the other?' said Lennie. 'Maybe we're crazy to even think of having Dad here, with private nurses and things.'

'The nurse Alison – you know the one we gave a lift to? She's longing to stop nursing in Glasgow and being near where she lives,' said Alec.

'That's not the problem,' said Lennie. 'It's money!'

'We'll find it somehow. And if we don't buy back the land, we don't.' Alec was determined. 'I've wasted years of my life not spending time with my father, sulking, being difficult. I'm determined to make it up to him now.'

'Good for you!' said Lennie and Caro blinked away a tear. It was wonderful that father and son were becoming close at last.

'I'm just going to ring the hospital,' said Alec. 'See how Dad is. I might get to speak to someone who can tell us when we could possibly move him.' Alec went out of the room.

'I don't think his mobile works in here,' said Lennie, possibly a bit embarrassed by his abrupt exit.

'That's OK. No need to worry but—'

Lennie took the hint. 'Oh, my dear girl! You must be exhausted. You should go to bed.' She paused, obviously thinking. 'I think the pink room would be best although I'm afraid the bed isn't made ...'

'Don't worry,' said Caro. 'I know where the airing cupboard is. I'll do it. You've got things to do here. But I will go up if you don't mind.'

As Caro found sheets and other bedding and made up her bed she realised that all hope of getting together with Alec had gone. And although there were lots of practical reasons why he was showing no interest in her romantically, surely if he felt about her in the same way she felt about him, he'd have given some indication?

Although she was tired, she lay awake between the slightly bobbly sheets, on a mattress that had seen very much better days, on a bed that creaked every time she moved. The pillows were lumpy and smelt musty. She cursed herself for not bringing her own pillow, or at least some lavender oil to sprinkle on everything.

But it wasn't discomfort that kept her awake, it was deciding what to do with herself.

She had promised Scarlet she'd help with her wedding and it would be cruel to leave Lennie to do it unaided while Alec was obsessed with turning at least part of the house into a hospital. Which meant she had to stay.

Although it was late, she sent Frazer a text, telling him there was no change with Murdo.

She wished she hadn't. A text came back immediately saying, *Really? I might need to speed things up a bit.*

Immediately she was not only wide awake but extremely worried.

Eventually she got up and went downstairs. She knew there was a bottle of whisky in the kitchen cupboard in the same way that she knew that in Skye's house there was a bottle of Rescue Remedy. It was just one of those things.

She found the bottle and then made herself hot milk. A spoonful of honey and a big glug of whisky would almost guarantee she'd sleep. She'd sort out the world in the morning.

As she took her mug upstairs she wondered where Alec was. The cottage where he made the perfume?

Or was he in his but and ben? She didn't think it was in the house. Her female instincts would have told her.

As she woke properly, having slept badly, she realised she did need to find Alec and fast. She had to tell him about Frazer. She could have told his sister, but Lennie was flustered enough already, what with the prospect of her invalid father needing to be brought home and a celebrity wedding all going on in a house that hadn't seen a paintbrush in fifty years.

Having made a cup of tea and found some bread and butter – it was at least an hour before Heather would appear – Caro thought she'd have a walk round the estate. A walk would help to clear her head. And then she needed to find Alec.

Somehow she wasn't surprised to see the outline of a man and a dog on the foreshore of the loch. She might never be his soulmate but she was fairly in tune with him.

She put the mug which she'd taken out with her and was now empty into the pocket of the old mac she'd borrowed and went to join him. It was a beautiful morning. The loch was like glass with threads of mist touched pink by the rising sun.

'Hey!' he said softly as he heard her approach.

'Hey to you too,' she replied, unable to help herself smiling, revealing how ridiculously pleased she was to see him.

George, Murdo's disreputable dog, ran up to her.

'Don't you dare pee on me!' Caro said, greeting the dog but keeping out of range.

'What are you doing up so early?' asked Alec. 'I'm walking the dog and thinking, obviously.'

'It's so beautiful it would be worth coming just for this, but I came looking for you. I had a text from Frazer last night.'

'Oh?'

'Bit worrying. I'd texted him to tell him there was no change with Murdo and he said he thought maybe he should speed things up a bit.'

'God.' Alec didn't speak for some moments. 'The thing is, I've got an appointment with the solicitors this morning. We've got to sort out getting rid of this power of attorney he's set up.'

Caro sometimes wished she didn't have such a strong sense of duty; now was one of those times. 'Would you like me to go in and sit with him?'

He brightened. 'Could you? That would be amazing. But do you really want to go all that way and sit with the old man?'

'Now he's awake he's quite entertaining,' she said, 'although we'll have to think of something to tell him so he doesn't think I'm minding him. I'm sure something will occur to me.'

'I'll ask Ewan to drive you in.'

'It would be better if I drove myself. I expect I could borrow a car? Then I could come back when I want.'

'Of course you can borrow a car but supposing Frazer turns up and things get nasty?' He frowned, his concern obvious.

'I'll manage,' said Caro. 'There are always people around in a hospital. But it would be far safer if we could get Murdo into the cottage hospital. He can't come home until the room is ready, and it would be so much easier now if he wasn't three hours away.'

'I'll see what I can do,' said Alec, leaving Caro in no doubt that Murdo would be in the cottage hospital very soon.

Caro tried not to think about the many, many things she'd rather be doing on a beautiful morning in Scotland than driving to Glasgow to guard a sick man. They did run through her head, of course, and one of them was getting the house ready for the wedding. Caro loved transforming things, and knew that getting rid of half a century of rubbish and keeping only the good pieces would be her idea of top fun.

She'd been with Murdo for several hours and was wondering if she could go back to Glen Liddell – Murdo was asleep and all seemed quiet – when a nurse came in.

'Oh! It's Alison, isn't it?' said Caro, recognising her.

'Yes! Hello, Caro. Everything's been arranged; we're moving him. It's a good time, we're not busy and we could do with this bed,' she said.

They were chatting gently about the move, how Murdo would respond and other such things when Frazer appeared at the door.

'Did I hear you say you were moving him?' he asked.

Alison and Caro stared at him. Then Caro got her brain into gear. 'Yes! Let me tell you about it.' She took him by the arm and whispered, 'I don't want to talk in front of the nurse. Come into the day room; there shouldn't be anyone there just now. Actually,' she went on, thinking quickly, 'it would be better if we went right outside then I can talk freely.'

Luckily, Frazer seemed content to follow Caro outside into the car park.

'They're moving him!' she said as if imparting information he didn't already have. 'As an emergency!'

Frazer didn't bother to hide his satisfaction at this piece of news. 'Oh! Why?'

Caro shrugged extravagantly. 'I don't know the medical details but they're trying to save his life!'

'Do you know where they're taking him?'

'Edinburgh.'

'Which hospital?'

Caro had no idea about hospitals in Edinburgh. She bit her lip and shook her head. 'They did say which one but I can't remember. I'll know it if I hear it.'

'The Royal Infirmary?'

'That's it. But you need to get off soon. They said something about blue lighting him.'

'Are you going too?'

Caro shook her head. 'I've got to report to the family and they'll go. Which is why you've got to get off now! The hospital will be ringing them and they'll set straight off!'

When at last Caro saw Frazer leave for what she sincerely hoped was the Royal Infirmary at Edinburgh, she called Alec and told him what was going on.

'I'll stay with Murdo until I've seen him safely in the ambulance. But honestly, I deserve an Oscar for that little performance.'

'I'll arrange it,' he said warmly. 'And I – we – are really, really grateful for this. You could have literally saved the old man's life.'

'I don't want gratitude,' Caro said but didn't finish her sentence. I did it for love, she said in her head.

Chapter Eighteen

The kitchen was crowded when Caro went down the following morning. Heather was there as well as Lennie, Rowan and Aaron. (Aaron had come for some cow's milk – he didn't fancy hemp, or any of the other plant milks that Skye's fridge supplied.)

After the greetings, hugs, questions, answers and oft-repeated thank yous, Caro eventually sat at the kitchen table with wholemeal toast and Marmite. Lennie sat down opposite.

'While you were guarding Murdo, I was in conversation with Scarlet on the phone. She is so nice! Who'd have thought she'd be so normal?'

'I know. And when you see just how lovely she is, it's even more amazing.'

'Well, I will see her soon. They'll be here about midday. I managed to get them the best room at the hotel, which, I imagine, is being cleaned to within an inch of its life.' Lennie sipped her tea. 'Their usual trade is a bit more rustic.'

Caro considered. 'David and Scarlet do seem really relaxed and they were fine on the barge but maybe when they actually see what it's like up here they may think it's just too – authentic.'

'Oh, I hope not! Now I've got my head round it, I'm really looking forward to putting on a wedding. It's the sort of thing I'd never have considered when Murdo was at full strength but with him safely in the cottage hospital – near but not in the house – it seems a really good idea. We have the scenery and we could always have a marquee, with midge netting for when the little devils get bad.'

Caro could tell that Lennie had been thinking about it a lot. 'The thing about being a wedding venue is, you'd only need to have as many as you want. One or two a year if it seems too much hassle.'

'Oh no!' said Lennie. 'I see it as a major source of income for the future. Locals could do B and B – it could be really lucrative.' She paused, her enthusiasm suddenly dimmed. 'But we really need that bit of land back. It should never have been sold. It's such an important part of the estate.'

'How's that going?'

'Well, Alec has spoken to the man who bought it and he's quite happy to sell it back, but as you know, there's a shortfall.'

'The wedding may be enough?'

'I hope so, but of course, the money we could get for the wedding wouldn't all be profit by any means.'

Caro wanted another bite of toast but felt crunching might make her look unsympathetic. 'And how is Alec getting on with the solicitors?'

'OK, I think. Thankfully they're prepared to wait to be paid.'

'It'll be all right, Lennie,' said Caro. 'We'll make it all right.' To her surprise she saw tears at the corner of this normally down-to-earth woman's eyes.

'Thank you. I usually relish challenges like this but I suppose I've been so worried about Murdo, and that ghastly Frazer and everything, and my daughter, thousands of miles away with her first baby.'

'But she's OK?' Caro wondered how she would feel if she'd just left Posy and a new baby in a completely different country.

'She's absolutely fine! Getting on far better without me, I'm sure.'

'You have had a lot to worry about and it's dreadful to think of someone selling your home from under you, so to speak.'

Lennie nodded. 'Yes, and Scarlet is going to come and see what a shabby old home it is. Then she'll go away and have her wedding somewhere else. In a proper castle, with carpet not held together with tape.'

This was a very real possibility; after all, the pictures Scarlet had seen had been hand drawn by Rowan – the real 'big hoose' by the loch might not seem nearly so charming in reality. 'Well, we can't completely redecorate before she comes at twelve, but maybe we should look at the church? Will there be flowers?'

'No. We only put flowers there when there's going to be a service and that's only once a month.'

'Let's do that then. It'll make a difference and it's doable. And more importantly, Lennie, it'll take your mind off things!'

The church was a simple, white-painted building, with very little adornment apart from one stained-glass window dedicated to the family.

They filled two vases with leaves and wild flowers, including foxgloves, broom and loosestrife.

'It's a shame that the bluebells are completely over now,' said Caro. 'I know we shouldn't pick them but the scent is so heavenly.'

'Do bluebells smell?' asked Lennie, surprised. 'I don't think I've ever noticed.'

As they went back to the house Caro understood a little better why Alec had been so keen to keep his passion for perfume secret from his family. Yes, bluebells smell! They had a divine fragrance!

Before Scarlet and David arrived it was all Caro could do to stop Lennie getting the staff (that was

Heather, Ewan and Rab from the smokery) to line up and doff their caps. Lennie was convinced that Hollywood royalty would expect that. And to be fair, Caro realised, some of them probably would.

Scarlet, however, didn't expect any ceremony. From the moment she arrived she was delighted by everything.

'Oh, it's just like a film I saw as a child! With heads on the wall and everything falling apart. I love it! How many people could we accommodate?'

Lennie was about to offer the entire house, including the bedrooms, so Caro stepped in.

'Well, obviously it's up to Lennie, but most of the downstairs rooms and two bedrooms upstairs.'

'Let me explore some more,' said Scarlet. 'David? What do you think?'

'I think whatever you want is exactly what I want.'

'If only all men were as amenable!' said Lennie. 'Although my darling Tarquin was pretty amenable.' She gave the briefest sigh and then said, 'Let me take you to the library – bursting with atmosphere.'

A little later, possibly slightly tired of inspecting wood-panelled rooms full of furniture, David paused. 'Where is Alec? I have the sample of perfume here.' He addressed Caro, who looked questioningly at Lennie.

'He dashed off early to a meeting with solicitors but he hopes to be back very soon.' Lennie sounded apologetic.

'Coffee anyone?' Heather appeared with a tray. 'The shortbread is home-made.'

Scarlet, diverted from her need to visit every room in the house, followed everyone else into the drawing room.

'This shortbread is amazing!' said David.

'Could we have this at the wedding?' said Scarlet.

'Or maybe we could have it for your wedding favours?' said Caro. 'So people really get to appreciate it? It could be packaged beautifully and it would be a lovely present from you both to your guests.'

'How many people do you think you could manage here?' asked Scarlet. 'We want to keep it small but you know how these things are, they always end up bigger than you hope for.'

While Lennie was dealing with Scarlet's queries (extremely efficiently, Caro thought), Caro was looking out of the window. She saw Alec's car pull up, spraying gravel.

She got up to forestall him. He'd find it embarrassing to walk into a room full of people he wasn't quite expecting.

'Caro!' he said as she appeared in the doorway. 'God, how good to see you, I can't tell you.'

'Good to see you too,' she said, amazed by her ability to disguise her joy. 'David and Scarlet are here, talking about the wedding. How did you get on?'

'Good! Really good! It's sorted. Frazer's power of attorney is no more and I have it instead.'

'Oh! Can you arrange that without Murdo's say-so?'

He smiled. 'Murdo said so! We all trooped into the cottage hospital and he signed everything he was asked to sign. Really, all these years we've been like two bulls going head-to-head and now he's turned into a lamb.'

Caro couldn't help laughing, partly from happiness that this horrible threat no longer hung over the family. 'I'd never describe him as a lamb, Alec.'

'Perhaps that is a bit of an exaggeration, but we reached an understanding that we never have before. He was so appreciative of our efforts to get him into the hospital near home.'

'You didn't tell him it was to make sure he wasn't bumped off by Frazer? Where the nurses all know him and won't let him be alone for a second?'

'Too much information! But I did say we'd get him home as soon as possible. Honestly, I thought I saw a tear in the corner of his eye. Something that never happens unless a dog's died.'

'Aw ...' said Caro. 'Talking of dogs, where is George?'

'You'll never guess. Ewan took him in to see Dad in hospital. They were so pleased to see each other, I can't tell you.'

'There can't be many hospitals where they let you bring your dog in to visit.'

'It was all a bit under the radar, but it was wonderful for the old man. Of course, when he's at home, George sleeps on Murdo's bed all the time.'

'Maybe get David and Scarlet's wedding over before you bring him home? And they've got the perfume! You can smell for yourself if it's different or not.'

'Well, we weren't happy with it when we had to leave, so certainly adjustments will have to be made.'

They went into the house together, Alec's use of the word 'we' making Caro feel as if she was walking on air, not very worn-out tartan carpet.

David and Alec exchanged manly hugs and back-patting and, possibly hearing voices, Scarlet came tripping down the stairs. Caro couldn't help noticing how much like a Disney princess she was to look at.

'I love your house!' said Scarlet. 'It's just perfect!'

'Er – isn't it a bit, well, shabby?' said Alec, pleased but a bit taken aback.

'It's darling! Oh, sorry, that makes me sound like a ditz?'

'Not at all,' said Lennie. 'You're a very discerning client.' She seemed more relaxed now, which was good. 'But you need to see the Michael Kirk. Caro and I put flowers in it, to make it special.'

'Is that a walk or a ride away?' asked David.

'A ride,' said Caro after a second's thought. 'Although I wonder ... Alec? Lennie? Do you know anyone who could arrange David and Scarlet to get from there to here by pony and trap for their wedding?'

'My God, that would be amazing!' said Scarlet, hands pressed against her cheeks.

'We have a shooting brake,' said Alec. 'It's pretty dusty but I'm sure we could have it brought up to scratch.'

'My brother means, *I* will find someone to bring it up to scratch,' said Lennie. 'And I will. We know a very pretty Highland pony – dappled grey – to pull it.'

'It sounds heaven!' said Scarlet. 'Now let's go and see the church.'

Alec stayed behind but Caro went with the party to inspect the little church on the hill. It was beautiful and while Caro never really thought about getting married these days, she decided this spot would be perfect. Close friends and family only and then a gentle walk down the hill to the house, walking behind the bride and groom.

Lennie told Scarlet all she needed to know about visiting the minister and the technical side of weddings (a friend's daughter had got married in the kirk the previous year and so she was up to date on such matters) while Caro was consulted on all things aesthetic. Simplicity was to be the watch-word because it was appropriate, subtle and stylish, and a lot easier to arrange.

As soon as they got back to the house Caro could see Lennie worrying about lunch. There was a vat of Scotch broth large enough to feed a troop of Boy Scouts, but was this a suitable repast for a starlet and her beau?

David saved the situation. 'Honey? We have a table booked for lunch and besides, we must bring Alec the perfume so he can finish making it.'

'When would you like to have it?' Alec said.

'Which? The wedding or the perfume?' said David. 'Ideally in about a fortnight.'

'That's hardly time to get a dress organised!' said Scarlet. 'But I know you're shooting soon and need to be back home.'

For a starlet presumably used to getting her own way, Scarlet was being very calm about having her nuptials so rushed. Caro supposed it was because she knew about the film business and was prepared to make sacrifices. She might look like a Disney princess but she didn't have to be treated as one.

'We'll come back after lunch with the perfume,' said David to Alec. 'Will you be here?'

'I'll be back by three at the latest. See you then?'

The arrangement made, Scarlet and David shot off in their hired car.

To Caro's disappointment, Alec didn't even wait to have soup. 'I have to be at the bank. I'm arranging a short-term loan so we can buy back the land immediately. I won't feel safe until it's ours again.'

'Have you put the police on to Frazer?' asked Caro.

'We're not actually sure what he's done is illegal. It was done with Murdo's consent, after all. It's more important to make sure he knows he can't sell the land now and if he knows what's good for him, he'll keep well away from Glen Liddell and its environs in future.'

'You sound very fierce,' she said.

'Do I? Well, I mean it.'

'Good for you! And I'll see you later.'

She went back into the house, not wanting to see him drive away. She was never quite sure if or when she'd see him again and, inevitably, this made her sad.

In the kitchen, Lennie was full of wedding plans, which for her meant decorating plans.

'I know Scarlet says she loves it all just as it is, but this is my home. I'm determined it should look its best. We won't change anything, much, but it has to look clean, at least.'

'Are you going to prepare a room for Murdo?' asked Caro.

'I'd prefer to keep him in hospital until afterwards, frankly, but if Alec insists, and he's well enough, I won't do anything to stop him coming home.'

Heather put a bowl of soup in front of Caro. 'It's grand to see them getting on when they've been at odds all these years.'

'It is,' said Lennie. 'It would be awful for Alec if Murdo died when they weren't on speaking terms. He'd never get over it.'

'That's very philosophical, Lennie,' said Caro, impressed.

She beamed. 'It is, isn't it? I can be, when I try. Now, Heather, how many lads can we get in to do the painting, do you think?'

'And we mustn't forget the pony and cart,' said Ewan. 'Shall I undertake to arrange that?'

Usually Caro would have relished all this discussion and would have longed to put on a boiler suit and move furniture and rearrange rooms, but this time her mind was on Alec. Soon, he would be smelling the perfume that Scarlet had brought with her and taking it to France to finish the recreation they had worked so hard on together. Pascal had everything he would need there, while if Alec stayed at home he'd have to send off for fragrances and wait for them to arrive. When the perfume was perfect he would come back and that would be that. Would she play any part in his life again? Murdo didn't need anyone to guard him; Rowan seemed on the way to being reconciled with her mother. Caro would be around for the wedding, of course; she had promised Scarlet. Would she then just go home to the barge, back to her old life? It would seem very dull.

David and Scarlet had arrived back from lunch so Caro went to greet them. She happened to walk back into the drawing room just as Scarlet was speaking.

'I'm so sorry. You must think I'm dreadfully senti-mental, but I can't be parted from that little bottle again.'

Caro saw the glass vial sitting on the table. Alec, David and Lennie were all looking at Scarlet, who seemed embarrassed and potentially tearful.

'It's going to be hard for Alec to match the fragrance exactly if he hasn't got the original to work from,' said David gently.

'I know, but I'm getting married. It's a stressful time. I need my grandmother with me and she's in that bottle.' Scarlet tucked an escaping curl behind her ear and sniffed.

'Maybe I should just finish it as I planned before?' suggested Alec. 'It's a really lovely scent and Caro says it would suit you beautifully.'

'It wouldn't be the same,' said Scarlet, 'and that won't work for me.'

'Then what's to be done?' said David. 'We haven't got time to go to France with Alec.'

'We don't need to,' said Scarlet. 'Caro will go. She can remember fragrances. She will know when it's right.'

Everyone seemed to relax a little except Alec and Caro. 'Well?' he said to Caro. 'Will you come?'

There was urgency and supplication in his expression as he asked her. He wasn't taking her for granted.

She shook her head. She couldn't go. She had promised Scarlet she would be there for her wedding, which included the preparations, and also Lennie. How would Lennie cope without her there to promise that everything would be all right? 'I don't see how I can go. There's so much to organise here.'

'Really,' said Scarlet, surprisingly firm all of a sudden, 'the perfume is more important than whether the moose head is cobweb-free when it comes to the wedding breakfast. We call cobwebs hammocks for fairies in the States.' Her serious expression made everyone laugh.

'Of course you can go!' said Lennie. 'We can manage. And you won't be long, will you?'

'I hope not,' said Alec. 'We were nearly there with the perfume when we had to leave.'

'But maybe don't hang around and go immediately?' suggested David. 'I'll sort out flights, Caro, you go and pack, and Alec, why don't you ring Pascal so he's ready for you when you arrive?'

He didn't so much give orders as make suggestions that no one would query. And as Caro went upstairs to do her part – and her packing – she understood why Scarlet loved him so. He made her feel safe, looked after, loved; and it was an irresistible combination.

Scarlet joined Caro in the spare room shortly after Caro got there. 'David's on flight duty, Alec's talking to Pascal and Lennie's going to bring you up a drink.' She sat on the bed, a very different young woman from the girl who couldn't be parted from her grandmother's perfume.

'Scarlet, are you sure you won't let Alec take the perfume to France?'

Scarlet's eyes opened wide. 'Honey! If he took the perfume he wouldn't take you! It was a no-brainer.' Her smile was conspiratorial. 'I was good, wasn't I?'

'You were very good!' said Caro a second later as she realised that Scarlet had just put on a show and while she did love her grandmother and her perfume she wasn't quite as attached to it as her performance downstairs had led everyone to believe.

'I had to make sure that you got to go with Alec. You know what men are like. They need a bit of help now and again.'

'Golly! Supposing he doesn't want me?' Caro was stricken. She wanted this so much but did Alec feel the same?

'He wants you! He just didn't know how to make it happen. So.' Scarlet turned her attention to Caro's carry-on. 'I thought France was hotter than here, mostly?'

'It is! I packed in a hurry and for Scottish weather.'

'I don't have many clothes with me or I'd offer to lend you something.' Scarlet was obviously bothered by the humdrum nature of Caro's jeans and sweaters, and not just worrying about her being hot.

At that moment Lennie appeared with two glasses of whisky. She handed one to Caro. 'Are you sure you don't want anything?' she said to Scarlet.

'I don't need a thing but Caro needs some clothes suitable for the Côte d'Azur. Can you help?'

'Scarlet—' Caro began and then stopped. Scarlet wasn't listening and nor was Lennie.

'I'd be more than happy to lend Caro anything she'd like,' Lennie was saying. 'Let's go and have a rummage in the wardrobe.'

The contents of Lennie's wardrobe was pretty much as Caro expected. Lots of skirts and tops, the skirts being mostly tartan. They were nice clothes, and suited Lennie, but they were not Caro's style and she wouldn't feel comfortable in them even if they had been any cooler than her own clothes.

'These clothes are pretty much for winter, no?' said Scarlet.

'Summer, actually, but in Scotland you very often can't tell the difference,' said Lennie. She paused. 'Really, you're probably better off asking Skye if she's got anything. As long as you're not allergic to cheesecloth, that is.'

Caro would rather have sweltered in a tartan pleated skirt and Fair Isle sweater from Lennie than ask Skye if she could borrow so much as a scarf. 'I'm sure there's something here—' she said, sounding as unconvinced as she felt.

'I can see that none of this is really suitable but let's have a look in another cupboard. It's in the dressing room.'

The dressing room was mostly taken up with a huge old Victorian wardrobe consisting of two mirrored cupboards and a chest of drawers in the middle. Opposite was a dressing table, obviously part of the same set.

Lennie opened one of the cupboards. 'This is where I keep things that I'm never going to get into again but can't face getting rid of.'

'Oh my God!' Scarlet squealed and almost jumped up and down in excitement. 'A Laura Ashley! You have a genuine Laura Ashley in your cupboard!'

'I'm surprised you've heard of Laura Ashley,' said Lennie, taking out the source of Scarlet's delight and holding it up. 'I wore this the first time I met darling Tarquin, in the early eighties.'

It was a sundress in fine cotton in a flowery print in shades of violet, lavender and pale green. It was fitted at the waist and was divinely pretty.

'I wore it with a big net petticoat – that's some-where here – and it's slightly boned.'

'Can you wear a bra with it?' asked Caro.

'Oh yes. The straps are quite wide. Try it on!' Lennie held it out to Caro. 'It's a lovely dress.'

'But even if I could fit into it, I'm not sure my arms are up to being bare, and how would I get it into my case?' said Caro, looking longingly at the delicate print.

'Try it on!' said Lennie and Scarlet in unison, which made their demands difficult to ignore.

Feeling slightly like a bride, Caro was zipped into the dress, which fitted perfectly. Lennie found the net petticoat and Caro stepped into this too. Scarlet twitched and tugged and made sure the dress was on properly.

'Now look!' Scarlet said, and pushed Caro gently towards the mirror.

It was a lovely dress. Caro felt pretty, girlish and, oddly, considering how quintessentially English the dress was, slightly French.

'Mutton dressed as lamb?' she asked her reflection.

'No!' said Scarlet.

'Don't wear the petticoat if you're worried,' said Lennie.

'What about my arms?' Caro turned to one side to see if they looked fat.

'Wave!' ordered Scarlet. 'Fine. Not a wobble.'

'I avoid waving now,' said Lennie. 'I've cleared tables with my bingo wings. But you've got lovely arms.'

'Well, I love the dress, Lennie, and I am really touched you're willing to lend it to me, but I'll never get it in my case,' said Caro, trying not to sound wistful.

'Leave that to me,' said Lennie, 'packing is my special skill. Let's have a look at your luggage!'

Chapter Nineteen

Less than an hour later, Alec and Caro were seated in the back of the vast, fast and luxurious hire vehicle, on their way to the airport. Alec had protested but as Lennie had said she'd drive David and Scarlet to their nearby hotel whenever they wanted to go, his protests were brushed aside.

'It's really kind of you,' said Caro before Alec could think up any more reasons why they shouldn't take David up on his kind offer. She loved the thought of sitting in the back of the car with Alec on the journey to Glasgow.

Now Caro and Alec settled themselves in the car, but, possibly inhibited by the presence of a driver, neither of them wanted to talk much. Caro looked out of the window thinking about the whirlwind that had her on her way to France in such a rush. She had two fairy godmothers who had facilitated it. There was Scarlet, with her insistence that her perfume couldn't leave her person, and Lennie who had a very pretty dress she insisted on packing into Caro's case. Caro hadn't had the heart to say she might not get a chance to wear it. Lennie and Scarlet had been so excited about it fitting her, and (Caro had to admit) it had looked so good on her. But would Alec even notice if she wore it? Was she just useful to him? Or did he care a bit? There was that kiss they'd shared in France. Perhaps going back there would recreate that mood? Although, she realised, that could just have been sex. However much she loved and wanted him, she didn't want to be wanted just because she was handy.

She woke to find her little finger touching Alec's on the seat. She glanced up to find him looking out of the window. For a tiny moment she had allowed herself to wonder whether this was deliberate; then she closed her eyes again.

Pascal was at the barrier to meet them at the airport. He was smiling, relaxed and his presence put Caro back into French mode instantly. They embraced warmly.

'I admire you, Caro, being able to fit all you need into this small case,' he said, taking it and wheeling it along for her. 'Neither my girlfriend nor my sister could ever manage that.'

Caro was certain he meant to be complimentary but she felt a bit deflated. She shouldn't be the sort of woman who could fit everything into a carry-on. She should demand proper luggage and take the kitchen sink (or its cosmetic equivalent) with her wherever she went. Then she would be glamorous, or, if that was beyond her, more like Frenchwomen generally.

'Well, we're here to work!' she said gaily. 'As long as I can borrow a lab coat, I'll be fine.'

'No work tonight,' said Pascal firmly. 'But I'm afraid I'm going to steal Alec for a meeting with some other perfumiers. They've heard the story about the lost scent and want details. But Amalie is looking forward to a cosy little dinner with you, Caro.'

Caro was very fond of Pascal but her hackles rose. She was just as capable of giving details as Alec was – in fact, she felt, she was somewhat better. However, she was too tired to make an issue of it.

'That sounds exactly what I want,' she said, and it was nearly true.

'Yes,' said Alec. 'We need to start as early as possible tomorrow. We need to get back to Scotland as soon as we can.'

Pascal put his hand on Alec's shoulder. 'Your father is still very ill, I am sorry.'

'And Caro has a celebrity wedding to organise,' Alec added more brightly.

'Amalie will be delighted to hear all about that, I'm sure.'

Pascal, although handsome and charming, had rather limited ideas about what women were interested in, Caro concluded, and was relieved to remember that Amalie wasn't the sort of woman likely to fall on her wanting celebrity gossip.

A delicious but fairly light meal with a couple of glasses of wine turned out to be just what Caro felt like. She and Amalie ate at a small table on the *terrasse*, occasionally hearing bursts of male laughter through the windows of another room.

'Pascal is part of a group of perfumiers who get together from time to time. It could be very useful for Alec to get to know them or I would have told Pascal to change the venue.'

Caro, her attitude possibly affected by the wine and the food, reverted to liking Pascal. He obviously had Alec's business interests at heart.

The next morning, Caro awoke early, showered and dressed and then went down to the kitchen in search of coffee. Breakfast could come later but she needed caffeine now.

Alec was there and seemed pleased to see her. 'Oh, great that you're up! Pascal has given me a key; we can go to the lab whenever we're ready. Are you going to have breakfast?'

'Well, I wouldn't mind a bit of bread and butter,' she said, although she knew he wanted her to say no. 'But as you're obviously in a hurry, I could take it with me and eat it in the car.' She frowned. 'Have we got a car?'

'Um – er – no,' said Alec.

'Shall we ring a cab, then?' She glanced at her phone, which told her it was only seven in the morning.

'No. We do have transport, it's just it's not a car. It's a motorbike.'

'Oh my God!' There was once a time when Caro would have been eager to please her love-object. But those days were long gone. 'I have never been on a motorbike and I don't want to start now.'

'Pascal has lent me leathers for us both and helmets. I thought it would be fun, whizzing through the French countryside.'

'It's the word "whizzing" I'm worrying about.'

He put his hand on her arm and smiled at her. 'I promise I won't whizz.'

Alec didn't smile quite often enough in Caro's opinion, but when he did, she found it very hard to resist.

'I'll give it a go until the end of the drive, but if I don't like it, I won't go any further.'

'I'll make sure you like it. And when we get to the lab, I'll bring you the best croissants you've ever tasted, I promise.'

As she climbed into the leathers, which, to her huge relief, were actually a bit big for her, Caro recalled forbidding Posy to ever go on the back of a motorbike. As she zipped the all-in-one suit over the long linen shorts that Lennie had put into her bag without mentioning them, she resolved that Posy would never hear about this trip.

Alec drove very sedately to the end of the drive, which was fairly long and so a reasonable test. After her initial terror, Caro found herself relaxing into it a bit. And the romantic in her did appreciate clinging on to the man she loved, even if he didn't appear to love her quite as much in return.

He put his feet on the ground when the bike had stopped. 'Well? Are you up for it?'

She nodded. 'As long as you don't go really fast the minute you're on the road.'

'I promise to look after you. And if you think I'm going to fast, just squeeze my waist.'

'Alec, I'm going to be clinging on for grim death. You won't notice an extra squeeze.'

'Well, shout. And I'll check back often, until I'm sure you're really happy.' He paused. 'I really do appreciate you doing this. I did try to borrow a car but there was nothing available.'

'It's OK,' said Caro. 'Now let's go before I lose my nerve.'

She tried hard to channel her inner Audrey Hepburn, imagining she was in Rome on the back of a Vespa, *Roman Holiday* being one of her favourite films. Sadly, they were travelling quite a bit faster than that Vespa had been capable of.

However, she did what Joe had once told her to do when she was nervous about something, and breathed deeply. It helped and soon she didn't have to pretend to be Audrey to enjoy it – she genuinely was enjoying herself. And the last part of the journey, through the narrow and steep streets of Grasse, had been quite like the film.

She was a bit shaky, though. Her fingers struggled to unclip the helmet. Alec took over and removed it from her head when he had released the fastener. He ruffled her hair. 'Don't want the world to know you've been on a bike. Even I know "helmet hair" is bad.' He grinned at her. 'You did really well! I'll make a biker chick out of you yet.'

Caro tried to think of a slick response but failed. Her legs were wobbly and she had to hang on to him.

'Let's get you upstairs to the lab and then I'll get breakfast. Would you like a brandy in your coffee?'

'Actually, I would!' she said, thinking: Only in France!

'Here,' said Alec. 'This should be it. Is it really so different?'

Caro closed her eyes and inhaled the perfume. 'It's not hugely different but – I'm sorry! – it's not the same.'

The trouble was, although she could remember the fragrance in Scarlet's ancient bottle, she didn't know what needed to be added to the one she was smelling now in order to recreate Scarlet's sample. She also understood it was hard for Alec, who had all the technical knowledge but not her super-memory for fragrance.

He sniffed again. 'Maybe it's the top notes that are a bit different. What do we think? Something a little bitter? Vetiver? Petitgrain?'

'I don't know!' said Caro.

'Tell you what, why don't you go and buy us some lunch? You need a break. Take some time and come back with something substantial to eat.'

'Not something nice? Just something filling?'

He nodded. 'I'm afraid I'm starving!'

It was nice to get out of the warmth of the lab, to clear her head and her nose. The sun was bright and while it was pleasant to feel it on her face, she wanted to get lunch before allowing herself a few minutes to relax and enjoy it.

She cut down a narrow alley she knew led into the main street. Here there was a large circular fountain, the water sparkling in the sunshine, cafés with their outside tables busy with people having lunch. She had seen people were hurrying along with their lunchtime baguettes under their arms before, some stopping to chat to friends, others just waving or briefly kissing (three times) their acquaintances before continuing on their errands. Now she was among them and it felt delightfully foreign – as if she'd relocated to France.

There was a row of scooters that reminded Caro of their journey on the motorbike and she found she was smiling. She had enjoyed that trip once she'd stopped being terrified. The fountain drew her in and while gazing mindlessly at the drops of water she spotted a little delicatessen and went over to look in the window.

It seemed to sell mainly charcuterie – salami, ham, innumerable sausages – and cheeses. She spotted a rack of *flûtes*, which she knew would be fresh and would be delicious with cheese and pâté. She couldn't resist buying a bottle of rosé although she knew they probably wouldn't drink it.

Slightly regretting adding the weight of the wine to her bag, Caro wandered out of the street and up the steps to the higher level. Grasse wasn't a glamorous Côte d'Azur town like Nice or Antibes but she liked its workaday atmosphere. It was a place where people lived and worked and there were some very beautiful villas tucked behind tall gates and walls.

Now she had bought their lunch she could find a bench to sit on and shut her eyes and turn her face to the sun. This would restore her and then she could go back to the lab and the problem of the perfume.

She found a bench and settled herself for a few moments' sunbathing. But while she was feeling the blessed warmth which would soon become too hot she was aware of an odour assaulting her nose.

She kept her eyes shut as she tried to identify it. It was sweet and a little bit sickly, and it reminded her of the smell of lilies which she never knew if she loved or hated. But as she breathed in the fragrance, hardly daring to move in case it went away, she realised it might well be the missing element of Scarlet's perfume. This could be the thing that would make it perfect.

The trouble was, the two samples from the original smelt very subtly different from each other. It was probably to do with how they had been stored but Caro felt the one Scarlet knew was the one they should recreate. And she was sure she'd just sniffed the smell that would make their creation perfect.

She opened her eyes, feeling brave. She looked up at the foliage around her and at first she could see nothing. Then she spotted it. Curled up and nearly brown she saw some sprigs of jasmine. She had to climb on to the bench to check it was the source of the smell and was relieved when she found it was. But she couldn't just go back to Alec and say the scent needed gone-over jasmine, she needed to bring a sample.

A quick glance around told her she was alone so she reached up to the sprigs of jasmine. Two seconds later she was wondering if it was worth going to buy some scissors, the stalks of the jasmine were so tough. But she persevered and eventually got a couple of sprigs although her hands suffered in the process.

When she arrived at the lab at the top of the stairs, lunch banging painfully against her leg, she was out of breath and very thirsty. It was only after she'd had a drink of water that she could speak.

'I think I've found it!' she said.

'What?'

'What's missing from Scarlet's perfume.'

'There's nothing missing. We added the final ingredient before you went for lunch. You know we did. You checked it off the list.'

'But it's not right. It doesn't smell the same as Scarlet's own version. But I was sitting in the sunshine when I realised I could smell something and I just knew it was what we needed.'

Alec made a good attempt at believing her but Caro could tell he wasn't really convinced. He was the trained perfumier, she was just (she felt) a gifted amateur, and although making scent was an art it was firmly based in science. 'How can you be sure?'

She wiped away the perspiration that was gathering at her hairline and felt another drop running down her spine. 'Indulge me. We need two batches, one with jasmine – slightly going over, with that slight smell of decay it always has – and one without.'

He wasn't paying attention. 'Your hands! What have you done to them?'

'Just scratched them a bit picking the jasmine – those stems are bloody tough – but never mind about that. Take a sample of what you've got now and add a tiny bit of jasmine and see what we've got.'

'Let me see to your hands first.' He took her over to the little sink and turned on the tap. 'You must be very convinced to actually injure yourself to prove a point.'

'I'm not proving a point,' she said, annoyed even while she enjoyed seeing her hands in his big brown ones, feeling his fingers rub away at the dried blood. 'I just want it to be perfect.'

'So do I,' he said, turning off the tap and handing her a towel. 'Two batches it is.'

It was late afternoon, they were both very tired and Caro still wasn't happy with Scarlet's version of the fragrance. Alec had taken tiny quantities of the perfume as far as they'd got it and then added further fragrance. Caro recorded the amounts and the ingredients, but none of the new versions was right. Then, hot and tired, he let his finger slip on the bulb of the pipette and a large squirt of something was added into the mix.

He cursed softly and was about to discard the solution when Caro said, 'Hang on! Let me smell!'

He dipped a paper wand into it, waved it about for a few seconds and then handed it to her.

She shut her eyes, sent her memory back to Scarlet's treasured bottle of perfume and then inhaled the fragrance. 'That's it!' she said after a few seconds. 'That's perfect! For Scarlet's version. We've done it! Was it jasmine you just put in?'

'Hedione,' he said. 'Practically an aphrodisiac – remember? In fact, if you believe they exist, that's what it is. I thought it would be too strong or I'd have tried it before.' He sniffed the wand too. 'You're right, it's like jasmine but not quite. This is a lovely fragrance.'

'The trouble is, we don't know how much hedione we put in.'

'We can work it out,' said Alec, ever so slightly pityingly. 'We know how much the vial weighed before my hand slipped and we can weigh it now.' He paused. 'Perfume-making is chemistry, you know. Science.'

She smiled at him. 'It's also an art.'

Caro enjoyed the ride home. She was no longer frightened of the motorbike and Alec didn't speed. When he pointed the bike into the drive to the chateau and she knew her journey was nearly over she felt sad. And as she clambered off the back, staggering just a little, she wondered if, now they'd recreated the perfume, her journey with

Alec was over too. She shook the thought out of her mind quickly.

'Ah! You are back!' said Amalie as they walked into the hall, holding their helmets under their arms in a way that made Caro feel very edgy and cool.

'Didn't you expect us to come back?' said Caro. 'Did you think we'd fall off the bike?'

She shrugged. 'I thought you may well have ridden off into the sunset together. Now come and have a quick glass of champagne before you shower and change. I hope you don't feel ill at the thought but we are having a little celebration.'

Although Caro was deathly tired and the thought of a party did indeed make her feel a bit faint, if not actually ill, she smiled. 'How delightful! What are you celebrating?' she said, following Amalie into the kitchen where Pascal was pouring champagne.

'Well, we have managed to get our gîte done and into a very smart guidebook and we already have a booking,' said Amalie. 'But also – more relevant for you and Alec – another member of the group of perfumiers who were here last night has arrived. He's very important,' she added, her eyes widening to indicate just how important.

'Great,' said Caro weakly, anticipating an evening when her French would be under pressure. The trouble with that was, when she stopped being

332

able to understand or join in, she would start to yawn.

'Don't worry,' said Pascal, handing them each a full glass. 'If you drink some champagne and have dinner, honour will be satisfied. But Alec, you will have to meet Monsieur Moulin.'

Alec obviously knew the name and while he looked tired he did not appear to be unhappy at the prospect of dinner and champagne with a famous perfumier. 'We deserve a celebration too. Our day in your hot but extremely useful laboratory has not been wasted.'

'Did you manage to recreate the perfume?' asked Pascal, suddenly much more animated.

'Two versions of it,' said Alec. 'One made to M. Dolinière's recipe – as far as we could tell – and one that Caro says is slightly different, that Scarlet, our client, had a sample of.'

'You have this second one with you?' said Pascal. 'I would be interested to see the difference.'

'Sadly not,' said Alec. 'The client didn't want her original sample to leave her. But Caro is confident she knows the difference.'

'Without a sample?' Pascal was incredulous.

Caro felt defensive. 'I have a very good memory for smells,' she said. 'And I swear I can smell things on television.'

Pascal smiled in a way that caused Caro to make a conscious decision not to feel patronised. She was too tired to fight the feminist cause just then, although even she thought her smell thing was a little weird.

'I'll go and have a shower,' she said.

'I'll come up with you,' said Amalie. 'I'll bring your glass.' She refilled the glass before she picked it up.

Amalie followed Caro into the bedroom. Caro, having been so concerned with the perfume, had forgotten about the dress and now she wondered how it had survived the journey.

'It's a really lovely dress,' said Amalie as they both inspected it for creases. 'Shall I iron it for you? While you have a shower?'

'Oh no, it'll be fine.' Caro wasn't much of a one for ironing although she could see the once-crisp cotton was fairly crumpled.

'No, I will do it,' said Amalie. 'You wash; I will iron. You need to look your best.'

'Are the other guests important then?' asked Caro, suddenly longing for a repeat of the quiet dinner she and Amalie had enjoyed the previous evening.

'*Oui,*' said Amalie, unhooking the dress from its hanger. 'Pascal is hoping one of them will invest in his and Alec's business.'

'What business?' Alarm cut through Caro's fatigue.

'Did they not tell you? They want to set up in business together and Alec can work from Scotland if he invests a little money in a laboratory.'

Caro's alarm became deep gloom. She could see why Alec and Pascal would want to do this, but it was all going to happen without her.

'You have forty minutes to get ready,' Amalie told her. 'I will leave the dress here for you when I have ironed it.'

It would take me at least forty minutes to iron that dress, Caro thought as she made her way to the bathroom.

She was terribly tempted to just lie down on the bed and sleep when she came out of the bathroom wrapped in a towel. Instead she went to inspect the dress, which now looked as if it was fresh from the shop. Excitement began to bubble up inside her – this was an opportunity for her to show Alec she could scrub up and look glamorous – well, glamorous for her. She must do it!

She focused hard on getting her make-up right; then she put on the dress and looked at herself in the mirror and liked what she saw. She wasn't perfect but she was, she reckoned, the best version of herself that she could be. And this, as all the magazines insisted, was enough.

Her hair shone, even if it was a little damp. The dress looked lovely, even without the bouffant petticoat she had worn when she first tried it on. Her own ballet flats went with the dress and the bit of bronzer that had been among the large range of skin-care products that Amalie had provided made her shoulders and décolletage look sun-kissed and golden. She tried out a smile and decided while she would never be twenty again, she was a pretty good version of forty-one.

Chapter Twenty

Caro made her way downstairs and followed the sound of voices on the terrace. It was a delicious summer evening, she decided. The air was warm, the roses scented the air and there were beautiful, elegant French people talking and laughing in an elegant, French way. She was wearing a dress she felt good in and her hair was clean. Added to that she was two glasses of champagne up. No wonder she was excited and happy.

Alec noticed her approach and separated himself from the group to meet her.

For a moment he just gazed at her and then he said, 'Caro! You look amazing.' He went on looking at her, as if he'd never seen her before, and then shook his head slightly. 'Come and meet everyone.'

If she could have just stayed there forever, with him looking at her like that, she'd have done anything to make it possible. Instead she let him usher her into the group, his hand on her waist.

'Oh!' one woman said in very accented English. 'You are wearing a vintage Laura Ashley dress?'

'Yes,' Caro began, wondering if she should confess to it being borrowed.

'It is a very English look,' said the woman firmly, leaving Caro uncertain if this was good or bad.

Alec made the introductions and it seemed that all the guests were connected with the perfume business in some way or another. They had all heard the story of the lost perfume and how Alec had recreated it.

'So, what is it like?' asked one woman. 'And is the young woman it is being made for suitable? There is a reason why perfumes are made for individuals. Their body, their personality, their character, the essence of their womanhood. It has to be right. Maybe it would be preferable for this woman to have her own fragrance.'

'Well,' said Caro, who felt it was up to her to describe – and possibly defend – Scarlet, 'this woman is young but she has known this perfume all her life.'

'How so?' asked a man who, unlike the rest of the group, seemed more detached and was possibly a little arrogant.

'Her grandmother was Serena Swan's dresser – her maid. She had a small quantity of the perfume in her possession when Serena Swan died. She kept it all her life and was very close to Scarlet, which is why Scarlet loves it so much. She associates it with her grandmother.'

'I am not sure a woman should think of her grandmother when she smells a perfume,' the man went on. 'She should think of her lover, her husband.'

'In part I do agree with you,' said Caro, 'but as it is her fiancé who is giving her this special gift, a perfume that is only for her, I think she will think of him when she opens the bottle and applies it to her pulse points.'

'Alec,' said Pascal, who joined the group and refilled glasses. 'Describe the perfume.'

'Well,' said Alec, 'the base is quite spicy, cedar, must, amber ...' He looked across at Caro, obviously wanting to include her in the description.

'Jasmine, neroli, and hedione also,' she provided.

'And the top notes?' the man went on.

'Quite a lot of citrus,' said Alec, 'bergamot.'

'It sounds very classic,' said the slightly older woman.'

'It was created in the thirties,' said Caro. 'It will be of its time.'

'Will we be allowed to smell the finished article?' asked a man whose name Caro didn't know.

'We'll have to ask Scarlet about that,' said Alec firmly.

Caro silently applauded this attitude. He could have got a lot of kudos had he let these influential people see what he could do with regard to creating an original perfume, but he knew his first loyalty was to Scarlet and David who had given him this opportunity.

'Let us eat,' said Amalie, clapping her hands.

To her discomfort, Caro found she was separated from Alec and the joy went from the evening. The setting was still as lovely and she felt good in her dress – having the label recognised was a definite plus, even if it was 'a very English look' – but it was what she had feared: she had to concentrate very hard to follow the French and she was actually quite tired.

Alec was next to the older woman and near to another man, both of whom had shown a great deal of interest in the perfume. Amalie, when she had asked Caro to sit between two charming-seeming Frenchmen (hardly a hardship), had explained that Alec's dinner companions were interested in employing him, even before they had sampled Scarlet's perfume. Pascal, she discovered, had been telling people how good Alec was.

By the time the cheese was served, conversation had become general and animated. More wine was served with pudding and then brandy and liqueurs. Alec and Pascal were up the other end of the table.

Pascal was talking earnestly and Alec's face was in shadow. Caro couldn't help thinking that soon Alec would move to France and set up his perfume business. It would be so much easier for him there, with access to colleagues, and helped by the money he would earn from recreating Scarlet's original scent. Then she wouldn't see him, even if she kept in touch with Lennie and Rowan in Scotland.

She twisted the wire from a champagne cork into a little chair, wondering what she would do with her life when she went back to the barge, when she wasn't making perfume, protecting old gentlemen or sorting out rebellious teenagers. She'd miss it terribly.

Suddenly Alec was at her side, clicking his fingers with impatience. 'Excuse me,' he said to the group, 'but I need to talk to Caro without delay. Caro? May we have a word?'

Delighted to be relieved of trying to get her tired brain to remember all the French she had ever learned, Caro got up quickly and hastened to Alec's side.

'Come on!' he said urgently, setting off into the garden at a frantic lick.

She hurried after him, anxiety increasing with her pace. 'Alec! Slow down! What's the matter? Is it Murdo? Has something gone wrong with the perfume?'

Alec stopped suddenly.

'It's not the blasted perfume,' he said fiercely, 'it's you! I can't put this off for another second.' Then he pulled her into his arms.

When they had kissed each other breathless, he said, panting slightly, 'I'm sorry, but I just kept thinking of the hours slipping away talking about perfume—'

'Which is your passion—'

'But Caro – we're here in France, away from all the other worries and distractions – we can't spend every minute of it thinking about base notes and synthetic ambergris!'

She laughed, happiness bubbling up from inside. 'You'd better go and say goodnight to everyone. These people could be important to your future career.' She pushed away the shadow caused by the thought of his career which might well mean he moved to France if making perfume in Scotland wasn't feasible. This was a night for joy.

He looked down at her and nodded. 'I should. Now wait here,' he said firmly. 'I'll be back.'

He set off but after a couple of paces he turned round and came back, took her face in his hands and kissed her again before setting off towards the party.

Caro stood still, anticipation sharpening every sensation. The fragrance of the evening was stronger, the faint sounds of birds and small creatures were louder, the stars were brighter and the surface of her skin was hypersensitive. The slightest touch and she would catch fire.

Alec was back with her very shortly. 'Come on!' he said, and took her hand.

It had been a while since her last relationship but she was so certain this was right, she wanted Alec so much the butterflies in her stomach were excitement, not anxiety.

If she'd allowed herself time to think about it she would have realised there was a glimmer of sadness among the joyful anticipation. This might be their only night together before their ways were parted by circumstances, but she wasn't going to let that spoil it.

He kissed her again when they were just inside the bedroom door. 'This is what you want too, isn't it?' he said.

'Yes!' she said, breathless from kissing.

'It's what should have happened when we met, all those years ago on that Greek island.'

He pushed the strap of her dress down and kissed her shoulder. 'You have got lovely shoulders.'

'Thank you.'

'And you smell lovely, too.'

The amount she'd spent on her perfume she jolly well should smell lovely, she felt.

'I can't wait to make a perfume just for you,' he said, breathing in her fragrance. 'I know what you wear already was what made me recognise you, but

I want to make you something entirely yours. I'd start with something woody, cedar possibly, and then—'

'Alec? Please? Can we not do this now? If you tell me every ingredient, I'll feel obliged to write it down and there are things I'd rather do instead.'

His laugh was a low rumble as he unzipped her. 'True.'

Her dress crumpled to her feet and she stepped out of it, standing before him in her underwear.

The way he looked at her made her forget she was wearing a rather tired bra and chain-store knickers. She felt beautiful.

It was late morning when Alec and Caro went down to the kitchen and Caro really hoped that Amalie, who was there, couldn't instantly tell what they'd been up to. But Amalie's knowing smile told her this was a vain hope.

'*Bonjour!*' she said, kissing them both three times. 'I will make you an omelette. Some protein for breakfast. Essential!'

Alec and Caro exchanged rueful glances. 'Please don't go to any extra trouble,' said Alec. 'Bread and butter will be fine.'

But Amalie wouldn't have it. She insisted on making omelettes and giving them large bowls of coffee to restore their energies.

She joined them for the coffee. 'Pascal would like a word and, like me, wonders how long you can stay? I would love to have you for as long as possible.'

'I'm afraid we'll have to go back later today,' said Alec. 'Now we've made the perfume, we must get it to our client and Caro is helping my sister organise Scarlet and David's wedding.'

'It will be very good for you, Alec, having a such an important celebrity client,' said Amalie knowingly.

'I hope so.' Alec picked up his coffee bowl and had a sip.

'It is partly why you are being so sought after at the moment,' Amalie went on.

'I wouldn't have had the client if it wasn't for Caro,' he said. 'Now we need to get our things together. Could we order a taxi? While I'd be more than happy to take the motorbike to the airport, I think Caro would prefer a car.'

'Very boring of me,' Caro said, secretly thrilled that Alec hadn't forgotten how he acquired his prestigious client.

'But you'll be back? Amalie asked Caro.

'I really hope so,' she replied, not sure what her future held.

On the journey back Caro was prepared for Alec to tell her of his future plans and that those plans might not involve her. She couldn't bring herself to mention it – the moment never seemed right. It was not something you could ask in the queue for security, or while they were taking their shoes on and off. Caro spent most of the flight dozing with her head on Alec's shoulder. She guessed that Alec, like her, was wondering what the future held for them.

At last the flight and all procedures were over and Ewan was there to drive them home. Caro closed her eyes again and let Ewan and Alec chat about estate matters without her joining in. She was glad she'd had this extra rest because the moment they pulled up, Lennie came rushing out of the house to greet them.

'You're back! Thank goodness! There's so much going on!'

'We've only been away for about forty-eight hours, Len!' said Alec, sounding tired. 'Surely not that much can have happened.'

'You'd be surprised!'

Alec gave his sister a quick, comforting hug. 'Just let us get in the door – please?'

A meal and a certain amount of good Scotch whisky later and things were a lot clearer. David and Scarlet were due to arrive the following day, which was part of the reason Lennie was a bit overexcited. They wanted to stay in the house, not the local hotel. It was a trial before the wedding.

'So I'm afraid I've put you in the box room, Caro, as your room was the only one halfway decent,' Lennie said apologetically.

'Caro can stay with me,' said Alec.

'What? In the but and ben?' said Lennie.

'No, in the cottage,' said Alec. He seemed a bit sheepish. 'I moved there to be nearer the house. For Dad ...' He didn't seem to know where he was going with this and looked relieved when Lennie spoke.

'But it's only got one bedroom,' she said.

Caro found herself blushing. It was ridiculous. She was forty-one years old, single, and there was no reason whatever that she couldn't sleep with a similarly single consenting adult, and yet she felt hugely embarrassed.

'I hope I'm not speaking out of turn,' said Alec. 'But Caro and I are together.' His eyes met hers and his expression was warm, amused and just a little bit questioning. 'Aren't we?'

Caro smiled and nodded. 'Yes we are. And I'm very happy to share the cottage with Alec.'

'Oh!' said Lennie. 'Well, I'm delighted obviously ...' She hesitated, obviously wondering if this was going to affect her plans in any way.

'You don't need to think about it,' said Caro. 'It'll just save making up a bed.'

'OK,' said Lennie, still a bit unsettled. 'In other news, you have more solicitors' appointments to go

347

to, Alec. It's to do with setting up the new lasting power of attorney. I have to be there too.'

Alec sighed. 'Got to be done, I suppose. Although I thought we'd signed everything in the hospital the other day.'

'And, Caro? Will you be able to help me with David and Scarlet?'

'Of course. Anything you need.' Caro smiled firmly, hoping to give Lennie the message that while in Facebook terms her status might have changed to 'in a relationship', she was still the helpful woman she was before.

'It's not quite a chateau,' said Alec as they approached the cottage.

'It's delightful, and so much better than a caravan,' said Caro.

He squeezed her arm apologetically. 'I'll get the fire going. We can have a nightcap.'

'It's summer!' said Caro.

'I love fires in summer. There's something faintly decadent about them. And we need something to take the chill off. I'm not entirely confident about my sheets.'

Caro laughed, beside herself with happiness. 'It doesn't take long to get down to the basics, does it?'

He kissed her.

'Maybe a hot-water bottle?' suggested Caro. 'If the sheets are damp?'

'A fire and some whisky first,' said Alec firmly. 'A hot-water bottle only if we're desperate.'

Caro was delighted to be in the cottage legitimately. She loved it. It was very traditional, with whitewashed stone walls and low, beamed ceilings. There were rugs and sheepskins draped over the furniture and floor, turning austerity into luxury.

'This is what I was promised when I first came here,' she said.

'I still feel bad about that,' said Alec.

'You can make it up to me later.'

'It'll be my pleasure,' he said with the warm, twinkling smile that turned her insides upside down.

As they hurried along to the main house at five to eight the following morning, Caro remembered that today Scarlet would smell the two versions of her perfume. While it didn't really matter which one she liked best, as long as she liked one of them, her pride was at stake. She had insisted Alec made two versions and wouldn't let him just replicate the recipe from M. Dolinière. She was going to feel a bit silly if Scarlet couldn't tell the difference.

Skye and Joe were in the kitchen, obviously waiting for Alec and Caro. They were holding hands.

'Oh, hello!' said Caro, unable to keep the surprise out of her voice. It was a bit of a shock but a pleasure to see they were still together, although meeting them in the kitchen was unexpected.

'We've come to ask a favour,' said Joe, relaxed and very happy. 'Could we go and stay on the barge for a few days?'

'Of course,' said Caro. 'Help yourselves. Joe, you know where the sheets are kept.'

'What about Rowan?' asked Alec.

'Rowan and Aaron are staying here,' said Skye, very slightly defensive. 'They're going to help with the wedding.'

'And I'm going to show Skye London, so she doesn't go on thinking of it as the armpit of hell.'

Caro laughed gently. 'Well, that's a good idea. London is great, really.'

'It is,' said Joe. 'And while it's really beautiful here, I'm not sure it could ever be home for me, I don't think.'

Alec opened his mouth and then shut it again. Caro was willing to bet he was about to say something about it being a bit soon for them to be thinking about where they wanted to live. Instead he turned to Caro. 'Could you live up here? Or would you miss London?'

'There'd be times I'd miss it, I'm sure, but being able to visit from time to time would be enough. I don't think I need to live there.'

Lennie, who had a lot on her mind, interrupted. 'Are you two joining us for breakfast?' she said to Skye and Joe. 'There's porridge.'

'We've had breakfast, thank you,' said Joe, his smile making Lennie relax a little. 'We won't keep you. We just wanted to ask Caro about going to the barge for a while after the wedding.'

Caro was lowering her spoon into the large grey mass that was her breakfast when it occurred to her to wonder how long 'a while' meant, in this instance.

'So,' said Lennie, putting down the teapot. 'Caro? Can you help me get the spare room ready for David and Scarlet?'

Caro understood why Lennie was so panicky. 'Of course I can help!'

'Heather is doing a cold lunch,' Lennie went on. 'Fish from the smokery, salad—'

'Goat's cheese and beetroot,' added Heather. 'In case they don't like smoked salmon. I want them to feel comfortable.'

Heather was obviously also anxious about the visitation so Caro hurried to reassure both women. 'I know David and Scarlet are stars but they're very easy. They've stayed with me on my barge. And while it's my home, and lovely, it is fairly scruffy.'

'So is this house, Caro,' said Heather crisply. 'Now, do you want a bit of haggis with eggs and bacon or has the porridge filled you up?'

*

Caro was glad that Heather was there to see Scarlet run into the house as if it was the only place she wanted to be. Heather was extra anxious because Lennie was with the solicitors with Alec and she felt responsible.

Scarlet embraced Caro, hugging her tightly, and then also embraced Heather, who was a bit surprised, being a more reserved person. David followed her into the house a bit more slowly.

'I hope you guys are as pleased to see us as we are obviously pleased to see you.' Caro was pleased to see that his warm, self-deprecating smile and American accent were having a calming effect on Heather.

'We certainly are!' said Heather. 'Now, would you like to make yourselves comfortable before lunch?'

'I could show you to your room,' said Caro, 'unless Heather wants to?'

'Oh, Caro, you do it, please,' said Scarlet, giving her a meaningful look. 'I want to talk to you!'

Scarlet hardly looked at the bedroom that Heather and Lennie had taken such trouble with; she just wanted to know how things were with Alec.

'So?' she said. 'Did you wear the dress?'

Caro couldn't help giggling – she felt like a teenager. 'Yes! It was lovely. Everyone admired it because it's "veentage Laur-ah Ashlee",' she said in a bad French accent.

'And did Alec like it?'

'What you really want to know is, did we sleep together?'

'Yes!' said Scarlet.

'We did!' said Caro and Scarlet clapped her hands like the Disney princess she so obviously was not.

'So you're an item?' Scarlet went on.

'We are. We're sharing the little cottage – although we've only been back for one night.'

'Oh, that's so great! And what about the perfume? Did you make it? Is it the same as mine?'

'I'll let Alec tell you about that,' said Caro. 'He's longing to and he'll back early this afternoon. Now, have you got everything you need?'

Caro looked round the room, which she had seen earlier. There was water on both bedside tables, lavender oil, tissues and bedside lights. On the dressing table was a magnifying mirror with a very good light, more tissues, some lovely locally made hand cream, and some home-made Scottish tablet. (Heather's mother had provided that.)

'It's all amazing!' said Scarlet. 'Where's the en suite?'

'I'm afraid there isn't one,' said Caro, 'but there is a bathroom very near that is dedicated for your use. Let me show you.'

The bathroom was full of fine-milled Scottish soap, some shower gel made by the person who made the hand cream and lots of towels, new and fluffy but pre-washed. Heather had excelled herself.

'This is lovely!' said Scarlet, ignoring all the special touches and going straight to the window. 'Look at that view!'

'Well, you can lie in the bath and look at it if you want to,' said Caro, 'but not now because Heather is waiting to give you lunch.'

Ewan had sworn on his mother's life that the hot water wouldn't run out and so Caro felt safe making this promise.

'Perfect!' said Scarlet. 'I'll be down in five minutes.'

But the part of lunch that Scarlet was going to enjoy most, given she couldn't have her perfume yet, was Rowan and Aaron's imminent arrival. Caro sighed with pleasure. It should be a very jolly reunion.

Chapter Twenty-One

Scarlet reached the hall at the same time as Rowan and Aaron came in through the front door. There was a lot of squealing, jumping up and down and hugging. Caro looked on, delighted but also feeling a bit old. She exchanged glances with Heather and they smiled.

'I'm glad it's a cold lunch,' said Heather, 'otherwise it would be ruined.'

'I think they're pleased to see each other,' said David.

'So will you be my bridesmaid?' asked Scarlet. 'And you, Caro?'

Laughing, Caro shook her head. 'No, thank you. I'll be your surrogate mother – whatever I can do for you, I will do – but be in a line-up with you two beauties? No thank you.'

'I like a woman who knows her own mind,' said David, possibly anticipating a lot of protest from

Scarlet. 'Caro has been so kind already, honey. Let's not make her do anything she would obviously hate.'

'Thank you, David,' said Caro, giving him a warm smile. 'Now let's eat. Alec and Lennie will be back soon and then we can smell the perfume.'

At the beginning of the meal Caro worried about finding a suitable bridesmaid's dress for Rowan and then realised it was probably something Scarlet would arrange. She would ask her. But as the cheese appeared she began to worry about the perfume. Supposing Scarlet either didn't recognise it, or hated it? All that work for nothing. And although they hadn't discussed it, she knew that Alec was depending on being paid for the perfume to pay for the land. Although the wedding would cover part of it, it wouldn't be enough on its own. The kickback that Frazer had taken was the theft that kept on thieving, she felt. If it was only buying back the land it would have been fairly easy, given that they hadn't spent much of the money. But that bit extra could possibly take all the money that David might give Alec.

At last they heard car tyres on gravel and realised that Alec and Lennie were back. Caro yearned to rush out and fling herself at Alec but resisted. She had to at least appear to be sensible, however much she wanted to behave like Scarlet and Rowan had when they saw each other again.

*

Alec and Lennie slotted into the places made ready for them at the table. Alec's was next to Caro's. 'All well?' murmured Caro.

'Think so. All over bar the money now.' He put his hand briefly on hers and her heart leapt.

'So, Alec! My perfume? You made it?' Scarlet waited only long enough for Alec and Lennie to swallow two mouthfuls of smoked salmon before her excitement got the better of her.

'Yup, we did,' Alec replied. 'Caro was very much part of it.'

Scarlet sent Caro a look of satisfaction coupled with smugness and a touch of innuendo. 'But when can we smell it!' she said with a smile that made this seem less like a demand.

'When Alec and Lennie have finished their lunch,' said David. 'Never try to do business with a man with indigestion. It's one of my rules.'

Luckily for Scarlet (and Caro, although her desperate need to know about the perfume was better concealed), Alec ingested a smoked salmon sandwich at the speed of light, gulped down some water and said, 'Right. Let's do this. Meet me in the library in five minutes.'

The three of them, Scarlet, David and Caro, went into the library. Caro was worried that the smell of musty books might affect the smell of the perfume but Alec seemed to have no such qualms. There was a small table with a white cloth spread on it.

There were two little flasks and a pot of paper wands. Caro knew there was also a beautiful glass swan – a copy of the original bottle that was the container for Serena Swan's perfume. But which, if either, of the perfumes would go in it had yet to be decided.

'Oh God, I'm so nervous!' said Scarlet. 'Supposing I hate them both?'

'Then I won't have done my job properly,' said Alec calmly.

'Well, honey, let's try,' said David. 'And put everyone out of their misery.'

Caro could hardly breathe. She so wanted it to be right – for Scarlet, for Alec, for herself. This could be the moment that made Alec's career as a perfumier. There might have been people in France who wanted to employ him, and others who wanted to go into business with him, but he'd have to get this right first.

'OK, Scarlet,' said Alec, having dipped a wand in the first flask and waved it in the air for a couple of seconds. 'Try this.'

Scarlet closed her eyes and inhaled deeply. 'Oh, that's beautiful. I love it!'

'Now try this.' Alec passed her another wand.

'That's gorgeous too,' said Scarlet when she'd smelt it.

'So which one is most like your original perfume?' asked Caro, unable to keep silent any longer, although she was pleased she didn't think they were both the same.

'I'll have to go away and sniff it,' said Scarlet. 'Can you give me a few moments?'

Alec and Caro exchanged glances. Both had their pride at stake.

Scarlet took her bottle with only a few drops in it to the corner of the room and sniffed hard. Then she came back to the table. 'It's this one.' She put her hand on one of the flasks. 'This is the one I've known all my life.'

'Which is it, Alec?' asked Caro, wishing she'd arranged to know which one was which before Scarlet came near them.

His eyes met hers. 'It's your version,' he said. 'You remembered it correctly. Congratulations!'

She studied him intently. Did he mind? Did he mind her being able to remember the smell of Scarlet's so accurately?

'It's really not a problem for me,' he said quietly. 'We just want the perfume to be right.'

'Sorry, what are you talking about?' asked Scarlet.

'The perfume we recreated from the recipe, which was supposedly the one Serena Swan had, isn't exactly the same as the one you've got,' said Caro. 'Although it must have been wonderful, in its original Lalique swan-shaped bottle.'

Scarlet nodded. 'My grandmother told me about that bottle. I wish I could have one for my version.'

'Your wish is my command,' said Alec with a smile and a flourish, producing a very charming replica. 'It's not made by Lalique but it's a good likeness of the original. My French colleague had it made for you.'

Scarlet suddenly became tearful. 'That's amazing! I can't thank you guys enough!' She ran to Alec and hugged him hard, and then she hugged Caro.

'Caro remembered the smell of your example,' said Alec, 'which is very similar but not quite the same as the one kept by the grandson of the original maker, M. Dolinière. Caro has an excellent nose and knew the one she was smelling in France wasn't quite the same as yours.'

Caro wrinkled her very good nose. 'It's never let me down.'

'It would have been easier if we'd had your bottle to take with us when we made the fragrance,' Alec went on, 'but we did understand you not wanting to be parted from it.'

'Well,' said David, who obviously thought the finer points of the perfume had been discussed enough. 'We need to talk about money. Let's go somewhere else to do that. This is a present for Scarlet, after all.'

'Come into the study,' said Alec.

Aware she was being desperately British, Caro couldn't help feeling embarrassed at the thought of the financial part of the whole perfume adventure.

To distract herself she said to Scarlet, 'Have you seen over the whole house? We must decide which rooms to concentrate on for the wedding.'

'I have seen it, but I can't remember which rooms Lennie felt would be best. She wanted to redecorate the entire house, but I like it just as it is.'

'You are lovely, Scarlet,' said Caro. 'Just lovely.'

The two women were just pondering over a bit of architrave that had broken off – probably years ago – and wondering if it was rustic charm or unattractive deterioration when they heard David's voice.

'Scarlet? Caro? We're done!'

Scarlet ran out into the hall and flung herself at David. 'I am so, so lucky to have you in my life! Any man could buy me expensive presents but you're the only one I know who'd have realised how important this is to me. I love you!'

'And I love you too,' said David, looking down at his fiancée as if there was no one else in the whole world. 'And I'm so grateful that you've given me an opportunity to show you just how much I love you. This gift really expresses my feelings for you in a way that diamonds never could.'

Caro had to wipe away a tear; she felt she'd watched a private, very touching, wedding ceremony.

Alec cleared his throat. 'Caro? Would you come with me to visit Murdo? He'd love to see you.'

'I'll get a jacket,' she said.

*

In the car on the way Alec said, 'David has been incredibly generous. He said he'd researched how much a personally made perfume can cost and based his offer to me on that. I didn't argue! With what we'll get for the wedding, it's enough to pay back the difference between what we got for the land and what the buyer paid for it. I really want to tell Dad. I think he's been worrying about it.'

'That's amazing, Alec! Really, David and Scarlet have been terrific.'

'David told me how wonderful Scarlet thinks you are. He told me that Scarlet's mother really doesn't do anything a mother should and you're filling that role.'

'Not really. I've only treated her like any other young woman.'

'I think that's the point; no one else in her life does, really.'

Caro gave a satisfied sigh. 'Well, that's nice.' It was an understatement but given how emotional she'd felt earlier she thought it best not to elaborate.

'Do you miss Posy?' asked Alec.

Caro was startled. 'That's rather out of the blue, isn't it? Why do you ask?'

'I just thought you might be missing her. You're here, being a mother to Scarlet and not to your own daughter.'

Caro considered. 'You never stop being a mother, even if your child is thousands of miles away.'

'So you are missing her?'

'A bit, yes. But Scarlet is quite a good substitute. And Rowan. I love young women. I think they're ...' She searched for a word. 'Life-enhancing!'

Alec laughed softly. 'I love that you're not jealous of them. Skye has always had a problem with other women – even Rowan, I think. She has to be the most beautiful person and she hates anyone who threatens that.'

Caro's laugh was properly amused. 'That's the difference between me and Skye – she's beautiful and I'm not!'

Alec glanced at her before steering the car round a bend. 'That's a matter of opinion.'

For the rest of the journey Caro thought about her daughter. She did miss her. They hadn't Skyped as often she'd have liked – life had been so weird and topsy-turvy lately. And she hadn't mentioned Alec in a romantic way. Telling your daughter you have a significant other wasn't something to do via email. You needed to be face-to-face. And it might come as a bit of a shock. Maybe she should write a proper letter. Or maybe she'd just see how things went. There was no point in involving Posy if Alec was going back to France and didn't invite her to go with him. She could tell her when Posy was back home and they could share a bottle of wine and possibly a few tears.

*

363

Murdo was very pleased to see them both. He was sitting in a chair doing a crossword and he tossed it aside the moment they appeared. 'Can't do nine down. Driving me mad.'

Caro picked up the paper. 'It's "wasp",' she said after a few moments' thought.

'Of course it is,' said Murdo. 'I've missed you, gel! Hope you're not here to say goodbye?'

'We've got good news, Dad,' said Alec, pulling up a chair. 'I told you we're negotiating to buy back that bit of land – the nature reserve?'

Murdo nodded. Caro could have guessed, even if she hadn't known, that there'd been rows about this after it had been sold and that neither Alec nor Murdo wanted to go back to the dark place when their relationship had been so difficult.

'But there was a shortfall – the amount of money—' Alec broke off, not wanting to remind Murdo of Frazer Neal and how he had nearly contrived to steal a large chunk of the estate, and possibly wouldn't have stopped with a chunk if he could have got away with it.

Murdo wasn't so tactful. 'The amount of money that scoundrel swindled is what you're not saying, Alexander!'

'Yes, that,' Alec went on, more calmly than his father. 'Well, I've got it now.'

'And how have you acquired this money?'

Murdo's tone was combative and Caro could see how and why father and son had become estranged.

'Perfectly honestly, Murdo,' said Alec, calm but on his guard.

Caro also noticed that Alec called his father by his given name when he was not feeling so warm towards him. She took a breath, trying to think of something to say to calm these two males battling for ascendancy. 'He was paid for a unique perfume he's created.'

'Perfume!' said Murdo, sounding outraged. 'In my day we called it scent!'

'Mine too,' said Caro, 'but standards have dropped recently.'

This did make Murdo twitch his lip in what could have been a smile. 'Well, I suppose it's good that you can make money out of these things but I'm still not happy about it.'

'For goodness' sake, Murdo!' said Alec. 'We're not in a position to be fussy about where the money comes from.'

'Yes we are,' said Murdo. 'I'm not taking your perfume money.'

'Dad!'

'I'll pay for the shortfall myself,' he announced.

There was a silence that Caro longed to fill but she couldn't. She knew that there wasn't the money in the estate without selling something that was profitable, like the smokery. And that would be such a bad thing to do. Heather had told her it was just beginning to do well.

'There's not the money, Dad,' said Alec gently. 'I thought we'd been through it all.' He glanced at Caro, looking distressed. She could tell he was wondering if Murdo's brain was beginning to be affected by old age and illness. She'd wondered the same thing about her own father towards the end and knew how distressing it was.

'I know what you've told me, boy,' said Murdo. 'But you don't know everything. I'm going to sell m'guns.'

Another shocked silence. 'Your guns?' Alec said it as if Murdo had suggested selling George.

'Never wanted to before,' Murdo went on. 'Always thought they were a sacred family heirloom that shouldn't be touched. But you're never going to shoot, Rowan's never going to shoot and the land is more precious than they'll ever be.'

'But you love those guns,' said Alec.

'I did love them, but I love other things now. They're quite valuable.' He turned to Caro. 'They're a pair of Holland and Holland side by sides. Although I know that won't mean a thing to you.'

Caro contrived to look impressed. 'I know Holland and Holland are a very good make,' she said.

'Don't suppose you have the faintest idea how much they're worth though,' said Murdo, sounding very slightly smug. 'Nor you, Alec.'

'I do know that guns can fetch hundreds of pounds,' said Caro. She kept this figure low, she didn't want to pre-empt the old man. She hoped they'd be worth a couple of thousand.

'I got one of the nurses here to look them up for me on the Internet,' he said.

'And?' said Alec.

'At the right auction, they could make nearly three hundred thousand pounds.'

'Three hundred thousand pounds? For a pair of guns?' sad Alec.

'Not saying mine would reach that much, but they could.'

Alec was pale with shock, whether because the guns were potentially so valuable or because Murdo was willing to sell them, Caro couldn't tell. 'Dad! Your guns are important to you, they always have been, and to Grandpapa before you. Don't sell them.'

'My land is important to me and it's important to you. If you give all the money you've earned making scent' – he managed to make it sound a very dubious occupation – 'to buying back the land that I was foolish enough to sell, I wouldn't think it quite fair. And you'll need that to put into your business.'

There was yet another strained silence. Murdo's suggestion seemed reasonable to Caro. How would it feel to Alec? Would he suddenly become proud and stuffy about it? But she needn't have worried.

'That would be amazing, Dad,' he said at last. 'If I didn't have to use the money David has given me for the perfume I could set up a proper lab here in Glen Liddell. I wouldn't have to go to France.'

Caro's heart leapt with joy. He was staying in Scotland. Yet, although she and Alec were a couple, she still didn't really know where she stood with him. When Scarlet and David's wedding was over, would they be over too?

'We should arrange for them to be sold, then,' said Murdo. 'Now if you don't mind, I'm a bit tired, I need a nap.' The old man settled himself more comfortably and closed his eyes. Then he opened them again. 'But don't worry,' he said, 'I've no intention of dying just yet!'

Chapter Twenty-Two

It was the morning of the wedding, a beautiful, hazy day that promised to become hot later. Glen Liddell had put on its very best weather for its celebrity wedding and Caro was feeling emotional. Scarlet, sitting on the dressing-table stool in front of her, looked wonderful. Caro was adjusting her veil over her dark curls.

'Most film stars would have a dresser to do this – a professional person,' said Caro.

Along with the emotion she felt a huge sense of responsibility. Scarlet and David hadn't gone for too many professionals to handle their wedding, but they had hired a photographer who was famous enough even for people up here to have heard of. If Scarlet didn't look right in those photographs, Caro felt it would be her fault.

'I didn't want a professional person,' said Scarlet. 'I had my hair done, didn't I?'

Caro nodded, glad of a reason to laugh so she wouldn't cry. 'I don't think that hairdresser will ever recover,' she said. 'She's more used to doing perms and shampoo and sets.'

'I'm not going to even ask you what a shampoo and set is,' said Scarlet. 'But when I showed her what to do with my tongs, she was fine.'

'You seem very calm for a bride. Not that I've had much to do with them in real life, but on television they're very shouty and demanding.'

'I'm just about to get married to the best man in the whole world in one of the most beautiful places I've ever seen. I don't need to be shouty and demanding.'

The twinkle in her eye told Caro that should the need arise, Scarlet could be as good a bridezilla as the rest of them.

Rowan came in, wearing a long, simple dress similar to Scarlet's only without sleeves. Her rose-gold hair feathered round her face in kiss curls and just for a second, Caro regretted her losing the nearly waist-length hair she'd had when they first met.

'Oh, Scarlet,' said Rowan, 'you look amazing! Have we got time for me to do a few sketches?'

'I'm pretty much done here, but maybe we've time?' Scarlet looked at Caro for confirmation.

'If you're really quick,' said Caro. 'I need to do my make-up. Five minutes, tops.'

Caro was wearing Lennie's vintage Laura Ashley with a little cardigan and a small straw hat. Lennie had turned out to be good at hats and had converted something rather over-done and fussy bought in the local town into something stylish and pretty. It sat on top of Caro's self-coiffed head in a very pleasing way.

While Caro was seeing if yet another coat of mascara would stop her wishing she was wearing false eyelashes, Skye came into the room. She looked as beautiful as her daughter and even more dryad-like. Since Joe had been staying she'd softened a lot and happiness enhanced her natural beauty. Joe was hovering behind her looking very fine in a borrowed kilt. 'Wow! Look at you all! Don't you all look lovely? Caro, that hat is perfect. Lennie did such a good job customising it.'

Rowan turned to her. 'You look amazing too, Mum, and Joe.' She had blossomed under the effect of having a happy mother who didn't snip at people all the time.

'Come in, Joe,' said Scarlet. 'We're all decent.' She studied Joe, taking in the kilt. 'Wow, I'm glad I asked David to wear a kilt now. I wasn't sure but I think he'll look just heavenly.'

Caro laughed. 'He'll certainly look very handsome though possibly not celestial!' She was looking forward to seeing Alec in a kilt, herself. He was going to escort Scarlet down the aisle and, as part of the official wedding party, was adhering to the dress code.

When Scarlet had asked him if he would take the traditional father's role, he had asked her why she wanted him to.

'It's not a matter of you giving me away, as if you owned me,' she had explained, 'it's just having someone with me as a friend, on a big occasion. I did ask Caro first, but she said no.'

Caro had laughed. 'I'd much rather stay in the background and I may need to leave early to help Lennie. Far better if Alec does it.'

'Then I would be honoured,' he had said with a smile to turn less susceptible heads than Caro's.

'Shall we have a quick glass of fizz before we go?' suggested Skye.

'Excellent idea,' said Caro, retrieving a bottle of champagne from a bucket. 'Joe, would you care to open it for us?'

'I can open a bottle of champagne,' said Scarlet.

'So can I,' said Caro, 'but we don't want to risk it spraying on us. Joe's tartan will absorb any fizz that goes astray.

Alec appeared in the doorway just in time to be handed a glass.

'Very excellent timing on my part if I may say so!' he said. 'Let's toast the bride – the first of many more toasts to come.'

When glasses had been raised and hasty, bubbly gulps taken, he put his glass down and turned to Scarlet.

'Are ye ready, hen?' he said in a broad Scots accent and a twinkle, to make her smile.

'I think I am,' Scarlet said, getting up. 'Aren't I?' She glanced round to check that everyone agreed on this.

'Good,' Alec continued, 'because there's a wee pony all dressed up like a sore toe ready to take you to the kirk.'

'I can't wait!' said Scarlet. 'My very own coach to take me to my wedding.'

'The coach being cunningly disguised as a shooting brake,' said Alec, holding out his arm. 'And not a speedy vehicle.'

'Just what I wanted,' said Scarlet and put her hand on his arm; together they went down the stairs.

Safely out of the sight of Scarlet and Alec, Caro allowed herself a tear. Skye topped up her glass.

'You've been brilliant,' she said. 'You and Lennie. I never thought it was possible to turn this scruffy old house into something fit for a wedding.'

'Rowan's gift for painting really helped,' said Caro. 'I would never have thought of hiding the particularly dingy areas behind sheets with beautiful paintings on them.'

'And there's the marquee, too. There would never have been enough room in the house. Even Scarlet's cut-down guest list turned out to be quite a lot of people,' said Skye.

'It was a good call,' Caro agreed. 'Thank God for a bit of level lawn!'

'Right, I think we should be moving along,' said Joe. 'I know it'll take the pony ages to get to the church but we do need to make sure we're there first.'

Not so long ago this sort of timing issue would never have occurred to Joe, Caro thought. 'True,' she said. 'And I need to check with Lennie that everything is OK here.' She smiled at Joe. He too seemed to have benefited from being with Skye. He'd always been a good, kind man with a special sort of energy, but now he seemed more in the world, a little more grown-up.

'Where's Aaron?' said Skye.

'Helping with the pony,' said Rowan. 'He was brought up with horses.'

'That's nice,' said Skye, without a hint of the sarcasm that once tinged all her comments.

'*He's* nice,' said Caro.

'Actually, you guys,' said Skye. 'While we're all together, Joe and I have a bit of a favour to ask you, Caro.'

'Oh?' Joe and Skye had become such a good couple, she felt. Originally she'd assumed it was just sexual attraction but now she hoped it might be a proper, long-term relationship.

'So you're really OK about me going back to stay with Joe in London for a bit?'

'Oh! Yes, of course.' Caro heard the words coming out of her mouth even as misgivings flooded in. How long was 'a bit'? And although she and Skye had been getting on much better recently, could they share the barge?

'I mean, you'll probably be here anyway, won't you?' Skye went on. 'You and Alec seem to have coupled up in a very good way.'

Caro cleared her throat. Why was Skye so certain? Not so long ago she'd tried to convince her that Alec would never commit to someone like her.

'And the thing is,' Skye went on, 'if it was all right with you, Rowan could live with us on the barge while she goes to art school next year.'

'What about your yoga retreats?'

Skye shrugged. 'I can find a venue in London if I want to do one. But I'm thinking of doing something new. Not sure what,' she added, as if not wanting Caro to question her.

'Oh, OK, that sounds like a good idea.' Caro's feelings weren't as convinced as her words were, although it was good news for Rowan.

'The barge will always be your home though, Caro,' said Joe. 'Whatever happens, that won't change.'

'Of course,' agreed Skye. 'That's written in stone. Joe made that absolutely clear when he first suggested the idea.'

'Well, I think that's a lovely plan,' said Caro. 'But now we've got a wedding to go to!'

Before they all piled into one of the limousines that David had hired to move guests about from the church and the house, Caro checked with Lennie to make sure she was happy with everything.

'I think it's going to be all right,' said Lennie. 'And if it's not, the amount of alcohol that David has ordered will mean no one notices anything bad. All the locals are going to be waiting staff and the house looks its very best!'

Caro laughed and put her hand on Lennie's arm. 'Murdo won't recognise the old place when he comes out of hospital.'

'Which is tomorrow! So quite a quick turnaround. But it will be good to have him back home. George will be delighted – he peed on Heather's nephew yesterday, when he was repairing the door to the outside loo.'

'As long as he spares the guests it'll be OK.'

'He's never been known to pee on anyone in a kilt,' said Lennie, 'so that's half of them safe!'

'Have you got a spare kilt I could borrow?' said Caro.

Lennie pushed her gently. 'You stick to my Laura Ashley – it looks super on you. You look terrific!'

'All thanks to you, Lennie. Your dress, your skill with hats; without them I'd be wearing my jeans and a beret.'

Lennie laughed, obviously pleased. 'You'd look very French. And if you don't go now, Scarlet will be there before you. We gave Becky extra oats this morning so she had the energy to go up the hill to the kirk. Now scoot!'

The car took the back route to the kirk and everyone was out of it and ready just as the bridal party were on the last stretch. The little Highland pony had white ribbons in her mane and the old shooting brake was similarly garlanded. Little posies of flowers were pinned at strategic places and the whole equipage looked enchanting as it came up the hill.

The photographer, a friend of David and Scarlet's from Hollywood, took what seemed like a million pictures as the cart drew up and Aaron jumped down from behind to hold Becky the pony. There was also a top cameraman doing a video. There was going to be a strictly limited number of photos taken in the church.

Caro slipped into the vestry so she'd be ready to adjust Scarlet's veil and nearly bumped into someone dressed in vivid turquoise who looked very like Scarlet. She was wearing a hat that proclaimed her the Mother of the Bride and all her clothes were matching, down to her shoes and handbag.

'I am Scarlet's mother,' said this well-preserved, imperious woman. 'And you must be Caro. I know it was arranged that you would help her, but I'm here to do it now.' She looked very strained and unsure of her welcome.

Caro decided to make it clear that she was very welcome. 'Well, I am delighted to meet you, Mrs Lloyd!' she said, hoping that Lloyd wasn't a stage name. 'It's just fabulous that you're here. Did we know you were coming?'

'It was a last-minute decision. Sadly my husband isn't well enough to travel with us but my two sisters and their daughters are here.' Mrs Lloyd smiled, just the tiniest amount.

'Scarlet will be so thrilled to see you,' said Caro, hoping it was true. 'And she'll be here any moment.'

As if on cue, Alec and Scarlet arrived and Caro whisked Scarlet into the vestry. She whisked herself out of it as mother and daughter recognised each other and opened their arms.

Caro slid into the seat next to Skye, who was armed with Rescue Remedy and tissues. 'We might need to do some repairs to Scarlet's make-up,' she whispered. 'Her mother is here!'

'So those overdressed women in the front row must be Scarlet's relatives?' said Skye.

Caro nodded, a tiny bit pleased that love hadn't completely suppressed Skye's inner bitch.

Scarlet's mother must have had a make-up repair kit of her own because after she had moved quickly down to the front of the church to be with her family, and Scarlet emerged from the vestry, she had only the slightest sign of smudged mascara. And the smile of happiness on her face more than made up for that.

Rowan slipped in behind her, picking up the long train of Scarlet's dress.

Caro tried hard to hold it together as she watched Scarlet and Alec, with Rowan behind, process down the aisle to a tune that always made her cry at even the least emotional of times. The unexpected arrival of Scarlet's family made it all more special somehow. Aaron sweetly squeezed her hand and passed over a tissue. She and Aaron were going to slip out the moment the service was over to help Lennie, who was at the house.

Caro had never thought much about getting married. It wasn't something she'd felt she'd do now – she was forty-one, she had a lovely daughter, why would she? And yet seeing Scarlet on Alec's arm being escorted to a waiting David, devastatingly handsome in his Highland dress, made her yearn to be Scarlet. Not because she envied her David – she just wanted to walk down the aisle with Alec.

Caro saw a couple arriving late. He was tall, very tanned and handsome and she was wearing red, a hatinator making her look very smart but hiding half her face. One of Scarlet's Hollywood friends, no doubt, thought Caro and concentrated on the service.

A piper played 'Marie's Wedding' as the happy couple emerged from the church and the guests threw dried rose petals over them. Caro saw the girl in red again, just as she came over to her.

It took Caro a moment – she was so out of context – but then they rushed towards each other and embraced so hard the girl's hat fell off.

'Posy! What are you doing here?' said Caro, looking at her daughter, so brown and adult-looking.

'Well, Joe got in touch and a man called Alec or something paid for our tickets. He said you needed to see me and guessed there'd be two of us.'

Caro dragged her eyes away from her daughter to look at the man with her. She waited for him to speak with an Australian accent, already trying to get her head round the fact that Posy would live in Australia permanently.

'Hello,' said the man, sounding very English and for a moment Caro was even more confused. Posy had gone to Australia and this was the boyfriend she'd met there. He shouldn't be English.

'This is Mike,' said Posy.

'But you don't sound Australian – at least not very,' she said. She was completely thrown by the delightful shock of seeing Posy and was not completely coherent.

'That's because I'm not Australian,' he said. 'I'm from Kent,' he explained. 'Posy and I were both working in the same bar, which is how we met.'

Caro hugged him briefly before hugging Posy again. There was plenty of time to find out if it was just a casual romance or something more meaningful – they were both so young after all. 'Come on,' she said briskly. 'Let's get you to the house. You may have to walk but it's not far. You probably want the loo before you eat or drink. There's one there, Posy, and, Mike, there's a Gents outside. Follow the signs.'

'You are such a mum!' said Posy, laughing and hugging her again. 'You'll be reminding us to wash our hands afterwards any minute!'

'Do you need reminding?' she asked, and then laughed. 'But as for being a mum, you don't ever stop being one, you know. Once you have a baby you've got one for ever. Even when they do grow up.'

It turned out that everyone except Caro had known about the plan to bring Posy and Mike over for the wedding.

'It's a bit of a thank-you present,' said Alec, 'for all you've done for this family. Reuniting you with your family seemed fitting, somehow. Even if your little girl does seem to be very grown up!'

Caro turned her gaze to Posy yet again (she'd hardly been able to keep her eyes off her since she arrived) and realised that yes, she had grown up. She'd been quite mature and sensible when she set off across the world but she seemed even more so now in her tomato-coloured outfit.

'And it's no fun going to a wedding without a date,' said Scarlet mischievously, 'so I suggested Alec needed two tickets. I'm not sure how well Mike and Posy know each other—'

'It's a pretty long flight,' said Posy. 'We know each other a lot better now.' She sent him a sparkling glance. 'And I knew he wanted to get home. I think I might go back to Oz to finish my year, though.'

'You don't have to decide anything just now. We're at a wedding, after all,' said Caro firmly.

Lennie nodded. 'We are indeed, and if I could gather everybody for the speeches, in the marquee, that would be helpful.' Lennie was a good wedding planner, it turned out, and so far that day people were mostly doing as she asked them.

'Speeches!' said Scarlet. 'Really?'

'There won't be many, honey,' said David. 'I just want to thank everybody and I expect you do too.'

'Of course I do! And Dad will need to see speeches or he won't believe we're legally married.' She paused. 'Honey? It was so cool of you to arrange for Mom and my aunts and cousins to come.'

'I hope you didn't mind it being a secret. When I left them after I'd visited them at your home they weren't sure, so I thought it better not to tell you in case it didn't come off.'

Caro understood this. It was really wonderful that Scarlet's mother had come to her wedding but David couldn't have been certain about it.

'Well, I know now that while I don't always like my mom, she's my mom and I'll always love her.'

Posy grabbed hold of Caro and hugged her. 'That's so sweet!' she squeaked.

'Come on, guys,' said Scarlet.' 'The party can't get started until we get in the tent!' And she picked up her skirts and led the way.

Sometime later, Alec appeared at Caro's side. 'Let's go and get some air.'

The marquee was full of reeling guests, some of whom actually knew the steps. It was hot and the music was loud. Caro had only just managed to extricate herself from the dancers and the thought of escaping for a few minutes was welcome.

'OK, but maybe I should tell Posy, in case she's looking for me.'

He laughed. 'I think you'll find her with her young man in the middle of that scrum!' He indicated a group of dancers who were handling each other in a way that gave a whole new meaning to the expression 'highland fling'.

Caro managed to catch her daughter's eye and mimed that she was popping out. Posy made a thumbs-up sign before being spun around yet again.

Caro expected them to just step outside the marquee but Alec led her to the old Land Rover which had had its canvas top removed and white ribbons draped wherever they could be.

'Blimey!' said Caro. 'Is there a vehicle in the place that hasn't been decorated for the wedding?'

'No,' said Alec, 'but I like to think that the ribbons on the Landy bring out its natural beauty.'

Caro laughed. She was so tired she could have slept propped up against one the posts holding up the marquee but now she was alone with Alec she felt re-energised.

He opened the door. 'Climb in,' he said, holding out his arm and helping her clamber up.

Alec walked round to the driver's side and swung himself in. He had a day pack with him which he put on the back seat. It clanked encouragingly.

'Where are we going?' said Caro.

'I want to look at the nature reserve. It's going to be properly ours again soon.'

Although it was late it never got very dark in summer in Scotland but Alec put the headlights on as they drove through the forest to the track that led up to the lochan. Caro thought how happy she was. She was absolutely focused on living in the moment. She wasn't going to think about how she'd miss all this later – not to mention how much she'd miss Alec.

Although Caro'd been there before, when they came out of the forest into the light and she saw the silver water with the mountains behind, it took her by surprise. Neither of them spoke for several long seconds. 'I had forgotten quite how beautiful it was.'

'Come on!' he said, picking up his pack and swinging it over his shoulder. 'Can you walk in those shoes? It's drier now; we shouldn't need walking boots.'

She stumbled a little and he took her arm, clamping her to his side. She felt very strong and supported.

'Look!' he said when they'd walked for a few minutes. 'No barbed wire!'

'And a handy boulder we can sit on not far off!' said Caro. 'I don't know about you but the wedding has exhausted me.'

'It's been fantastic though, hasn't it?' said Alec. 'You and Lennie did a wonderful job. Scarlet and David are obviously delighted.'

'Yes. They liked it all being a bit haphazard and quirky.' She smiled. 'The house lends itself to haphazard and quirky.'

'Though with a bit of investment it won't need to be quite so eccentric,' he said, smiling down at her.

'And thanks to Murdo being willing to sell his guns, there'll be money for that.' Caro was concentrating on being practical, talking about the house, the estate, the wedding, so she wouldn't have to talk to Alec about what she should do next. Really, she didn't want to talk at all.

Alec obviously felt the same because he just said, 'Mm.'

They reached the boulder and Caro discovered wild roses were growing up all round it. 'How lovely!' she said and bent her head so she could inhale their scent. 'They smell gorgeous and not the same as the roses in France, somehow. It's a more innocent sort of fragrance. What do you think?'

He looked down at her. 'Really? I think I don't want to talk about roses just now. I want to talk about something much more important.'

Caro suddenly felt slightly sick. She realised she was nervous but wasn't sure why.

'Will you marry me?' Alec said. 'I know it's an old-fashioned concept but seeing Scarlet and David declare their love for each other in front of family and friends I felt I wanted to do that too. I want to tell the world how much I love you.'

Caro put a hand on the boulder to steady herself. 'You could try telling me, first,' she said huskily, hoping she wasn't going to cry.

'Don't you know how precious you are to me? Since you came into my life it's been like having a prop – a special support. You make the impossible, possible. I love you so much more than I thought I could love anyone. I just didn't know how infinite love could be.' He smiled gently. 'When Rowan was little I used to tell her that I loved her as much as that lochan was full of water. She said it was only a little loch and so didn't have much water in it. I told her – and it's true – that it's very very deep. Nearly as deep as my love for you, Caro.'

Caro couldn't speak. She'd wanted this for so long she couldn't quite believe it was really happening. Eventually she cleared her throat. 'What have you got in your pack? If it's champagne, I think you should open it.'

'As a celebration or consolation?'

Although she thought her response was clear she realised he was diffident. She hadn't made it clear how much she loved him. 'Celebration! I'd be delighted to marry you.'

'I am so relieved! I'm afraid I rang Pascal and Amalie a little while ago and booked their honeymoon suite. They were utterly delighted.'

'It sounds the perfect place. I love the chateau. But maybe we should get married here quickly? Before the new paint gets chipped and while it's all looking lovely? The house, I mean,' she added quickly. 'Glen Liddell will always be beautiful.'

'And so will you,' said Alec, and he kissed her.

It's the season of new beginnings for Helena and Gilly.

Gilly runs her own B&B business from her much-loved family home, which she doesn't want to part with – at any price.

But that's before she meets handsome estate agent Leo. Soon he has her wondering whether it's finally time to sell up and try something new in life.

Meanwhile Gilly's daughter **Helena** has a budding romance of her own. A talented weaver, she's becoming very close to her new landlord Jago, who's offered to help her at an upcoming craft fair that could give her career a major boost.

It's what friends do, and they are just friends. Aren't they?

With spring in full bloom, Helena and Gilly begin to ask themselves the same question:

Could their new loves lead to their happily ever after?

OUT IN HARDBACK 20TH FEBRUARY 2020

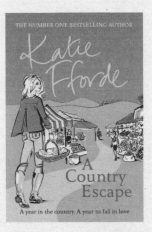

Emily is happy with her life just as it is.

She has a career as a midwife that she loves. She enjoys living on her own as a single woman. But she also feels it's time for a change and a spot of some sea air.

So when her best friend Rebecca asks whether she'd like to spend the summer cooking on a 'puffer' boat just off the Scottish coast, she jumps at the chance.

But she barely has time to get to grips with the galley before she finds herself with a lot on her plate. And there's Alasdair, the handsome local doctor who Emily is desperately trying not to notice.

Because if she falls in love with him, as he appears to be falling for her, will she ever want her old life back again?

'A lovely warm, escapist read'
Choice Magazine

ORDER YOUR COPY NOW